MW00794883

PSYCHO IN PARADISE

PARADISE SERIES

BOOK 15

DEBORAH BROWN

PSYCHO IN PARADISE
All Rights Reserved
Copyright © 2018 Deborah Brown

ISBN-13: 978-0-9984404-6-0

Cover: Natasha Brown

PRINTED IN THE UNITED STATES OF AMERICA

PSYCHO IN PARADISE

Chapter One

The sun glittered off the Tarpon Cove sign, touching everything around it. Baby blue skies straight off a postcard, fluffy clouds, and the scent of the salty water in the air—just another day in the Florida Keys.

Traffic on the Overseas Highway was light, and glancing in the rearview mirror, I was surprised to see flashing red lights bearing down on me. I checked the speedometer before easing off the gas. Speeding wasn't the issue, as I'd been holding steady at a couple of miles an hour under the speed limit.

Just great. I've only had this SUV for a couple of days and already my first ticket. But for what?

I eased to the side of the road, the cop car pulling up just behind me. The officer didn't get out right away. Shutting off the engine, I rolled down the window, keeping one eye on the rearview mirror and the other on the side mirror. Absently, I reached for my wallet, grabbing it off the passenger seat and extracting my ID. It surprised me to see two more police cruisers roll up behind the first cop.

The newest arrivals exited their cars, moving up and joining their colleague behind his open driver's side door.

The first officer lifted a megaphone into view. "Throw your keys out the window," he ordered.

What the hell?

"Put both hands out the window. Use one to open the door from the outside."

This was no speeding-ticket stop.

As soon as I opened the door, another officer directed me to get out. "Stop. Get down on both knees and lie face down on the ground, hands extended outward."

An officer approached from behind and handcuffed me, then patted me down. I assumed they were looking for weapons or drugs… or whatever. I had no clue.

"Stand," he ordered, grabbing my upper arm and leading me to the first police car, where he directed me into the back seat.

"Why did you pull me over?"

"The car you're driving may have been involved in a serious crime." The officer held up a search warrant. At a quick glance, I saw that they were searching for a body and any evidence that a body may have been in the car — hair, blood, fibers.

Picking the keys up off the ground, one of the officers hit the button for the liftgate.

To my utter shock, something that closely resembled a black body bag lay in the back… and judging by the shape, chances were good there was a body inside.

After several more vehicles arrived on the scene, including the coroner's van, the officer slid behind the wheel. He made eye contact with me in the rearview mirror. "You're being taken into custody on suspicion of murder."

* * *

The door of JS Auto Body flew open and banged against the wall. Located in a seedy part of the dock area, the car repair business was owned by Jimmy Spoon, who ran it strictly by appointment only and for a select clientele with high-end autos.

"Well, if it isn't the jailbird, Brad Westin." Spoon's baritone laugh filled the room. The big man leaned back in his chair, feet on the desk. "What are you doing slumming down in this neighborhood?"

"I need a change of scenery." Brad came through the door, glancing briefly over his shoulder before applying his foot and shoving it closed, then hitting the lock. "Every time I pass a police car, I think I'm going to see it make a u-turn and come after me for another ride to jail."

The two men were both over six feet, but that was where the similarities ended. Brad had once resembled the boy next door... until he was kidnapped by his deranged ex, who'd had plans to live in wedded bliss with her husband tied to a bedpost.

Brad's old beach boy persona had been replaced by a more serious version. He'd been in good shape before, but now his workouts had taken on a different intensity; his abs were rock hard and he'd honed his kick-ass skills, carrying himself like a man you didn't mess with. He'd tossed the tropical shorts and shirts he'd often donned as a commercial fishing captain, replacing them with tailor-made suits and opting for a new career in real estate development. The black suit he wore was fitted and well made, showing off his lean physique. His sun-bleached hair had a slightly messy look.

Jimmy Spoon, on the other hand... a mere squint from him sent any sane-minded person scurrying in the opposite direction. His mean-ass reputation preceded him—little did people know he'd been tamed... somewhat. He cleaned up well, in large part due to his wife, who loved to shop for him. He wore tan linen slacks, a short-sleeved silk shirt, and Gucci loafers. His dark hair was tied back, not one speck of dirt or grease on him, and it even looked like he'd had a manicure.

"What brings you here?" Spoon asked.

"No one would look for me here, not even the cops," Brad said in a tone meant to irritate Spoon, a slight smile at the corners of his mouth. He crossed to one of the chairs in front of

Spoon's desk. Kicking it back, he sat and stretched out, putting one foot on the corner of the desk.

Spoon flipped him the finger.

Brad returned the gesture. "I'd ask for a beer, but it would be a bad idea to drink and drive, even if it is only one." He lifted his pant leg, showing off the ankle monitor. "The cops can find me pretty easily, and I don't want to give them any reason to arrest me and run the risk of revoking my bail. I'll take a soda."

"Just because I'm married to your mother doesn't mean I'm going to wait on your ass like she does. Get your own drink," Spoon grumped.

I slid quietly off the couch where I'd been lying since my brother blew through the door, oblivious to his surroundings, retrieved a Coke from the fridge, which held an array of drinking options, tiptoed the few feet to Brad, and pressed the can on his cheek from behind.

Brad leaped from the chair. "What...!" he yelled. Catching sight of me, he relaxed slightly. "Hey, sis."

"Don't you 'hey, sis' me. Why wasn't I your first call after your lovely mugshot and fingerprints were taken?" I cuffed the side of his head.

"Ouch."

"I'm hoping you didn't growl at the officer behind the camera." I swung again out of sheer annoyance at his stupidity, but he caught my hand just before it made contact a second time and hugged me hard.

"Madison, sit down," Spoon ordered. "A judge might revoke his bail if he shows up at his next hearing all beat up."

"You really need a keeper." I threw myself in the chair next to his. "You don't scope out your surroundings wherever you go? You didn't even notice me stretched out on the couch."

"In case you haven't heard, I've got a lot on my mind."

I swung out to cuff him again. His foot hit the floor, and he leaned back out of reach.

"Aren't you going to ask me if I murdered Patty?"

"I'd be more likely to dispatch that horrid woman to the beyond than you. And if you *did*, the last place you'd store the body is in the back of your *new* car."

"No whiff of dead-body scent when you got behind the wheel?" Spoon asked.

Brad shook his head.

Patty Thorson—the ex-girlfriend from hell that wouldn't go away, not even in death—still had her tentacles extended, even from the afterlife. Someone had murdered her—certainly not my brother—and wanted to frame him for it. But who?

"What I'd like to know is how she got out of the mental institution," I said. "Surely she wasn't declared sane *again*."

"Get ready for this — she escaped over a month ago." Brad sighed in exasperation. "Not one word from the authorities that she was on the loose. Surprised me she didn't make a beeline for my doorstep."

The door to the mechanics' bays opened, cutting off conversation. A fierce-looking man in his mid-forties stuck his head inside, the noises of a busy shop audible behind him. "Miss Westin, your Hummer is ready."

I smiled at him as he crossed the office, handing off a sheaf of papers to his boss, then leaving.

The front door opened with less fanfare than when Brad entered, and Fab wiggled across the threshold in a pair of skinny silk ankle pants. She pocketed her lockpick and kicked the door closed with her stiletto, sending a reverberation throughout the office.

Spoon came out of his chair and barked, "Next. Time. Knock."

Fab looked over her shoulder as though she didn't know who he was talking to. She pulled a card out of her back pocket. "Here, you need a security update. You qualify for the family discount." She pasted on a phony smile, handing it to Spoon.

Fabiana Merceau, my best friend and roommate, had recently opened her own security agency. She always had a business card in hand and never failed to point out the weaknesses in people's systems in the most creative ways.

"If it isn't the criminal..." Fab reached out and ruffled Brad's hair before sitting down. "I'm here to pick up my car. You can bill Madison; I'll take the keys."

"It's not your car—it's registered to Madison, and if I had my way, you'd walk home," Spoon said irritably.

Fab ignored Spoon, instead asking Brad, "How was your jail stay? You and your cellmate, Bubba, get friendly?"

Hard as I tried to bite it back, I laughed, which earned me glares from Brad and Spoon.

"Bubba and I didn't share life stories... except that he really did kill someone and wasn't the least bit remorseful. Besides, he kept busy knitting. Ugly sock things." Brad wrinkled his nose.

"Assuming you slept, it was brave of you to close your eyes around someone with a needle." Fab smiled, enjoying Brad's frown. "Who knows what he might've poked out."

Brad covered his ears.

I pulled his hand away. "Back to why you didn't call and why I had to track you down. One nice thing about being a guest of the county— your ilk is all housed in the same place. I tried to book a visit, but the clerk on the phone informed me the joint would be closed for a few days. Thinking to be funny, I threw out riot as the reason. Surprised me when she said, 'Good news has a way of getting around.'"

"Stop," Brad admonished. "I'm not in the mood for your humor."

"In case you didn't know, your sister knows everyone," Fab said in a tone meant for a six-year-old.

"You're not a lawyer," Brad responded in a huff, as though I might need a reminder. "Told the officer I needed the number for Cruz Campion, and he laughed. 'Pretty fancy lawyer,' was his response. Spoke to Cruz's assistant, and she assured me she'd relay the message. Never heard from him. For my first appearance, I got assigned a public defender, an overworked fellow, and that's when it sank in that I might never get out of jail for a crime I didn't commit."

"Hope you were smart enough not to talk to the cops," Spoon grumbled.

"After they read me my rights and I asked for a lawyer, they were pretty cool. One asked the questions you might expect. Did I know Patty? Any clue how the body got in my car? And my favorite, 'did you kill her?' I answered honestly, then was led back to a cell."

I hadn't shaken my exasperation with how everything went down. "You were lucky to get another bail hearing."

"Phil came through and got me Ruthie Grace. I was skeptical at first—the smell of incense was off-putting—but she handled herself like the seasoned pro that it turns out she is. I did some research on her when I got home."

"That girlfriend of yours didn't have jack squat to do with you getting out of jail." Spoon kicked the desk hard enough a picture frame fell over. "That stupid woman planned to represent you herself—apparently she forgot that she specializes in contract law."

"Phil said..." Brad paused.

"Let me guess, the esteemed Philipa Grey took all the credit," I said, making a fake shocked face. "Once I heard about your arrest from *Mother*, she and I worked together to spring you. Ruthie was my idea—she's equal to Cruz in talent and has a stellar win-record, and all she expects in return is her bill paid, as opposed to free favors for an extended family of nine hundred. Also, Phil thought using the Bub Brothers for bail was a good idea? They're thieves with exorbitant interest rates, and you'd be in debt to them until they got bored collecting and you were found on the side of the highway—dead. I got you a much better option. But why did you have to borrow money at all? What's up with your partner and new bestie; he couldn't pony up the cash?" I asked in disgust.

"Bordello's in Chicago, in negotiations on a big deal, and Phil didn't want to bother her brother."

I knew I should inform Brad about the confrontation Phil and I'd had in the hallway at the courthouse but decided his girlfriend could do the telling. "Of course she didn't." I didn't know if Phil had honestly thought she could handle it herself or just didn't care if Brad ended up in prison for life, but he was sure headed that way before I stepped in.

Phil got off the elevator on the third floor of the courthouse and sauntered down the hall, blending in with her brethren in her black suit. I was also in a suit, as I'd made it a point to look professional, and caught sight of the woman as I sat waiting for the door to the courtroom to be unlocked.

Nose in the air, Phil was about to pass me by when I reached out and grabbed her arm, indicating that she should sit on the bench next to me. I swiveled in her direction. "You listen to me — you stand up in that courtroom and utter one word about representing my brother, and I'll see you disbarred."

"To think we were friends," Phil seethed.

"We were never friends. You had your own agenda from day one." I waved off her response. "Ruthie Grace will be representing Brad, and I've got the bail covered. You get in the way, and if they don't make mincemeat of you, I will."

She stood, tossed me a glare, and without a word, stomped into the courtroom, where she waved at Brad, seated at the defendant's table in a blue jail uniform, and claimed a seat in front.

I stayed until the judge went over Brad's list of restrictions and he was led back into custody to await his bail being posted.

That had gone down yesterday, and Brad had holed up in his condo as soon as he got out. He'd talked to Mother and sent me a text.

Brad checked his watch and stood. "I've got to go. I've got fifteen minutes to get back home. Got a conference call, and I'd rather be early than late."

I stood and hugged him. "Mother's planning a dinner for tomorrow and invited your lawyer. See you then."

"Yeah, great." He laughed humorlessly. "See you there."

The door opened again, and Liam walked in, a smirk on his face.

Liam was, hands down, the favorite of the family. Now a student at the University of Miami, he'd been informally adopted into the family in his teenage years when his mother dated Brad.

"You better not have used a lockpick," Spoon growled. "Because if trouble over here—" He glanced at Fab. "—taught you, then my wife has now honed the skill."

Liam laughed.

"Well?" Spoon demanded.

"Grandmother loves being in trouble with you, and I'm not about to ruin her fun."

"Gotta go." Brad headed to the door.

"I'm right behind you," Liam said. "I'm turning your place into a party house after you've swum up the river."

Everyone laughed except Brad.

"No swimming involved," I said. "It's a free bus ride."

Chapter Two

It wasn't often that Fab and I shared the island countertop in the kitchen, papers spread out beside our laptops. But she'd informed me that she wasn't going into the office and I could move the heck over.

I ogled my boyfriend, Creole, over the rim of my coffee cup when his booted feet hit the tiles and he clomped into the kitchen, Didier behind him. Both were over six feet and dressed for construction work. I wanted to tease them about their usually groomed dark hair sticking up on end.

The cats, Jazz and Snow, must have cracked an eye open and noticed Didier in the kitchen. He was their go-to soft touch for treats. The two single-filed into the kitchen and sat at his feet, Jazz's howling translating to "hurry it up."

Creole stepped over the cats and pulled up a stool next to me. He cast a glance over my pile of paperwork, his eyebrows going up.

"I'm trying to gather as much information on Brad's case as I can before dinner tonight. I called my information guy—he's got an in to find out what the cops know that we don't."

"When do I get to meet this guy, GC?"

GC was short for Gunz's Connection, Gunz being a shady friend of Fab's.

"You know he's holed up in a basement somewhere, working his magic. *I* haven't even met him, if that makes you feel better."

"It doesn't."

I bent forward and brushed Creole's lips with my own. "Don't worry so much. He's really good at his job, and he did come highly recommended."

Fab pushed her paperwork aside, making room for Didier, and nodded in my direction. "If you guys need help down at the docks, I volunteer the two of us. I nominate myself as supervisor, with the understanding that I'll be the one telling you what to do."

The guys laughed.

"We've got a small section of one of the docks to repair before inspection tomorrow," Didier said. "I've got hopes that by the weekend, all the slips will be leased. It was a good decision to increase the amount of available space and double the size of the guest dock."

A mutual friend, Corndog (beware: when you enter a hotdog-eating contest and win, the moniker could be with you forever), owned the highly sought-after dock area, which had stood empty and rundown for years. Despite being pressured to sell, which included threats and bodily harm, he opted to renovate it himself instead. I'd met him when he hired me to investigate who was pressuring him to sell, and when I realized he needed a partner for the renovation, I'd suggested Didier.

"All thanks to Madison's friend in the building department," Creole said. "Turns out the man had more than a few good ideas."

"Another great connection from my aunt's phone book." I often thought she'd left it with her personal papers knowing I would need it. "It's nice of you to volunteer."

"I need the exercise." Creole flexed his muscles. He'd been asked by Didier to come in on the project because he needed someone he trusted and could work well with.

Didier reached for the coffee pot that he'd refilled earlier, filling everyone's mug except mine. Their strong brews were too much for me, and besides, I didn't need hair on my chest.

"What are you two up to today?" Didier's blue eyes bored into Fab and me.

"I've got a new client. I'm meeting him at his office in Miami," Fab said.

"New client" always gave me a bad feeling. Even if they were millionaires with penthouse views of the water, they were trouble and asked for the most outrageous services, almost always illegal ones.

"Let me guess, rich guy got caught in his mistress's bed and left his pants behind, and he's hiring you to sneak past sixteen layers of security and retrieve them." I mentally applauded myself for not ending in an eyeroll.

Didier banged his fist on the countertop. "Once again, I'm having to remind you of your promise to run these jobs by me *before* you make a commitment."

"You didn't share every detail of this dock project with me." Fab's whiney voice told everyone that she already knew there was something hinky about the job.

"As a matter of fact, I did," Didier said evenly. "Guess you weren't listening."

Fab flinched.

"I thought I made it quite clear that the sharing of details was to be before the job and not when you were on your way to jail." Didier stood and crossed to the sink, rinsing out his mug. "Don't let me stand in your way. If it's that important, go ahead." He headed to the front door, pausing to pick up his briefcase. "I'll meet you at the office," he said over his shoulder to Creole.

Fab vaulted off her stool and ran out the door after him.

I swiveled on my stool, wrapping my legs around Creole's waist. "Want to place a wager that they make up before he leaves the driveway?"

"You think you're marrying a stupid man?" He lifted my right hand and kissed my knuckles right above the "friendship" ring.

Creole had proposed a few months ago but was adamant that he didn't want a large wedding attended by people we didn't know. He wanted us to elope and say our I-do's on the beach with the sand between our toes. I wholeheartedly agreed, except for the elopement part. I couldn't do that to my mother and told Creole to figure it out with her. Thus far, he hadn't broached the subject. The engagement ring had become a "friendship ring," for which he took endless needling from my family.

"I'll remind you that Mother has never met a problem she couldn't find a solution to. You two can work it out so everyone is happy and you don't end up dead with Mother in prison."

"I'm working on a plan." He grinned.

"That scares me," I murmured against his lips. "But to show my love, I'm in."

"That's why I love you." He looked over my shoulder, surveying the driveway through the garden window over the sink. "I consider myself lucky that you're not as crazy as she is. They're kissing. That means Fab promised… again. Didier's not going to back down when it comes to her safety. I don't with you. Have I thanked you lately for not being as shifty as your friend?"

"There's enough crazy going on around here—we need a few sane moments." I tried for a smile, but when I thought of my brother and his pending trial, it had me renewing my oath not to leave any stone unturned.

"On my way to the docks, I'll give the chief a call and see if he'll put out a few feelers. You're one of his favorites, so I can't imagine that he'd say no. Though my old team has mostly retired — moving on to less stressful, more pleasurable jobs — I've still got a couple of friends on the force that can kick over a rock or two."

Creole had been an undercover cop for the Miami Police Department until his partner died in a shootout and he nearly did too.

"Didier just pulled out." Creole stood, bringing me with him, kissed me thoroughly, and set my feet on the floor. "Here comes Fab."

At that moment, the front door banged open. Fab blew in and ran upstairs.

I slipped my hand in Creole's. "I'll walk you out so we can smooch again before you leave."

Creole and I made our way down the driveway, sliding between Fab's Porsche and my Hummer to cross the street to where Creole and Didier parked their vehicles in the driveway of the neighbor's seldom-used vacation home.

"Have a good day, honey." I waved as he drove off.

Going back across the street and up the driveway of my white, two-story Key West-style house, I saw that Fab had come back into the kitchen and poked her head between two plants in the garden window. From this distance, the fierce look on her face clearly telegraphed, "Hurry up."

When I opened the door, Fab stood in the entry, purse slung over her shoulder.

"You might as well sit." I crooked my finger and pointed to a stool at the island as I passed her. "We need to have a talk."

She huffed and grumbled the few steps across the kitchen and paused in front of the coffee pot, casting me a glance.

"Fill your cup to the top."

Fab took my suggestion and sat across from me, sighing. "I've had a rocky morning."

"Do you want to stay made-up with Didier or not?"

"Of course I do."

"Share the details about this new client of yours and the job I'm certain you've already accepted."

Exasperation poured out of her. She hated it when I could see straight through her schemes. "Mr. Worth is experiencing some security issues that he believes I'm a perfect fit to solve."

"What a bunch of drivel. Let's skip to the illegal part. After picking the lock, disarming the security — assuming the building isn't a high-rise with a guard, which is breaking and entering — and, let's see..." I rubbed my chin. "Theft? There must be a couple of other *felonies* to choose from. They escape me at the moment."

"There are times..."

"I know, you don't like me. That's old news. Now stop stalling."

"This case doesn't involve the litany of activities you just ran down. Maybe." Fab paused. "Mr. Worth's girlfriend stole three million dollars' worth of gold from his personal safe."

I whistled, trying to imagine what that kind of a haul would look like. Bars? Coins?

"Girlfriend didn't make any attempt to cover up what she'd done either. He wants her found… or more accurately, he wants his money."

"That couldn't have happened unless he gave her the combination." I shook my head. "Why? There's some stupidity that hiring a security expert can't fix." It must have been some safe to hold all that gold.

"I can hardly point that out to him in such succinct terms."

"When you find said girlfriend, then what? You break into her place and hope that she's also stupid and kept the gold in her possession? If, after ransacking it, you come up with zip, then what? You bring out your bag of torture tricks?"

Fab grimaced. "Too messy for me. Before you ask, I'm not going to have any part in turning her or anyone else over to be hurt. My luck, the person would die, and prison for me."

"Easy fix. You meet with your client and go over his expectations. Better yet, all of this can be taken care of in a phone call. In the meantime, I'll give the woman's name to GC. He can track her down with a few keystrokes."

Fab not making eye contact meant there was more.

"What else?" I asked.

"You were right about Mr. Worth wanting her apartment searched. First priority is the gold, and the second is to make sure that there's nothing left behind that would suggest a relationship of any kind between the two. Seems I wasn't his first choice—he hired another firm, but without a key, they wouldn't go in."

I grabbed her mug and mine and put them in the sink. "You need to follow their example. Where do you find these clients? They have the worst taste in mistresses, and when they end the relationship, they tend to leave behind incriminating evidence. How did they get to be bazillionaire businessmen with stupidity like that? Just goes to show that, no matter their net worth, they tend to think with their little brain."

Bored with my observations, Fab checked her watch. "I've got just enough time to make my meeting with Mr. Worth."

I leaned against the counter and crossed my arms.

Fab glanced into the entry. "You steal the keys again?"

"Both sets." I smiled smugly. "Enjoy your walk." After she was done growling, I said, "Call Worthless. Tell him you'll do your best to track the girlfriend down. If she's left any kind of trail, you'll find it. As for the breaking and entering part — forget it."

Frustration poured out of her.

"If you need some extra incentive, you have a wedding coming up once you and Mother stop giggling over the details and make some decisions." I tended to tune out those discussions, liking Creole's elopement idea better every day.

My phone rang, interrupting her response, but I knew I'd gotten through to her. Mac's face popped on the screen. Macklin Lane was the manager of The Cottages, a beach property that I owned. Somehow, the units had a tendency to fill up with misfits, and it was her job to keep them in line, which she mostly succeeded at. But every once in a while…

"Good news first," I answered.

"That will have to wait until later." Mac whistled and yelled, "Over here."

"That's my ear," I grouched.

"The cops are here, and they've surrounded Miss January's cottage."

Chapter Three

Before racing upstairs to change into a jean skirt and tennis shoes, I reached inside my bra and took out Fab's car keys, handing them over. Halfway up, I yelled, "I wish you'd wait until I get back to meet with your client. It's much faster to post bail if I'm close by when you get in trouble."

In record time, I was taking the steps back down two at a time and running out to the SUV, where Fab waited impatiently behind the wheel.

I slammed the car door, and Fab shot me a disgruntled look. Did she think the door would fall off? "I'm coming with you," she said. "I took your suggestion and called Mr. Worthless. I wish you'd stop giving people rude names. I have a hard enough time remembering names as it is."

"And he said?"

In true Fab fashion, she squealed out of the driveway and up to the corner. "The call took all of a minute. He had nothing new to add. What a colossal waste of time it would have been to drive to Miami for a meeting. Once I assured him I'd get right on it, he seemed satisfied and told me the next phone call better be to say that I retrieved the gold."

"I've got more free advice." I took my phone out of my pocket. "Tell Didier the job could be done in-house. That's the truth." I hit redial. Voicemail. *I'm going to kill her.* Just figuratively, as Mac was too good at her job and life would be darn dull without her. I texted, "On my way."

"This should be interesting." Fab raced through a yellow light. "What do you suppose that feeble old woman could do that would require more than one cop?"

I'd inherited Miss January as a tenant along with the property. Yes, she was feeble, but not old—she only looked it. Cancer had ravaged her body, and it didn't help that she medicated with cigarettes and alcohol. Her favorite was a fifth of vodka, which got delivered midday and she drank until she passed out.

"I'm sure it's all a misunderstanding." One could hope. "Not that she wouldn't commit some crime, but she'd have no idea that whatever it was could get her in trouble. We can hope she gets a sympathetic judge who'll consider that flimsy excuse."

Fab laughed, cutting through a field, swerving around a pile of beer bottles, and turning into a driveway that turned out to be an alley, another shortcut that shortened drive time.

The street to The Cottages was blocked by a police car. Fab parked around the corner, and we cut down the walkway alongside one of the houses, where she claimed to know the owner. "Know" was used loosely — probably an older gentleman she flirted shamelessly with before going on her way, leaving him with high hopes that she'd come around again.

Mac slid around the side of the duplex that she and her friend had bought across the street from The Cottages. Her commute time to work was less than a minute. She'd told me once that it was the ideal location for spying on the late-night activities that often took place across the street.

Wearing a colorful muumuu that a friend had brought her back from Hawaii, she waved frantically, hurrying in our direction. Her clothing and shoe choices seldom made sense — instead of a pair of sandals on this warm day, she had donned a pair of high-top, fur-trimmed rubber boots.

"Kevin drew the short straw."

Instead of the whisper I suspected she was going for, her words came out in a shriek that had the man turning, a glare on his face — a familiar look to everyone that knew him.

"Surrounded?" I snapped. "There's two cars here."

"Is that all?" Now standing next to me at the end of her driveway, Mac looked up and down the street.

Kevin Cory, a local sheriff's deputy and also a tenant of The Cottages, was still looking at us from where he stood conferring with another officer at the end of the driveway of the u-shaped, ten-unit property. Miss January's cottage was in the middle.

"Where did your friend go?" Mac tossed her head in the direction we'd come from.

I turned, and the street was empty. I needed a wrist leash to keep track of Fab—she had a habit of vanishing.

"Stay back," Kevin ordered.

"If this has to do with Miss January, I can help and no one needs to get hurt." I surveyed my property. All was quiet. My guess was that as soon as one cop car drove up, anyone outside bolted back inside. "Please don't shoot her."

Kevin rolled his eyes at me. "I've got a warrant for Nestor. My partner knocked respectfully, and someone poked a gun between the blinds. My money's on Nestor."

"Yeah," Mac said. "This time of day, Miss January usually takes a snooze, getting rested up for her next drunk-on."

The officer who'd knocked, and was now standing on Miss January's porch, waved and shook his head.

Out of the corner of my eye, I caught a glimpse of Fab running across the street at the corner. She reappeared a minute later from the back of Mac's house.

I ran over to her. "They're looking for Nestor. Is he still in there?"

Fab smiled coyly.

"You make my head hurt. Don't even pretend you don't know."

Fab cut around me and approached Kevin. "I'll deny it if you tell anyone you heard it from me."

What part of "he's a cop" did she forget?

"Nestor somehow shoved his butt out the bathroom window, and he's en route to the beach."

Kevin's face registered disbelief.

"Seriously, he's headed that way." Fab pointed. "Probably over the fence by now."

"Mike," Kevin boomed as he took off running and met up with his partner. After a short discussion, Kevin cut over to the pool area, disappearing through the gate that opened onto the beach.

I moved closer to Mac, standing shoulder to shoulder. There wasn't anyone in hearing distance, but I didn't want to take a chance. "Tell me Nestor isn't wanted for murder or some other heinous crime."

"The warrant is for hit and run and car theft. He got an extra charge for the drugs in the trunk."

"How did you find out?"

"My super-secret confidential source." She beamed.

"If the snack bill goes up, I'll know it was Kevin. He can be bought." Fab smirked at Mac.

Mac looked ready to lunge. I grabbed her arm. "What else?"

"Nothing." She crossed her arms over her chest.

"Fab's just jealous you got the info before her."

Appeased, Mac grinned. "Nestor's been using a phony ID. His real name is actually Rupert Talbot. In fact, he's used several aliases and has a rap sheet a mile long."

"Kevin's been suspicious for months. No wonder he couldn't come up with anything — assumed name and all."

"Nestor left the wrong person for dead. When the cops couldn't find him, the 'presumed victim' put an investigator on it and tracked him here. The information was delivered to someone high up." Mac relished dishing the details.

"I'm worried about Miss January. Nestor was an ass to us, but he took good care of her." In my opinion, the twosome resembled a remake of an old movie — teenage boyfriend/old woman girlfriend.

"I'll keep an eye on her," Mac said on a sigh. "When she asks, I'm telling her the truth — that her boyfriend is a criminal. Otherwise, she'll hear about it from someone else. This way, I can comfort her."

"Call your mother." Fab nudged me. "Have her start the hunt for Miss January's next boyfriend."

"I dare *you* to make the call."

Mother's matchmaking attempts were often joked about... unless you were the one she decided to fix up.

"Look who's back," Mac said.

Kevin had Nestor in cuffs, one hand gripping his biceps as he led him across the pool area. Nestor fought him at every step.

Mike, the officer who'd been standing guard at Miss January's, met them in the driveway, grabbing hold of his other arm, and the two dragged him to Mike's patrol car.

Kevin was clearly not happy, looking disheveled from his run down the beach. Having seen Kevin in shorts and a t-shirt, I knew out-of-shape Nestor hadn't stood a chance. "You are aware that you're not to interfere in police investigations?" he said to Fab.

"What?" Fab threw her hands up. "I was walking down the street, minding my own business, when I happened to notice Nestor making his break. A little 'thank you' would be nice." She sniffed. "You wanted to stand out here all night? Maybe teargas an old woman?"

"Yeah, thanks. Next time, do as you're told and stand back, or better yet, get in your car and leave." Kevin stomped over to his patrol car.

"Go smooth things over with Kevin," I whispered to Mac.

She turned on me, brows raised. "Why me?"

"You lost the coin toss," I said. "Besides, it's better coming from you, since he likes you better than either of us."

Mac took a step and paused, turning slightly. "Do I get a raise?"

"You get my heartfelt thanks." I put my hand on my chest. "That's worth so much more."

"I'd rather have the money," she grumbled before walking over to Kevin, who sat in his car, window down.

"I'm thinking I'll make her a 'get out of jail free' card. Saw the idea on the internet — gift ideas for those hard-to-buy-for people."

"I want one," Fab said.

"It's understood between us. Our pact regarding breaking each other out has no expiration date, if it comes to that."

A breath of air grazed my cheek, and I jumped. Fab had blown on me.

"I want to go now. The fun is over."

Chapter Four

After Fab and I got home, we disappeared into our bedrooms and didn't reappear until it was time to leave for family dinner night, an evening meant to show support for Brad.

Creole and Fab no longer played tug-of-war over who was driving. Creole and I climbed into the back seat of the SUV, I stretched out and laid my head in his lap, and we talked, ignoring Fab and Didier in the front.

The Westins didn't have a reputation for being on their best behavior at these get-togethers, especially me, often egged on by Fab.

Pulling up in front of the condo complex, we followed another car through the security gate. Spoon had pitched a fit at our use of lockpicks as acceptable methods of entry, and Mother asked us to stop. "You have a key," she'd huffed. Fab buzzed through the security panel as we passed, and when Spoon's voice boomed through, she blew in it. I laughed, and the guys frowned.

When the elevator arrived at the top floor, the doors opened on Spoon, leaning against the jam, smirk firmly in place.

I was happy to see Ruthie Grace already seated in the living room. Good, she hadn't thought better of coming. I had a lukewarm relationship with the woman, and when Mother and I had teamed up to help Brad, I sicced Mother on her to unleash that maternal charm of hers. They'd since become friends.

No sign of Phil. I wondered if she had a good excuse, such as a sudden case of ptomaine poisoning. I'd ask Brad, but another time. For now, I'd ignore the fact that she wasn't here with everyone else. Tonight was not about annoying him.

Spoon offered Fab and Didier a drink, and they followed him over to the bar cart. Brad came out of the kitchen, an apron around his waist, and waved a greeting. He got Didier's attention, motioning him over to the counter.

Creole tugged on my arm. "Are you going to behave tonight?"

"It depends on whether there's a pitcher of margaritas with my name on it... or wine." I wrinkled my nose. "Promise, if you see me teetering on the edge of making a scene, that you'll grab me back."

"Break it up, you two," Mother said with a laugh, enveloping us in a hug. "Everyone is here except for Phil. She had a business meeting."

Liam stuck his head out of the kitchen and waved.

I left Mother with Creole and crossed the room

for a hug. "I'm surprised to see you here on a school night."

"It's the best way to stay in the loop. Besides, I'll end up with food to take back to the dorm."

"You're a true Westin—loving those leftovers."

"Met Brad's attorney. Not quite what I expected." Liam eyed the dark-haired woman in her colorful caftan.

"That's most people's first impression. I've seen in her court. In her tailor-made suit, she comes off as approachable with a spine of steel and has a way of putting people at ease." I gave him another hug. "I need to go kiss up to the woman. It comes in handy to have an attorney on speed dial, especially a good one."

Creole appeared at my side, wine glass in hand, which he handed to me. I frowned at it but took it anyway.

"Now that you're practically part of the family, does this mean you'll take my phone calls, Counselor Grace?" I greeted her. When we first met, she'd emphasized to Fab and I that she preferred that moniker.

"Please call me Ruthie." She tipped her wine glass at me. "Are you also in need of a lawyer? As for your brother's case, you can't ask any questions—keep in mind that pesky little thing called client confidentiality."

Fab, who'd left the guys at the bar, reached my side in time to hear the last part of the conversation.

"Neither of us has been arrested this week." I nudged Fab. "I'm volunteering both our services for my brother's case."

"Not to be rude…" *But* hung in the air. Ruthie flashed us a professional smile. "I'm not in need of an unlicensed investigator. Or a licensed one. I'm fortunate to have a good one I've been using for years."

You could hear a pin drop.

I'd missed the moment when the room had gone silent and all ears tuned into our conversation.

Brad hustled across the room, putting his arm around my shoulders. "I'm sure everyone here is in agreement that Ruthie's investigator can do all the digging. I don't want you getting hurt."

"Who tracked your ass down when Patty kidnapped you? And the faith you had in me not to give up until you were found, where did that go?" I managed to say evenly; no yelling about how stupid he was being.

Patty had drugged him and taken him to a foreclosed house, where she tied him up and shared her delusional rantings about marriage, starting a family, and living happy ever after. Fab, Creole, Didier, and I worked together to track down his location, calling in the cops after we found him.

"Really, Madison." Mother shook her head.

I didn't remind her that we were all adults and every one of us had heard the word "ass" before.

"What have you got so far?" Ruthie asked. From her tone, she didn't expect it to be anything useful.

"Client confidentiality. If Brad were to sign a permission slip, then I could share." I eyed Brad in challenge, and when he didn't say anything, I said, "I'm going to be part of this case whether you like it or not because you are *not* going to jail." My voice was loud enough that no one had to strain to hear.

Spoon refilled Ruthie's glass. "Westins never let you wonder what's on their minds."

Fab stood and stretched, which I'd never seen her do. My guess was she wanted all eyes on her, and she succeeded. "If Brad doesn't want your help, then fine," she said to me. "We'll take the reports and go." She picked up my tote, which Creole had set down next to a barstool.

Ruthie perked up. "What reports?" she and Brad asked at the same time.

Mother patted Ruthie's hand. "It really does save time if we can be kept up to date together and not have to bother Brad, since he's a busy man."

"Well?" I stared straight at Brad.

"You need all the help you can get, dude." Liam clapped him on the back.

"Okay, fine," Brad ground out. "You need my

permission, you've got it. Your safety is top priority, and yours too." He turned his glare to include Fab.

"According to the coroner, Patty was strangled manually." I put my hands around my neck, making a choking noise.

Spoon grinned.

"I'm sure this is all old news, huh, Counselor?" Fab asked. "We're not that hungry, so we'll get take-out on the way home, although we'd like our dessert to go. We'll leave you to your tidbit-sharing."

Fab and Ruthie exchanged dirty looks. "The report hasn't been released yet." Ruthie looked at me with new interest.

The guys looked down, shoulders shaking.

"No one is going *anywhere*." Mother used her no-nonsense voice. "I didn't slave all day in the kitchen to have everyone leave before eating." More laughter. Everyone in the room knew that Mother didn't *slave* over anything but the to-go menus. She continued, "New family rule: No intense discussions until after we eat."

Brad was the first to ignore the new rule. "Patty looked like she'd blow away in a stiff wind, but physically, she was strong. She engaged in an intense workout routine every day. Someone would have to catch her off guard, get the jump on her."

"Had to be someone she trusted. Who? My money's on a man." I turned to Fab. "You're pretty kick-butt, do you think you could…"

"I'd have shot her." Fab made a couple of popping noises.

Didier laughed and winked at her.

Fab beamed back.

"I'd like to hear what you've got," Ruthie said.

Fab waved me off before I could answer. "First you agree, if you need any information with regards to Brad, that you'll call us first. And to share anything that would help us in pursuit of additional information."

All eyes went to Brad, who hesitated.

"We're talking ferreting out info, not house-to-house searches," I said. That would come if we found any viable persons of interest.

"I'll sign anything you need me to," Brad said to his lawyer.

"We'll shake on it, figuratively speaking." Fab stuck her hand out an inch in front of her chest, and I copied her.

From the grouchy look on Ruthie's face, she wasn't in the mood for the symbolic handshake. "I reserve the right to withhold information when it's in the best interests of my client."

"Dinner's ready," Mother announced. "Any more legal maneuverings can wait until after we eat."

* * *

After dinner, we stayed seated at the dining

table, which had been moved in front of the floor-to-ceiling windows, giving us a spectacular view of the lights glistening off the water below. The conversation around the table remained light.

Mother directed me to clear dishes while Spoon refilled glasses and Didier and Creole put away the leftovers.

Once we were all reseated, Ruthie asked, "Anything else of importance?"

"A couple of months ago, Patty escaped the nuthouse. Actually, a local emergency room," I said, unsure what she knew, as her expression wasn't easy to read.

"You'd think, since I was a victim of hers and agreed to her going to a mental institution instead of fighting for a state prison sentence, that I'd get a call," Brad said in pure frustration.

"Even if you were alerted, chances are it wouldn't have changed the outcome," I said. "Patty's clever. There's no way that her escape wasn't planned down to the last detail. Here's what I know so far. Patty got transported to the local emergency room and, not long after, traded her hospital gown for street clothes and walked out. At the curb, a car was waiting, an older model that we've yet to identify. I'm working on getting a better photo to get the license tag."

"No one here knows cars better than I do," Spoon said. "If you need an ID on the make and model, I'm your man."

"You'd do that?" I asked sweetly.

Brad laughed. "She got you."

I'd moved my tote next to my chair and now reached in, pulling out a grainy 8x10 and holding it out. "Here you go."

Spoon stood, shaking his head, and came around the table to grab it out of my hand, holding it under a nearby lamp. "Early sixties Rambler. Haven't seen one of these on the road in a long time."

"Mail your bill directly to Brad," I said.

Creole scrutinized the picture. "I'll call a couple of guys I know who live local and tell them to keep an eye out. It won't be hard to spot."

"You got any more car questions, call me first," Spoon offered. "If I don't know, which isn't likely, I can find out."

"The photo might be a wild goose chase," Ruthie said. "Have you verified where it came from?"

"It came from the security camera right outside the hospital," I said.

"And you got your hands on that how?" Ruthie asked. "That takes a warrant, and you couldn't possibly have gotten one of those."

Creole and Didier turned to Fab.

Fab shrugged. "Not me."

"Friend of a friend type of thing," I said, not about to disclose GC's activities to anyone. "I've got a man unearthing Patty's life, before and after Brad, and after she skipped out of the hospital. Where she went, what she did, and who she was doing it with. She's from South Carolina, and I've got a man on that—maybe her family would be willing to share something helpful. Surely they'll want the real killer behind bars. I'm hoping my guy can turn up something that will answer the question of who really killed her."

"Sounds like you've got everything covered," Ruthie said, conveying that she didn't believe I did.

"I personally assigned the man who's tracking Patty," Fab said. "He acts like he's a mental patient, so he's a perfect fit for the job."

Brad arched his brow.

Toady, I mouthed.

He grimaced.

Toady was Brad's neighbor out in Alligator Alley, where he owned a second home. Toady discouraged trespassers of the two-legged variety from coming onto the property with the incentive of the shotgun he carried everywhere. The fascination that area held for Brad escaped everyone in the family.

"Don't forget the mental patient that Patty hung out with in the hospital. Apparently, they have coed events." Fab smiled, enjoying the telling of that tidbit.

"Patty was a model patient and kept to herself. She mostly hung out with her roommate, who she got along well with, and another patient, Leo Main," I said. "Leo checked out four months ago, and as it turns out, he relocated to California and is living with his mother. Also, there was a man who made regular visits that stopped a couple of days before she escaped. Coincidence? Who believes in those? I'm working on getting his name and picture." I wondered if I'd sufficiently impressed the lawyer, proving I could do the job. "Once I get back the complete background report on Patty, I'll check out anyone linked to her."

"Good job." Creole squeezed my shoulder.

"I have to admit you've got good information," Ruthie said. "Can I get the name and number of your information person? I might be able to throw some work his way."

Not going to happen.

Fab spoke up. "We'll give him your information, and he can contact you. He likes to maintain his anonymity."

I didn't make eye contact with Fab. We both knew GC wouldn't take her on as a client.

Chapter Five

Fab pulled up in front of the Bakery Café, finding a parking spot right in front of our favorite table, the last one at the end of the sidewalk.

"I didn't think we'd ever get here," I complained. "Coffee is the juice of life."

"I don't know where you got that nonsense from, but you need to stop." Fab grabbed my arm as I reached for the door handle. "That's Cara. Three tables down." She pointed.

We'd rescued Cara when her grandmother got arrested running an illegal dog-fighting operation and delivered her to the other set of grandparents, who lived north of Miami.

"What's Cara doing down here?" I asked. "Better yet, who's the man?" At a quick glance, he appeared to be in his fifties and short on fashion sense, in a ratty Hawaiian shirt, his safari fedora pulled down low.

"We're about to find out." Fab grabbed her phone and snapped pictures. "In case he's a runner."

It was my turn to grab her arm. "If this turns out to be some kind of weird hook-up, you will not shoot him, as much as that would be your first choice. We're calling the police."

"As long as he hasn't touched her." Fab removed her Walther from the back of her waistband and moved it to the front. The door slammed, and she was standing in front of the table in a blink.

I hustled to catch up and came up behind Fab in time to hear her say, "Hi Cara, want to introduce us?"

Deer in the headlights was a good description as Cara turned and made eye contact with Fab. Seeing me, she gave a short wave.

"This is, uh… He's a friend," Cara mumbled.

My guess was she was trying to come up with a name other than the man's real one. She got extra points, from me anyway, for not being good at being sneaky.

Close up, the man wasn't in his fifties — actually his thirties somewhere — and probably prided himself on his disguise from the thrift store. The shirt was frayed around the edges and would fit a man twice his size. Between the hat and the reflector sunglasses, he'd done a good job of covering his face.

"Does your friend have a name?" Fab casually tucked her shirt in behind the butt of her gun.

"He's too old to be a friend." I pulled out a chair and sat down next to Cara. "If you don't come up with something better than that, then I'm calling the police." I held up my phone. "I'm telling you now, if you're a perv, I may rethink calling the cops and instead call the coroner for a body bag."

The man nodded slightly to Cara.

Her blue eyes were imploring. "This is Alex, and he's a family friend. My grandparents know I'm here. He takes me out every couple of weeks to do something fun and catch up with what I'm doing, make sure I'm staying out of trouble. Like an uncle." She grimaced. "We're not doing anything wrong."

"Didn't say *you* were," I said. "You know Fab and I care about you a lot. We're just looking out for your safety."

Fab bumped the man's shoulder and, at the same time, snatched the hat off his head. "You have anything to say?"

He swayed slightly in his chair and, in a quick move, retrieved his hat from Fab's hand and jammed it back on his head, growling, low and gruff, "Get lost."

I leaned back, arms crossed, a huge smirk on my face, and stared at the man in question. I'd know that growl anywhere.

"Please, I don't want any trouble," Cara said, her anxiety on the rise. "Call my grandparents—they can straighten everything out."

"That won't be necessary." I reached over and squeezed Cara's shoulder. "I'll vouch for the man."

"You'll what?" Fab screeched. People from the tables around us turned to stare.

"My ears." I rubbed them. "Sit down. You're making a scene."

Cara giggled.

"Where do you know this old perv from?" Fab dragged a chair from another table without asking, earning a glare from the two girls sitting there.

"You wouldn't want to miss out on a free cup of coffee," I said. "I'm sure he's buying."

"You'd be wrong," he growled.

"You could be a little nicer. If Fab had shown up by herself, you'd be missing your nuts already," I said with a grin.

"This is my fault." Cara covered her head with her hands.

"It's all good," I reassured the pre-teen, then motioned to the waiter, ordering for Fab and me. "Refill?" I asked Cara, who shook her head. "Shall we wait for our drinks to toast finally meeting the elusive GC?"

"No!" Fab squealed and leaned forward, almost nose to nose with the man. GC held up his hands to ward her off. "A few wardrobe tips, and you just might be... acceptable."

"Now there's a compliment," I said.

"I've seen him all cleaned up, and he's hot," Cara vouched.

The server showed up, dropping off our drinks. I took a long sip of my iced latte and sighed.

"Your number will be disconnected tonight," GC barked.

"Oh, get over yourself," I said. "It was bound to happen sooner or later. Saves Fab and I from setting a trap."

"Your secret is safe," Fab told him. "Which is what exactly? You have a first name?"

Fab and Cara laughed.

"Great, I'm being ganged up on now. You two can go."

Fab leaped out of her chair and snapped a close-up of GC. Ready for him, she jumped back as his hand shot out to grab the phone.

"What the hell?" GC roared, kicking back his chair. "Delete it, now!"

"You two are making a scene. Half the outside diners are staring." I jumped up and pulled Cara with me. "If you take another step, I'll nick you in the butt."

"You'd get life," GC snapped.

Fab pocketed her camera and headed for the car, ignoring GC's shouted, "Get back here."

I stepped in front of GC, giving Fab plenty of time to get the doors locked, and turned to Cara. "You've got Fab and I on speed dial. Don't hesitate—ever—to call one of us." I turned GC. "Talk to you soon."

"I wouldn't count on that."

"Ignore me and I'll hunt you down." That was a threat I wasn't sure I could follow through on, but it garnered me a creepy smile. "As for your secret..." I locked my lips with an imaginary key.

Cara and I did a convoluted handshake that she had to slow down so I could keep up. I got to the car the same time as the waiter, who handed Fab one of their signature pink boxes through the window. I suspected cookies for the guys.

Fab deposited the box in the back, then turned to stare over the steering wheel. "Where did those two disappear to?" She craned her neck as she pulled out, scanning the sidewalk, and drove slowly, surveying the parking spaces. No one was coming or going or hanging out in their car.

I knelt on the seat, peering out the back window. "Now that's impressive."

Fab humphed. "I planned to get his license tag and a description of the car."

"GC's good—he's got a few tricks up his sleeve. Had you figured out and pulled his disappearing act at the first opportunity."

"How are we going to find him now?"

"Whatever we decide, we won't be breaking the trust we have with Cara to do it."

Fab turned at the corner and headed back to the restaurant, grabbing the same parking spot. She snatched cash out of the ashtray. "Be right back." She jumped out and flagged down the server that usually waited on us when we sat outside.

Their chat lasted less than a minute. Then she handed him money, and he waved as she walked back and slid behind the wheel. "GC's a regular. Usually to-go."

"My guess is he won't be back anytime soon."

Chapter Six

Fab turned north on the Overseas, so we weren't going home. I should've known, when Fab lured me out with the offer of coffee, that she had something else on her agenda.

"I'm not sure where you're going," I said, having the sinking feeling she was dragging me to a job and would *surprise* me when we got there. "You need to turn around and take me home. You didn't book my time, and I'm busy with my own business."

Sheer exasperation poured through her fists clenching the steering wheel. Instead of slowing, she hit the gas, speeding up the open highway. "It can't be an emergency or you'd have mentioned it by now. Besides, it's too late now."

"Pull over. I can get back from here."

"Now you're being totally annoying, probably on purpose."

I turned and smiled out the window, happy she hadn't called my bluff. It would have been difficult to find a ride that didn't involve my thumb. "What's the job?" I asked over my shoulder.

"It's an easy one."

I bit back a snort, not bothering to remind her that there was no such thing as an easy case.

"You're riding along because you wouldn't want me going by myself, which I'm certain I don't have to remind you I promised Didier I wouldn't do."

Ignoring her, I pressed my face against the glass, which was another of her pet peeves and a surefire way to make her get to the good stuff.

Fab blew out a sigh loud enough to be heard across traffic. "We're on the way to Miami Beach, one of your favorites." She smiled when I turned my attention back to her. "Mr. Worth is due back tomorrow and expects a full report on what I've found out about his thieving girlfriend. I'm paying Reva Lee a visit; *maybe* I can broker a compromise."

"Not to be a downer but good luck. She's got her mitts on three million dollars—my guess is she's not letting go except under extreme duress. I thought you were dumping this case in Toady's lap."

"I can't send Toady to an upscale condo building; he'd stick out and garner unwanted attention. And even if he managed a meeting with Reva, he doesn't have the authority to negotiate."

Fab merged onto the Turnpike, staying out of the fast lane for once and avoiding a high-speed game of bumper tag between two sports cars.

"Your scenario sounds above board, but that's

assuming Reva answers the door and is open to your plan. I'm certain I already know the answer to my next question, but humor me—if she's not home?"

"I'll use my key."

"I don't believe I've ever heard a lockpick referred to as a key."

"Having thought this through..." Fab hesitated.

I rolled my eyes. Knowing her as well as I did, I knew she was currently coming up with an additional contingency plan or two. "What's my role?" Creole hated criminal activity, and I shuddered to think what his reaction would be. Not good. I'd have to tell him, as that was the kind of relationship we had and I wasn't about to mess it up with sneakiness.

"Stay in the car. The cops show up, message me and don't come to my rescue. I might surprise both of us and not use that *key* of mine." Fab glared at the car that cut her off. If the Hummer had steel bars on the front, the driver would be flying through the air down the off-ramp.

I stared as the white sandy beach rolled by. "If I were into condo living, this would be perfect—lots of shops and restaurants and a short walk to the beach."

Fab pulled into the parking lot of a giant high-rise, finding a spot in the visitor section.

"I'm surprised this joint isn't gated," I said,

looking around.

"There's not a lot of crime down here. Occasional car theft. They do have security — it rolls by in a golf cart."

"One last thing. While you're riding up in the elevator, think about marriage and happy ever after. Make your decisions with Didier in mind."

"Ten minutes." Fab slid out, grabbing my new sun hat, which she hadn't asked to use. She adjusted the brim to cover her face, checked her reflection in the glass, and dashed off with a thumbs up.

I watched as she used her "universal" security card to get into the building and thought back to lying in bed and telling Creole about the case. Even he was surprised by the amount of gold that Worth had on hand and his stupidity in revealing the combo. "Must have been some wild sex." Not knowing whether Worth kept his gold in bars or coin, we'd looked up the general specifications for each. No matter which one, or both, it had taken some work to haul it off.

Waiting was a practiced art that I hadn't perfected yet. I played with my phone but mostly ticked off the minutes staring at the dash clock. Late! And no sign of Fab. My phone buzzed. The message read, "Five more."

Reva Lee must be at home, and they were in negotiations. For what? Reva gives the gold back, and Mr. Worth doesn't call the cops? Or worse, she doesn't and she disappears without a trace.

He must have crossed the cops off his list or Fab wouldn't be here. And if he wanted Reva to disappear, he'd have yet another person on that list. A killer Fab wasn't, and she wouldn't send someone else to do it. And I knew Toady well enough to know he'd only shoot in self-defense.

Fab came through the glass doors with one minute to spare. Turning, she waved and crossed the sidewalk to the SUV. I unlocked the doors, and she slid behind the wheel.

Fab pulled out onto Ocean Boulevard, and I gave the glistening blue water one last look, wanting to go for a walk. I knew I had no chance of getting Fab to pull over.

"Reva's door stood open. What a mess." Fab shuddered. "Not tossed either. A flat-out pig."

I snapped my fingers.

"You're so impatient." She tossed her long brown mane in annoyance. "Back to my story." She tapped her chin as though she'd forgotten. "Stuck my head in the door and sniffed for telltale dead body signs before calling out."

Hideous stink. I scrunched up my nose.

"The maintenance guy came out of the bedroom, a middle-aged man full of information. Reva skipped," Fab said in a ta-da voice. "She up and left, and based on the date she vacated, she hit the road the day before Mr. Worth discovered his missing stash."

"Mr. Helpful have any clue where Reva went?"

Fab shook her head. "Judging by the way the woman left the place, she didn't leave a forwarding. I was allowed to take pictures of every room." She beamed. "Reva wasn't attached to her possessions, tossing quite a lot on the floor."

"When you steal millions, you can afford to buy new."

"Reva was renting the place and had a six-month lease that was about to expire. Quiet, kept to herself, and Mr. Helpful didn't recall seeing her at the pool or in the exercise room."

"How much did that info cost Mr. Worth?" I asked.

"Made an interesting deal."

"I bet," I murmured.

"It is," she insisted. "He got two hundred for the info and allowing me free access to the unit and an additional hundred to promise that, if he remembers anything, he'll call."

"Don't make deals like that with my money."

Fab ignored my sarcasm and picked up her phone. After punching in a number, she said, "I've got a job for you. Come to my office in the morning."

"Mr. Worth isn't going to be happy with a 'Reva skipped' report."

"That's why I'm siccing Toady on her tail. Here's where I'm drawing the line—when he locates her, he'll surveil her until Mr. Worth shows up to take care of his own problem."

Chapter Seven

Fab sped through town, bypassing the turn to our street without even a sideways glance. "I've got one more case, and I'm hoping you'll go with me."

"It would have been nice if you'd asked me before you blew by the Cove city limits."

"I knew you'd say yes." Her smile was so shifty, most people would do a double take.

"Your manipulation is going to come back to haunt you."

"We're doing a welfare check," Fab said.

"We? Now?"

"My client, Charles Newton, has a son that he's worried about. Name's Globe."

"Globe? Your client a stoner? Surprised the kid wasn't named Fig."

"Are you finished?"

I flourished my hand in a way that she took as a yes.

"He hasn't been able to reach Globe; his phone is turned off. Easy job—drive by, knock, and leave."

"You need to stop using the word easy," I grouched. "How old is this person, twelve? Can't be because a kid would notice their phone's off within seconds and turn it back on."

"He's a grown man, but his father worries when he doesn't stay in touch. He's a concerned parent."

"So he hires an investigator because..." I squinted at her, waiting for her to fill in the blank.

"He's rich and doesn't want to do it himself, I guess. Besides, Globe is a recluse. I'm to tell him to stay in touch if he doesn't enjoy these impromptu visits."

It was a beautiful sunny day, and instead of picking up shells on the beach, I'd spent the better part of the day on the highway between Miami and Plantation Key, where Fab had just veered off, handing me a piece of notepaper with an address scribbled on it.

"At least it's not in the middle of the weeds for a change," she said.

It was a few blocks down to the water. She turned on the last side street, easily finding the address. The houses all had long driveways, their front sides facing the beach and nothing to block the water view. The short wooden fence that ran across the driveway stood open, and she turned in, checking out the large property, and drove past the volleyball court on the right. An Olympic-size pool could be seen around the front.

Fab parked and motioned for me to follow,

pausing to peer through the glass of the back door, which opened into a small entry that curved out of sight to a set of steps off to one side. Instead of knocking, she made her way over to the brick pathway that ran along the side of the house and around to the front of the cream-color two-story house. It had been designed so that every window had a spectacular view of the open water. Fab rang the bell at the ornate front door, which was flanked by a series of glass French doors that could be pushed open to bring the outside in.

To the right, the doors opened into a gym with enough equipment to satisfy the pickiest workout enthusiast. On the opposite side of the door, an open space revealed a massive living room, dining room, and a glimpse of the kitchen off to the side.

If I had my way, I'd pull up a chair, sit down with an iced tea and a book in front of the pool, and enjoy the view. The patio was protected by a portico that ran the length of the house, and the backyard had a square of well-maintained green grass that was set up for a game of croquet.

While I relished the sunshine and water, Fab walked around the house, peering into windows. Soon she was back at the door, this time knocking — some would say banging — which got no response.

Standing back and shading my eyes with my hand, I momentarily forgot to be helpful and instead checked out the high-end finishes on the exterior. I didn't like the idea of pulling a peeping Tom act, especially if there was any chance I'd get caught staring in the windows. Moving closer, I pushed my sunglasses up, peering into the living room. Out of the corner of my eye, a movement from the dining room area caught my attention.

A person occupied one of the chairs, slumped sideways. Napping? From this angle, I couldn't make out whether it was a man or woman. My neck hair stood up in warning. If it was the man we'd come to check on, it couldn't be good news. Out of patience, Fab cop-knocked.

"Fab…"

"You're trespassing," a man decked out in "tropical cowboy" shouted as he came around the corner from the side of the house with the volleyball court. Shirtless, in board shorts and cowboy boots, he captured my attention, as did the holster strapped around his waist holding a pair of six-shooters, his hand on one of the butts in a draw stance.

"Globe?" Fab asked, pairing it with the smile she reserved for old men. "Your father wanted me to stop by and ask you to call. He was worried when he wasn't able to get ahold of you."

Certain that Globe hadn't seen me, as he'd passed me without a second look, I removed my Glock from my waistband, thankful that I'd chosen to wear a skirt and could tuck it into a fold unseen. Another movement from inside caught my attention. The person in the chair—a blond woman—had lifted her head, and there was no mistaking the gag wrapped around her mouth.

What the heck had we stepped into?

"Thanks for stopping by," Globe said amiably. "I'll give Dad a call."

I crept up behind Globe, sticking the muzzle of my gun in his back. "Get your hand off the damn gun. Unholster that thing and drop it to the ground."

The moment his hands flew up in the air, Fab drew her Walther. "What the heck?" she hissed.

"One wrong move, and I'll blow your arm off," I threatened, my tone letting the man know I wasn't bluffing. "I'm not going to tell you again to drop the holster." I turned to Fab. "There's a woman inside, and since she's gagged, I'm certain she's not here of her own free will."

Globe made a move for his gun, and Fab shot him through the forearm.

"Bitch," he hissed. He fumbled with the buckle of the holster, grunting. When he finally got it undone, it fell to the concrete.

"No name-calling." I shook my finger at him. "You've got bigger problems. If a neighbor heard the shot, the cops are on their way." I turned to Fab. "You need to call a paramedic."

"I'll deal with this." Fab closed the distance

between her and Globe, kicking the holster away. She picked it up and slung it over her shoulder. Glancing in my direction, she said. "You go check on what's going on inside." She pulled out her phone, punching in a number.

Entering the house, I crossed the wood floor to where the woman was tied to a chair, and untied the red bandana used for a gag. "You okay?"

She worked her jaw and nodded.

Examining the knots on her wrists, I knew that I didn't stand a chance of untying them. Globe had secured them tightly with no wiggle room. I'd need a knife, which had me wincing and rethinking the idea.

"Do you have a name?" I asked.

"Carly," she coughed. "You're not going to hurt him, are you?"

The last thing I wanted to hear was an excuse for Globe's behavior. "Fab," I yelled. "Your expertise is needed in here pronto."

"You don't understand. We have a special relationship. We play games, and this is one of those times." Carly's cheeks were turning pink.

It took a minute to click. "What's your safe word?" Mother wasn't the only one to sneak a peek at one of Fab's naughty books.

Carly didn't know what I was talking about and didn't bother to hide it.

"I'm not going to lecture you on your choices, but there are some things you should study up on before indulging in."

Carly didn't bother to make eye contact as she said, "I love Globe, and I know he feels the same. I don't want any police called." She added, "I have warrants and don't want to go to jail."

Well, swell!

Fab led a docile Globe through the French doors by his good arm. The other arm had paper towels wrapped around it, a find from the outdoor kitchen. His whole demeanor change had me suspicious.

"I have no skill untying knots." I pointed to Carly.

"Got Mr. Newton on the phone, filled him in, and he's on his way." Fab pushed Globe forward, since he'd dug in his feet suddenly.

After a slight hesitation, he broke into a run, straight to Carly, and threw himself at her feet. "Carly, don't leave me."

Fab whipped out a miniature switchblade. When she released the blade, Globe looked up and yelled, "Noo." He threw his arms around Carly.

"Calm down," Fab yelled. "I'm only going to cut the knots."

"I'll do it." Globe held out his hand.

"Get back," Fab ordered. "Carly gets so much as a scratch, and it will be due to your histrionics." She moved behind the woman's chair, waiting for him to back up, which he did, sort of, his good hand clenching the material of her pants.

Fab sliced through the knots, throwing the remnants of the rope on the floor.

Carly gathered Globe's head in her lap, stroking his hair.

Fab pulled me aside while the lovebirds spoke in quiet tones. "Globe lost his wife last year and flipped out. He was doing well with his recovery before he met Carly, who's a dead ringer for the deceased."

"During any part of this little adventure, did you or Mr. Newton wonder whether Carly's safety was in jeopardy?"

"Mr. Newton assured me that Globe's harmless."

The roar of a helicopter could be heard overhead. Fab and I watched out the window as the chopper landed on the volleyball court. The door opened, stairs came down, and an older gentleman got off first, followed by two other men, one with a small medical bag.

I sank into a chair that backed up to the wall next to a credenza, a prime spot to watch what would unfold next in the reunion of father and son while staying out of the way. Fab and her client met at the door and conferred in a tone that wasn't meant to be overheard.

The two men planted themselves on either side of Globe. One reached down and tried to pull him up off the floor, which turned difficult, as the man decided not to cooperate. "I'm not going anywhere without Carly," he whined, his arms wrapped around her legs.

It was clear the man had had enough of Globe's resistance. He leaned over and whispered in the other man's ear. Globe registered shock, then stood and claimed a chair next to Carly, who patted his hand. The man I assumed to be the doctor unwrapped the paper towel and checked the wound.

I overheard him say, "Clean exit."

He cleaned and bandaged Globe's arm, and while Globe was occupied in conversation with Carly, the doctor whipped out a hypodermic needle and injected him. Globe yipped and struggled, held fast by the other man. After a minute, he calmed. Each man grabbed an elbow and led him out to the waiting helicopter.

Another man strode around the back of the house. Judging by the uniform, he was a chauffeur... or resembled one anyway. It wasn't his first visit, as he helped himself to a soda and leaned against the patio table, downing half the can.

It surprised me when the helicopter took off with Globe and the two men, but without Carly or Mr. Newton. Carly sobbed, apparently caught off guard at being left behind.

Mr. Newton stepped away from Fab to take a call that lasted seconds, then crossed the room to talk to Carly.

I beelined to Fab's side. "Carly?"

"She's going to be fine. Mr. Newton promised

to help her with her problems. He's taking care of everything—getting her a lawyer, and the doctor that just left recommend she see a psychiatrist."

"Not that I don't trust your client..." Which I didn't. "But I'm going to speak to Carly. I want to know that she's agreeing to whatever Newton has planned of her own volition and isn't being coerced."

As I walked away, I heard Mr. Newton ask Fab, "Can you trust her?"

"You okay?" I asked Carly, sitting next to her.

"I'm fine." She twisted a lock of blond hair around her finger and tugged. "Mr. Newton says he can keep me out of jail, and all I have to do is not tell anyone about knowing his son or what happened here today. I'm good with that. I didn't want to agree not to contact Globe again, but I'd rather have my freedom."

Mr. Newton appeared in front of us and held his hand out to Carly. "Come, my dear, the limo is here." She stood, and he hooked his arm around her shoulders and led her outside and around the side of the house.

His paternal tone caught me off guard, and I wondered if he was sincere. If he wasn't, he'd perfected it to a tee. I might as well have not been standing there for all he acknowledged me—not so much as the slightest glance.

"I've finished locking up, so we're free to go," Fab said. On the way down the brick path, she

paused. "I don't think this needs to be said, but your appearance caught Mr. Newton off guard and he wanted me to stress that the confidentiality agreement I signed extends to you also."

"The only exception would be if Carly's name shows up in the news followed by a story about how she met with an unfortunate accident. You're lucky I can't swing you around by your hair for all the details you left out on this job."

Fab tossed her hair in my direction, laughed, and scooted out of my reach, running to the car.

Chapter Eight

"Not talking to me?" Fab sniffed as she headed back toward the Cove.

"Hard time shaking off how sad that case of yours was."

Someone laid on the horn and had me craning my neck around the headrest to see out the driver's side window. The limo next to us looked close enough to take out the entire side of the SUV.

"Is that driver drunk?" I asked in disgust.

Fab signaled and pulled onto the shoulder. "I'll be right back." She slid from behind the wheel. The limo had already pulled in front of us, the driver getting out and walking around to the passenger side to open the door. His jacket was open, holster visible. Fab stuck her head in the limo.

Another client? I groaned. *Who holds a business meeting alongside a busy highway?*

The conversation was short, and when Fab came back to the SUV, the limo driver continued to stand by the open door. Fab opened the driver's side door, reached behind the seat, and slid out her purse. She grabbed her phone from the console and tossed it in. "Don't worry. I'll catch up with you at home."

Fab slammed the door as I screamed, "Get back here." I reached over, and blasted the horn, which neither Fab nor the driver acknowledged as she climbed into the limo.

Having learned from the best, I retrieved my phone and captured a pic of the license plate as the limo driver slid back behind the wheel. Unhooking the seatbelt, I crawled over into the driver's seat.

"When I get my hands on her..." I merged into traffic and sped after the limo. It had a head start that I planned to remedy.

Who she was driving down the road with... I had no clue. I knew full well that if the shoes were reversed, she wouldn't let me disappear into the Keys. By now, she would've nudged the bumper of the limo a few times, each time with more pressure applied to the gas pedal. Speeding up behind the limo, I hit the brakes, planning to tailgate and hopefully not cause an accident.

The driver signaled, getting off on a side road, making a loop around, and heading back in the direction we came. Several miles later, he turned off again, this time winding through a residential airport community and pulling onto the landing strip a few feet from a helicopter. The security arm went up, and I followed close behind, parked next to the limo and jumped out.

Fab climbed gracefully out of the back, one

long leg after the other. "I told you…" she said in a huff.

"If you think you're going anywhere with whomever is in that car, think again." I held up my phone. "The license number has been forwarded to Creole. And guess what? He's on the phone right now." I'd hit speed dial before I got out of the car and knew he could hear me. "He has instructions to call the cops if he hears me scream."

A dark-haired man climbed out of the limo, towering over Fab by a foot. His blues eyes intently checked me over from head to toe.

"I warned you she wouldn't go away," Fab told the man.

Checking him out in the same bold way he did me, I realized the face looked familiar. A longtime client? Sixties… maybe… being in tip-top shape made it hard to tell. If Didier were here, he'd admire the tailor-made suit.

The man barked at Fab in French, and she laughed. Hooking her arm in his, she nudged him forward.

"Madison Westin." Fab's smile was bigger than before. "I'd like you to meet my father, Caspian Dumont." She kissed his cheek. "He knows all about you."

That makes one of us.

"Is it true that you've been instrumental in helping reign in my daughter's wild side?" There was no hiding the smug amusement in his voice.

"It's a full-time job and a thankless one."

He threw his head back and laughed.

"Excuse us." I grabbed Fab's hand, jerking her out of hearing distance. "Is this man really your father, or is this some weird client story you're concocting?" I already knew the answer, as father and daughter shared many of the same striking features. It would've been hard not to notice all the ways Fab resembled her father. "Dumont? Merceau?"

"It's a long story, and one I should've shared a long time ago." Fab sighed. "Caspian's in town for a few hours, and I'd like to spend them with him before he leaves."

"You're not setting foot in any direction until you tell me where you're going."

"Caspian purchased an island about ten miles off shore to be near his only daughter. We're helicoptering over."

"What do I tell Didier? If he calls, and I'm sure he will, I'm not lying to him." I grimaced, realizing I'd forgotten that Creole was still on the phone. I lifted it to my ear. "Babe, I'll call you back when I get in the car."

"Don't you dare disconnect." Creole unleashed a low, rumbling growl. "Just let Fab think you did."

I blew a kiss through the phone, and Fab rolled her eyes.

"Didier knows about Caspian. In fact, they've met several times and get along quite well. I called Didier in the limo, and he's on his way. He'll be here in about an hour, and the helicopter will be waiting."

Mr. Dumont had run out of patience, judging by his body language and tapping foot.

Fab grabbed my hand and pulled me back over to her father.

"It's a pleasure to meet you, Madison Westin." Mr. Dumont leaned forward and kissed my cheek.

"And you, Mr. Dumont."

"Please call me Caspian."

"You'll be home when?" I asked Fab.

"Didier and I are spending the night. We'll be home after we have breakfast with Caspian."

"You know I prefer Papa," he grumped.

"If you're not home by noon and I haven't received a call, I'm calling the police."

Caspian appeared amused at my bold warning, threat, however he wanted to take it. It was a promise.

"Really, Madison." Fab mimicked her father's disgruntled tone.

Ignoring her, I turned to Caspian. "You're lucky that our roles aren't reversed. Fab would've shot you by now and asked questions while you lay on the ground, blood coating the gravel."

Caspian laughed heartily. "That's my girl." He pulled Fab to his side, kissing her on the cheek. "When we meet again, Madison Westin, you can introduce me to the fine cuisine of Jake's and a round of poker." His eyes twinkled in amusement.

"Once my mother finds out, she'll be organizing a big dinner to introduce you to Fab's American family."

"I'm looking forward to it," Caspian said. He draped his arm across Fab's shoulders, leading her to the steps of the helicopter.

I watched as the duo climbed inside and the blades started whirling. The limo pulled out and headed to the exit. I got behind the wheel of my SUV, putting the phone to my ear. "You hang up?"

"Of course not," Creole said. "I'm thinking there's material for my next book in this."

"They're taking off." I grabbed a couple of pictures of the number on the tail. "You hear all that?"

"All the time we've known Fab and Didier, and not one mention of their families. Didier's got a lot of nerve calling Fab secretive. You think this story of hers is on the up and up?"

"Fab would be annoyed to be asked that question, but that comes from being creative with the truth."

Creole laughed. "Creative, huh?"

The helicopter could still be seen in the distance, cruising over the water. I started the engine and headed back to the highway.

"Side by side, it's impossible to miss the

resemblance. The open adoration when she smiled at him. I believe that he's her father and not some pervy client. Watching them together, I felt a pang, missing my own father, and I was in junior high when he died."

"Not having had a great dad, I always envied other kids for having a good relationship with theirs. I haven't thought about him much since his death. All my good memories are thanks to my mom." After a pause, he asked, "You headed this way?"

"I'll pick up food. You make the drinks, and I'm thinking hot tub," I said in a husky whisper.

"Done. Drive safe."

Chapter Nine

"I love you."

"Now that's the way I like to start the morning." I pressed into Creole's chest. "Love you back." We'd spent the night at Creole's and awoke to the morning sun glistening off the water, shining through the pocket doors.

"Thanks for including me in yesterday's adventure. Never a dull moment with Fab."

Fab had called the night before to let me know that she and Didier were out on Caspian's island and not to worry.

"It keeps me from getting in trouble." I mimicked his frown. "You know, the kind where you only half believe me and then remind yourself that I don't lie to you. Mostly anyway."

"Mostly." He nipped my neck.

"Who's ever one hundred percent?" I flashed a teasing smile.

Creole's phone dinged with a message alert. He reached over and grabbed the phone off the bedside table. "You up to having dinner with Fab and Didier?"

* * *

From the start, it had been established that whoever extended the invitation got to pick the restaurant. It surprised both Creole and I when Didier chose a restaurant in Marathon that was nestled around a marina, boasting of fresh catches by local fisherman, since both of us assumed we'd be staying local.

Entering the open-air restaurant, the first thing that caught our attention was the view of Florida Bay and the Gulf of Mexico. A cool breeze rippled off the open water through the wide-open space. Creole spotted the couple at a table on the deck that overlooked the water's edge and stopped the server who'd just left the table to add a margarita and a beer to the drink order.

Fab and Didier were smiling at one another, holding hands. Maybe he wasn't the last to know that Fab's father had moved to the Keys.

As we sat down, a man showed up at the table, introducing himself as the owner, and bent over Fab's hand, kissing it. He announced that the chef had prepared a special menu at the request of Caspian, who'd spoken to the man directly, and with a wave of his hands, our drinks were set in front of us.

"When Caspian heard that we were meeting the lovely Madison for dinner, he recommended this restaurant, promising first-class service," Didier said.

"This is fun," I said. "Can't beat this view. I'll have to tell Mother; she'd love it here."

Creole raised his glass. "To family."

"We spent the night out on the island." Fab shared a secret smile with Didier. "So beautiful — you would love it — and the views are amazing and endless. Didier and I talked about spending the day lazing around, but we both had to get back to work."

"Will we be meeting your mother?" I asked.

"That's a long story." Fab sighed. "Caspian..." She half-laughed. "He hates it when I call him that. He prefers Papa, and my telling him I'm too old to call him that gets me a stern look." Didier squeezed her shoulder. "Caspian is my biological father. Shortly after I was born, my parents divorced, and one day when I was snooping through private papers — even at a young age, I didn't mind my own business — I found my original birth certificate, naming Caspian Dumont and not the man I thought of as my father. I confronted Mother, and she informed me that Caspian was dead. I'm not sure why I didn't believe her. I tried asking questions, but Mother shut me down and told me to be happy that I had two parents who loved me. After all, a name on a birth certificate does not make a father and I was a lucky girl."

"You tracked him down, didn't you?" Feeling sad for her, I managed a smile.

Didier hugged her tighter, and from the naked adoration on his face, this wasn't the first he was hearing the story.

"Overly inquisitive, the nuns used to say." Fab squeezed Didier's hand. "Then they would add, 'Nothing good will come from your bad habit of snooping.' I'm certain they congratulated themselves, thinking they broke me of the habit, because over time, I stopped getting into trouble. What I did was hone my skills, got sneakier, craftier. I made a promise to myself as a pre-teen that I'd find out everything there was to know about my father."

A server cleared the center of the table, and another set down plates in front of us. A third delivered a platter of appetizers that looked mouth-watering and came close to taking up the entire table. The first one came back with a tray of drink refills.

"Smells so yummy." I eyed the shrimp, which was my favorite, and was happy that the squid and octopus—foods that Fab and Didier savored—were on the opposite end. Thankfully, the octopus's head was turned away so it wasn't looking at me. "If there's a main course coming, I hope they have doggie bags."

Fab snorted. "You mean to-go containers."

"Call it what you want as long as I don't have to stuff the food in my pockets." I took a bite of shrimp and almost sighed at how delicious the stuffing tasted.

"I never ate leftovers before I met you," Didier said, amusement in his eyes. "Now I'm hooked."

"Back to Fab's story," I said. "When did you

find out Caspian was alive?"

"High school." There was a sadness in Fab's eyes that she blinked away. "Finding out spun my sheltered life around, and I morphed into a wild child. Before, I'd managed to maintain my good girl image despite always pushing the rules; after, I gave up the pretense. To this day, my parents don't know what brought about the change." She downed her martini and held it up for a refill. "I couldn't wait to go to college. Freedom at last."

"How did you orchestrate your meeting with Caspian?" Creole asked.

"I hired my first information specialist to find Caspian, paying an exorbitant amount of cash. He found out that Caspian would be attending a film festival in Greece and hosting a party aboard his yacht."

"Let me guess," I said and smiled impishly at her. "Sans invitation—I mean, who needs one of those?—you wiggled on board, right under the eyes of watchful security guards that didn't have their eyes where they ought to."

"I had an invitation." At my raised eyebrow, she said, "One of the women found that hers had gone missing and made a scene. They escorted her away, and I snuck on board." She wiped a non-existent tear away with an unrepentant smile. "I made myself comfortable on the couch in his locked office and dozed off. Woke up when the door opened and slammed shut. He had his lips all over a young thing and was about to have his way with her on his desk, having shoved everything on the floor, when I cleared my throat, practically having to yell, and interrupted the tryst."

Creole choked out a laugh. "That was embarrassing. Once your papa got his clothes back on, then what happened?"

"You're so rude. It's not like he had his clothes off... although he did dispose of his shirt in record time." Fab blushed. "He pulled down the woman's skirt and sent her on her way, which she didn't take well. The door had barely closed when he crossed the room and pulled me into a crushing hug. No introductions necessary. We started talking and have stayed in touch ever since."

I looked down and chuckled, not able to imagine a more uncomfortable scene... unless... maybe I could, but I wisely didn't voice my thoughts.

The appetizer platter was whisked away and replaced by another, full of various grilled fishes and vegetables.

"Is there dessert?" I asked, trying not to groan.

"The chef's desserts are award-winning." The server smiled.

Creole leaned over and whispered, "Just take little bites and save the rest for breakfast."

I took Creole's suggestion and so did Fab, taking extra-small servings of everything.

"Caspian told her later that he wanted to hug and throttle her at the same time." Didier laughed.

"I'm sure he's had those feelings again since," Creole said.

"It's not like I planned to barge in on an intimate moment. I can't tell you how many times I rehearsed my introduction. Never pictured it the way it happened." Fab grimaced. "Caspian recognizing me instantly was the best feeling. The next was finding out that he'd kept track of my daily activities, grades... He claimed to know before Mother — and I believe him — that instead of signing up for ballet classes, I'd signed up for fencing." Fab shook her head as though throwing off an unpleasant memory. "Mother confronted me. It started out, 'How dare you...' and the lecture about unladylike behavior came next. My punishment was missing the last two classes and not being allowed to participate in the exhibition." She made a Z with her pretend sword.

"Do your other parents know that you found Caspian?" I asked.

"They have no idea," Fab said. "I didn't want to hurt them because I knew it would change our relationship, and in all honesty, it already had, the day I discovered Caspian was alive and I'd been lied to."

"You're such a part of the Westin family, and yet, I know so little about your family. I haven't wanted to pry."

"Secrets divide a family, and it was just easier not to think about it. It's not like they live in the next neighborhood over." Fab tipped her glass at me.

"Ideally, I'd like for you not to be estranged from your family. But I've never regretted you barreling into my life and taking over."

"I'd come clean with them now..." Fab smiled at Didier and brushed his hair back. "You're such a good influence. But Caspian still has feelings for Mother and doesn't want her hurt, so we've kept our relationship a secret. He also fears a 'him or them' choice and doesn't want to cause me that kind of pain. I discussed it with Didier and, with his support, decided to wait until the time is right. And if that never happens, that's fine, too."

The waiter came back to the table, clearing away dishes. When he picked up the platter, Didier said, "Would you pack up the extra food?" He cocked his head and winked at me. Another platter replaced the old one, along with more plates.

A man at the next table let out an ear-splitting belch. Several heads turned his way, and once people recovered from the shock, they laughed.

"Can I do that?" I asked innocently.

Fab's horrified face rewarded me for that prank. "You do, and I'll tell Madeline."

Creole and Didier laughed.

"How do you get along with your prospective father-in-law?" Creole asked Didier.

"Caspian and I hit it off immediately. We have real estate development in common, and I've enjoyed our talks and appreciate his perspective."

"They get along great." Fab leaned over and kissed Didier's cheek. "They've developed their own friendship, in which I think they trade ideas on how to keep me in line."

Creole roared with laughter. "How's that working out?"

Didier shot him a dirty look. "As you well know, some days aren't as frustrating as others." He winked at Fab.

"When did you meet Caspian?" I asked Didier. If it was too nosey, he could tell me. It wasn't yesterday, so when?

"We met shortly after Fab moved me into her life." Didier pulled Fab close, kissing the top of her head. "I had just finished up a business meeting at a restaurant in South Beach and was about to leave when Caspian approached with three bodyguards and wanted to talk. Make sure I was good enough to even look at his daughter."

"You must have passed muster, since you're sitting here," I half-joked.

"We parted on friendly terms with a warning not to get her into any kind of trouble. I laughed it off as him being a protective father, with no clue as to the adventure my life was about to become."

"Adventure. That's one word for it," Creole said. "A lesser man never would've survived."

Slightly embarrassed that I still had a hundred questions, I figured a couple more wouldn't hurt. I'd save the rest to grill Fab another day. "How long has Caspian been living here?"

"Normally, he flies in for a day or two, and then he's off—always another meeting that demands his attention. When I told him that Didier asked me to marry him and I said yes, he briefly mentioned buying a Florida getaway, and the next thing I hear is that he inked the deal for Caspian Island. It's hard to pass up a good deal, he said. I'd been adamant that Didier and I were not moving back to France."

Creole whistled. "Nice, naming an island after yourself."

There was no doubt that there were things I hadn't known about my friend, and I wondered how much more would come out.

The waiter appeared and waited patiently for our attention. "Another drink? Coffee with dessert?"

I groaned. "I have room for mine in my purse."

The waiter laughed. "It's a platter of assorted delicacies."

"A whole platter?" I asked in awe. "So mean of you not to warn us—we could've started with the *delicacies* first."

"Ignore her," Fab said with a shake of her head. "We'll take the largest dessert and four spoons. And the rest we'll take with us. All of us have a sweet tooth."

"Want to go for a midnight run?" Creole said to Didier.

"Let's run it off in the morning."

One more question nagged at me. "How did Caspian know that you were driving the SUV?"

"How many black Hummers are there in the Keys?"

Would there come a day when I knew as much about Caspian as I'd bet he knew about me? I couldn't imagine a sit-down of questions and answers. My guess was it would be tough to get any information that he didn't want you to know out of him. A lot like his daughter.

"We should throw a party," I said. "Welcome Caspian to the Keys. Maybe we can catch everyone on a night that they'll be on their best behavior."

"Love that idea. Caspian leaves tomorrow on business. I'll pin him down on a date when he plans to be back in the Keys."

Chapter Ten

A typical morning. Fab and Didier had left for the office early, both having appointments. Fab breezed past me, not sharing a single detail. I was kissing Creole, who had one foot out the door, when my phone started ringing. I raced back through the kitchen to snatch it up off the island.

"It's Jake's." I held it up so he could see the screen.

Creole leaned against the doorframe with a "hmpf."

"There's been an incident," Kelpie whispered hoarsely. "The cops are here."

"I'll be right there." I hung up and raced back into the entry, grabbed my bag and reached inside to grab my thigh holster. All Fab's admonitions not to leave home without protection had sunk in.

Creole's eyes narrowed as he watched me strap on my gun. "I'm coming. You can give me the details in the truck."

"*Incident* is all I know."

He grabbed my hand, and we ran down the driveway.

Creole managed to get us to Jake's in record time without scaring me. When he turned into the driveway of the tiki-style bar with its thatched roof and palm trees, there were three cop cars and two ambulances parked in front. He veered around to the back and found space next to the kitchen door.

I owned the entire block, which included Fab's lighthouse, which had mysteriously shown up in the middle of the night and was now used as office space by one of her dubious friends. Junker's, an antique garden store, sat on the opposite side of the lighthouse, and Twinkie Princesses, a roach coach, sat facing the curb, advertising that they'd fry anything... if they were ever open. What they all had in common was that their rent checks were on time and the cops never showed up.

Before getting out, Creole turned my face to his. "Law enforcement is here, so try to refrain from waving your gun around. I'm sure they have everything under control."

"You just suck the fun out of everything." I drew an imaginary gun and blew on the muzzle.

He brushed my lips with a kiss. "People think you're so normal."

"In comparison to whom?" I laughed. "Fab? I win hands down. Girlfriend is going to be sorry she missed the police drama. I'll try to grab a picture or two."

Creole got out and went around to help me out. The kitchen door stood open. I poked my head around Creole, and for the first time since I took over sole ownership of the place, Cook was nowhere to be seen. Come to think of it, his truck hadn't been parked outside.

It was a straight shot down the hall to the bar, and it was empty. Voices could be heard from the interior. A uniformed officer stepped into view, his back to us.

"Kevo," I called out.

He glanced over his shoulder, turned, and met us at the bar. "That's Deputy Kevin Cory to you." He smiled slightly, his irritation lessening. "Don't come any farther." He held up his hand.

We halted at the far end, which gave us a vantage point where we could see everything going on inside the bar and out on the deck.

My manager—Doodad, aka Charles Wingate III—sat, a tad lopsided, at a table next to the jukebox, a paramedic tending to his head.

Kelpie, our newest kick-butt bartender, sat sprawled in a chair on the opposite side of the miniscule dance floor, legs spread indecently (thank goodness for tights), arms crossed, her usually happy face radiating anger. She'd been dipping into the dye bottles again, and her naturally blond hair was lit up like a rainbow.

Two stretchers rolled out the door, each with a person strapped on—a man on one, a woman on the other—and after a quick glance, I was certain I'd never seen either of them before.

"What happened?" Creole asked Kevin.

It was my lucky day. Creole and I had gotten a slow start to the morning, which meant that he was still home when the call came in. His being a retired detective afforded him a different level of respect that meant Kevin would answer his questions. Me, he'd blow off or half-ass it at best.

"Those two..." Kevin pointed to the stretchers. "Husband and wife thieves. They overstayed their welcome last night. Instead of leaving at closing, they hid out, planning to rob the place. When all attempts to get the safe open with a hammer failed, they decided to have a sleepover and hold up the first employee who arrived. That lucky person was Doodad."

"I take it Doodad took them on, hence the bandage on his forehead." I had watched as the paramedic worked on him, and he appeared to grumble the whole time.

"The man's a pain in the behind," Kevin grouched. "He's refusing to go to the hospital and get checked out. Instead, he's whining like a kid. Too bad it's illegal to gag him."

"It was illegal back when I was a cop, too," Creole said with a laugh.

"I'm certain your *friend* wouldn't enjoy your assessment of him," I reminded Kevin.

"When I leave, I'm arresting Doodad and taking him to the hospital myself," Kevin said.

"Where he'll stay until a doctor releases him."

"Am I free to get back to work or what?" Kelpie bellowed from across the room.

Kevin rolled his eyes at her.

Kelpie jumped up, kicking her chair back, and managed to catch it with her toes before it hit the middle of another officer's back. She flounced over. "If boss chick has questions, shouldn't I be the one to answer them?"

Nice hiss! I grinned at Kelpie.

"I'll take a soda," Kevin ordered.

"Anyone else want a drink—non-alcoholic?" Kelpie's voice boomed through the room. She stomped behind the bar, hips shaking with every step.

Doodad ditched the paramedic. "Water for me," he hollered as he slid onto to one of bar stools. "I suppose you're wanting details?"

Creole edged a stool closer for me to sit. Standing behind me, he wrapped his arms around me.

"I always come through the front door, and there wasn't a single clue from the outside that there'd been a break-in," Doodad said. "Later, I found out that they slept over—that won't happen again. Bastard jumped me as soon as I cleared the entry. Caught sight of the beer bottle coming my way out of the corner of my eye, courtesy of the wife, but had no time to get out of the way." Doodad downed his water bottle, capped it, and pitched it in the trash.

"Ouch." I made a face.

"I came to lying face down on the stinkin' ground, chair on my back." Doodad grimaced. "Guess the two geniuses thought that would hold me." He barked a laugh. "Only plan I could come up with involved beating the two over the head with said chair."

"Told him that was a bad idea," Kevin said.

"When do I make my entrance?" Kelpie thrust her double D's out with a huff.

"Your turn." Doodad laughed.

"Da, da, daaa…" Kelpie jumped up, her arms in a victory salute over her head. "I waltzed in the door." She twirled. "Got me an eyeful and went into ninja mode." She air-boxed, kicking out one leg, then the other.

I winced as she came close to taking out a rack of glasses.

"Connected with the woman's midsection." Kelpie gave a demonstration, then grabbed her middle, making a groaning noise, acting out both sides of the drama. "The woman crumbled to the floor. Not only couldn't she stand, she had a hard time sucking in air."

"Isn't this where you invited her to 'bring it on, bitch'?" Doodad reminded her.

"If only she'd stood up…" Kelpie appeared miffed.

"Her partner?" Creole asked, amusement in his eyes. "Where was he in all this? Sneaking out the door?"

"His story is that Kelpie sucker-punched him, even though he had his hands up in surrender," Kevin said.

Kelpie leaned over the bar top, offering a bird's eye view of her assets all the way to her navel to anyone who cared to take a peek... or openly stare. "*I told you* I feared for my life and was only defending myself."

I'd never seen a man who could lose his train of thought over a pair of breasts faster than Kevin.

"Not a scratch on you," he observed after a moment.

Frightened. I managed to swallow my snicker. Most people would shake in their flip-flops with Kelpie bearing down on them, not the other way around.

"I bruised my knuckles, if that counts." Kelpie brought her hand to her lips, kissing them. Kevin staring.

"I'm surprised those two aren't dating," Creole whispered in my ear.

"Doodad, you're going to have to schedule extra help for the next week," I directed. "When word gets out that two people were brutally slain at Jake's and there was blood everywhere, it will be standing room only. Especially on Kelpie's shifts, since she's the heroine."

Creole and Kevin groaned.

"Anyone die?" A regular scooted through the door and up to the bar. "I'll have me some breakfast — a beer." He slapped his hand on the counter.

"Get out," Kevin yelled and pointed to the door.

The man flashed him the finger and hotfooted it out the door.

"A friend?" Creole laughed.

"Some days..." Kevin said irritably.

"How long are we going to be closed?" I asked. "Do I have time to get out the 'Active Crime Scene' sign that I keep in the office? That won't keep the drinkers away, though — they'll just insist on a table being moved out front so they can sit in the parking lot, guzzling a beer or six."

"How about 'This Rathole is Closed'?" Kevin laughed until he noticed he was the only one enjoying his humor. "Once we're done here, you'll be able to reopen. Shouldn't be much longer."

Before I could tell Kevin to stuff it, he got called away by the other officer. "I'm happy you called the cops," I said to Kelpie.

She shook her head, mouthing, *Not me.*

Doodad raised his hand. "It was me. I wouldn't have if they'd made a run for the door."

"All it would take is for one to die in the parking lot. Then try explaining why you didn't bother to make a phone call while you're on your way to jail," Creole said, letting Doodad know what he thought of that stupid idea.

"You okay?" I asked Kelpie. "We can flag the paramedic down before he leaves."

"I'm fine." She flexed her muscles. "Don't have to hit the gym after work now. No need to worry, I got this handled. The other cop told me we'd be able to reopen today. I'll get the place cleaned up, toss a little tomato juice on the floor, and hope it dries looking like blood."

"Just when I was about to say how happy I was that, in addition to no bullet holes in need of repair, there's no blood that needs cleaning up, necessitating a call to 'crime scene cleaner' dude," I said.

Creole stared up at the ceiling.

I nudged him. "If you see a patch, it's probably a bullet hole."

"You should've gotten up there and dated each one and wrote the shooter's name," Kelpie suggested.

"Next time," Doodad said with a laugh.

Creole shook his head. "Is this you two cooking up new entertainment? Not happening. Got it?" His blue eyes turned icy and bored into Doodad and Kelpie until they agreed. He didn't notice that Kelpie had one hand behind her back—her promise meant *maybe*.

"Doodad, take the rest of the day off and any more time that you need," I said.

"Snuck off a call to Cook when the cop had me corralled in a chair—told him we'd be reopening soon," Kelpie said. "He's on his way back with a couple of relatives in tow." Kelpie patted her girls and spun around. "Do I look okay?"

"You'd never know you took down two felons," Creole said, which had her grinning.

"We're leaving so you can get the bar ready to open, but before I go, is there anything else I should know about?"

Kelpie looked down before answering, which had me on alert. "Need some ideas for our next theme night."

"There's only so many times we can do wet t-shirt, even though it was super popular," Doodad said. "You come up with something good, toss it our way."

Creole hated anything that attracted trouble, and a room full of people drunker than usual fit that bill. He pinched my butt, and I struggled not jump.

Looking up, I asked, "You got any good ideas?"

"Nothing sissy," Kelpie said. Responding to Creole's glare, she added, "I'm sure it'll be great."

My shoulders shook. Creole tightened his hold.

The only officer left now was Kevin. He walked up to the bar and held out his hand. Kelpie put a soda in it. "You need me to open it?"

"Got it handled." Kevin smirked. "You're clear to open. If possible, take a rest from the 911 calls."

I slid off the stool. "You need *anything*, call."

Creole took my hand in his and pulled me down the hall. "Kelpie should come with a warning sign—a neon one. I can see why the regulars love her. She fits right in—as crazy as they are, only sober." He pulled me into a hug. "I'm happy we missed the action, although I know you hate to miss the good stuff."

Chapter Eleven

Fab's Porsche roared into the driveway, and I glanced up briefly from my stack of paperwork as she passed the garden window. The door blew open, and the first thing that caught my attention was the coffee cup holder from our favorite bakery.

"I'm home," she yelled at the top of her lungs, turning and flashing a cheeky smile before crossing the kitchen and handing me a cup.

Mimicking one of her tricks, I snapped off the lid and sniffed. "I smell a bribe."

"I'm playing phone tag with a potential client. Once I find out what it's all about, I'll need you for backup. The promise and all."

"You're always promising, and then you do whatever you want." If looks could kill… "Might not be available." I punched a button on my phone and waited for my call to go to voicemail. Again. "Brad, if you don't call me back in the next five minutes, I'm going to go pick up Mother and we're both coming over." I hung up.

"That was mean. Didier says the pressure of murder charges hanging over his head is getting to him. He tried to beg off working out with the guys, but they wouldn't let him."

My phone rang, and the picture on the screen made me smile.

"What?" Brad roared through the phone. "You're threatening me now?"

"You home?" I took his silence for a yes. "I'm coming over. I got a report back on Patty, and I have a couple of questions."

He sighed. "Let's do this next week."

"Pizza? I can pick it up on the way over. If you're not there, I'll track you down, and believe me, I'll find you."

"You kind of scare me."

"That's so sweet."

"Don't be stingy on the shrimp." He hung up.

Fab picked up one of the reports and fanned through the pages. "All this is about psycho Patty?"

"GC sent me information to follow up on that will hopefully lead to someone other than Brad. The Rambler that was used to pick Patty up was stolen and not recovered, but he did get me a lead on the guy that picked her up from the hospital, and I'll be finding out where they went. The threat of jail should loosen his lips, unless he's a repeat offender and sees it as a free-room-and-board op." I laughed at Fab's eyeroll.

"At least GC hasn't cut us off yet."

I gathered the reports together, plus another stack that I'd set aside for Brad. He couldn't say I wasn't keeping him updated. He might not open and read them right away, but eventually he would.

"Tell Brad that, if the worst happens, we'll break him out and find him a hiding place where even the cops won't look."

"He doesn't enjoy that kind of humor." I flashed a flinty smile.

* * *

Brad had given me a security card for the underground garage long ago, and thus far, I'd only used it once or twice. One of the perks of buying a unit in the building—two parking spaces and an additional guest space. I parked next to Brad's loaner car, an Escalade from Spoon, who'd joked he had a Pinto waiting for him. Brad had threatened to sell it for parts. Once the cops released his SUV, he planned to trade it in.

Grabbing my bags, I headed for the elevator, punching the button for the penthouse. Brad shared the floor with one other unit, which he and Didier had used for office space until they finished renovating the building and all the other units sold.

When the doors opened, my brother and a man I'd never seen before stood talking in the hall. If I hadn't been looking, I would've missed the scowl on the stranger's face—that was how fast it disappeared—and it took me by surprise.

My brother took the bags from my hand and introduced me. "This is my neighbor, Alexander Mark; my sister, Madison."

"Nice to meet you," I said, checking him over—similar to my brother in age, height, and sun-bleached brown hair.

"Likewise," he mumbled. "We'll talk later." He waved to Brad. Apparently, he couldn't get away fast enough.

Brad opened his door and disappeared inside. I stalled and openly stared as the neighbor hustled to his door, inserting the key. "Alex Mark," I said, loud enough for him to hear.

He looked up, and I winked.

Well, I'll be damned! My brother's neighbor is GC. I'd know that growl anywhere, since I talk to him almost every day. So much for my theory that he was a nerd who lived in his mother's basement.

I closed Brad's door and followed him into the kitchen. "Is Alex the original owner of that condo?"

He nodded. "We had a couple of offers but took his, since it was all cash. Investment Advisor. Perfect neighbor. Quiet, minds his own business."

"He's hot. If he needs a date, you should sic Mother on him. She hasn't meddled in anyone's personal life lately."

Brad barked an unamused laugh. "Let's eat before the good news. We wait until after, and I probably won't be able to stomach food." He ripped paper towels off the roll and served up the pizza.

Thinking he'd want beer, I asked, but he shook his head and indicated he wanted water before motioning me into the living room and dropping the pizza box on the coffee table. We sat on the couch, enjoying the view and eating in silence.

"Tell me you've got another suspect besides me," Brad said as he finished off the last piece.

"Working on that angle. Before Patty came to town the last time and kidnapped you, she was living with some guy named Folsom Diggs. I've ordered a background check that will hopefully include his present address. So much faster than having to go to previous addresses and shake down the neighbors."

"Folsom? Named after the prison?" He squeezed his eyes shut, taking a deep breath. "You be careful, you hear me?" I nodded. "Folsom's probably crazy, like Patty. Don't you have associates to foist these field trips off on?"

"Fab." I smiled. "Trust me—she's a match for any amount of craziness." I picked up the pizza box and carried it into the kitchen, putting it back in the shopping bag to take with me, so it wouldn't sit around. Coming back into the living room, I said, "We're going to find whoever did this."

Brad leaned back against the cushions. "It would be easy to think you're making this up to impress me, but I know you wouldn't do that to me… or any client."

"Hmm…"

"What?" Brad snapped.

"There's one more bit of information that you need to know."

He groaned and covered his eyes. "Talk about the girlfriend you can never get rid of. I'm being punished for my crappy choice in women."

"Stop." I reached over and attempted an awkward hug. "When you and Patty got together, you had no clue that she had issues. I'm not sure if you know this, but after your breakup, she was committed for one of many hospital stays. That time was different from the rest— turns out she was pregnant. Six months later, she gave birth to her daughter, Mila Thorson. She's currently in the foster care system."

"Are you saying I'm the father?"

"The time frame fits. Don't you want to know if she's yours or not?" I grabbed his hand and squeezed. "This little girl has haunted me ever since I found out about her."

"My guess is that she's not my child. If she were, Patty would've used her to manipulate me, starting long before she drew her first breath."

He had a point. But still. "Do I have your permission to check this out, get definitive proof?"

"This is really bothering you, isn't it?" Brad asked.

"If by chance she's a Westin…"

"We want her," Brad finished. "But if, like you said, chance and all... this isn't the best time. The reason being I'd like to get to know my kid from somewhere other than behind bars." He smiled sadly. "Knowing you, you've already checked this out."

I got up and retrieved my bag from beside the door, then sat back down. Reaching into it, I pulled out a stack of reports. On the top was a picture of Mila.

Brad stared for a long time before removing it from under the clip. "This is Mila?" He ran his finger over her hair. "She has the same light-brown hair I had as a kid."

"Same color eyes."

He held the picture next to his cheek. "Resemblance?"

"I'm not objective. The first time I laid eyes on her, I wanted to scoop her up and smother her with hugs." Tears threatened, but I breathed them back.

"Why wouldn't Patty tell me? Never mind. I know the answer," he spit out. "She wouldn't risk losing her bargaining chip, even at her child's expense. She was waiting for the perfect moment to spring her on me."

I scooted closer to Brad. "I've had some newly acquired experience dealing with Social Services and found out through numerous phone calls that a child's family takes priority. That's if they check out. It also takes patience—they move at their own speed, not to mention having a big caseload."

"My money's on you." Brad continued to stare at the picture. "You're a force to be reckoned with when you want something."

"If Mila turns out to be yours, you'd be expected to pay child support. They also wouldn't even consider the issue of you getting custody until you're cleared of the murder charges."

"If she *is* my daughter, I want her out of foster care, whatever it takes. And I want you taking care of my kid. You have no record, stellar references, and knowing you, one of your connections could cut through the paperwork. If only you were married." He glared down at the "friendship" ring.

"Creole would marry me tomorrow."

"He what?" Brad yelped. "You're holding out on me. Again. I better not be the last to find out."

"Super-pinkie, cross your heart, you'll tell no one." I held out my little finger.

"This must be good if you're resorting to our childhood 'under threat of death' promise." He looped pinkies, went through the ritual, and pulled me into a fierce hug.

"We're really engaged. But… Creole doesn't want to go through any wedding hoopla. He wants to elope."

Brad stared, open-mouthed, then threw his head back and laughed. "Enjoy the honeymoon because Mother will kill you both when you get back."

"Tell that to Creole. Don't forget your promise to keep the secret."

"Who else knows?"

"No one, not even Fab. And she'll kill me, or want to anyway, when she finds out. Secrets between friends—we've been doing that a lot lately." I told him about Caspian Dumont.

Brad whistled. "He's a billionaire? I know that island, and the asking price was twenty-six million, give or take a million."

"I haven't had the opportunity to grill her about her papa, his preferred title. I'd like to run a background check on him, but I suspect that's over-the-line nosey to do to my best friend."

"I'm not Caspian. I wouldn't have been able to stay away from my daughter and not be a part of her life." Brad closed his eyes, leaning back. "Wouldn't that be something, if I turned out to be Mila's dad? Could this case get any more complicated?"

"You've got the best on your team. Ruthie Grace's record is impressive, equal to Cruz, with a high percentage of wins."

"You know what she told me? 'If I can keep a man who surely deserved it from getting the death penalty, I can keep you out of prison for a murder I'm certain you didn't commit.'"

"I love that she believes in your innocence. We all do." I hugged him.

Chapter Twelve

Fab blew in the door, gun in hand. Catching sight of me sitting at the kitchen island, she peeked into the living room. Reappearing, she demanded, "It's just you?" I nodded, and she re-holstered her gun.

I gave her the once-over, head to toe. "Lose the pricey outfit. I suggest jeans and tennis shoes. And of course, don't forget your Walther."

As if, her glare conveyed. She stomped into the kitchen... as much as she could in stilettos. "What's the emergency?" She peered over my shoulder, checking out the patio. "You're not funny, summoning me home, and for what? You still haven't said."

"Are you finished ranting?"

Fab ignored me and reached into the refrigerator, pulling out a pitcher of fruit water. Pulling a glass from the cupboard, she filled it halfway, picking fruit out with her fingers.

"Cooties." I crossed my fingers in an X in front of my face. "The plan is to pay a visit to Cardio Gates, Patty's *friend,* introduce ourselves, and get the lowdown. Sadly, it's in a seedy part of town, so I'm not going by myself. I thought of you first."

"I'm busy," she said snootily.

"Don't think I won't stoop to blackmail. So be a good girlfriend and go upstairs and change— nothing too nice—and get back down here pronto."

* * *

Fab jumped into the entry, tapping her watch. "Five minutes. That might be a record."

I jiggled the keys in front of her face. Ready for her to grab them out of my fingers, I jerked them out of her reach and ran out the door. Her hand shot out, grabbing the back of my shirt, slowing my momentum. Plucking the address from my fingers, she jumped behind the wheel and entered it into the GPS.

She groaned when the map popped up, and instead of heading up the main highway to the interstate, she detoured in the direction of her office. She parked the SUV next to the white beater pickup, and we traded rides. It had been a good purchase and had come in handy a few times when we needed an unidentifiable ride.

"Does Creole know we're headed to this shady area, and that's putting it nicely?" The truck started right up—looks were deceiving; it might have looked like it was on its last tire, but it ran smoothly.

"According to GC, it's a generally safe area as long as we're careful. You know, not doing anything stupid that makes us a target, like carrying a map around. In general, act like we know what we're doing. Basic common sense, he wrote in big letters."

"What I got out of all that was blah, blah, blah and that our assigned phone number still works."

"He knows darn well that I'd just show up at his home and blackmail him, same as you."

"His home," Fab screeched and beat on the steering wheel. "How long have you been sitting on that information?"

"You have no respect for my ears." I rubbed them.

"*How. Long.*"

"He's hot without the crappy clothes and face-covering sunglasses," I said, enjoying being intentionally evasive.

"You're giving me a headache." She hit the gas and cut off a Porsche merging onto the Interstate. The driver didn't take it well, being bested by a beater truck, and cut around us. "Start at the beginning."

I related the details of meeting Brad's neighbor in dramatic detail, highlighting the fact that, as hard as GC tried to disguise his voice, I recognized the distinctive growl. "You're not to tell *anyone*, and that includes Didier, that GC is Alexander Mark. He wants us to continue using

GC. I suspect because he likes it. If the guys ever push the issue of meeting GC, we'll deal with it then. You can blame me."

Fab turned off the freeway and onto a residential street that consisted of two-story apartment buildings surrounded by rod-iron gates. Two women were out walking their dog. The corner store had a few men gathered around out front.

"You're going to be in so much trouble with Creole." Fab looked over at me. "Are you smiling?"

"A little trouble sounds fun. Keeps the relationship from being a total bore."

"It appears that I haven't rubbed off on you in a good way."

I ignored her gloating and pointed to a faded turquoise building. "It's that one. Here's the plan. Circle around to the far corner of the parking lot and park next to the stairs. Do we knock or pick the lock and barge in?"

"Do we know if he's even home?"

"According to the report, he's a recluse. No mention of employment."

"If we're not careful, the lockpick thing could get us a bullet. I can't believe I'm going to be the one to say this, but I vote for knocking. And no cop-knock. That will alert the neighbors or set off… What's his name?" Fab asked.

"'Hey you' will probably work. If not, then Cardio."

"When *Cardio* hollers from the other side of the door or peers out his peephole, we use his name, because it sounds friendly, and say we're friends of Patty, no matter how distasteful that is." Fab scrunched up her nose. "You've invaded my mind, and I hope you don't stay long."

"So now you're the cautious, law-abiding one..." I smiled at the dirty look she shot me. "I was going to say 'for a change' but probably for the first and last time."

The run-down building showed signs of age and neglect, but the outside was well-tended. There were a few clumps of dead grass, mostly weeds that appeared to have gotten a close shave.

Fab pulled around the perimeter of the property and lucked out, finding one empty space in front of the stairs.

Looking around, I saw all was quiet, the only movement one lone woman sitting outside on her porch.

Opening the car door, Fab jerked on my arm. "Once Hey You opens the door, you take the lead. I'll have my Walther ready for trouble. Chances are good that he's not operating with a full deck." She laughed, then laughed again. "I'm so funny."

"Ha, ha, ha." I shut the door on what I assumed would be a quick-witted response. "Left side, second door from the end. 212, if they're numbered." I tested the banister with a jerk, and despite the rot that showed in places, it didn't give way.

We got to the second level and saw the fire door had been propped open. I peeked down the darkened hall, where one light overhead cast a dim shadow. "No one hanging around looking for trouble."

When we reached the door to 212, Fab stood off to the side so Cardio wouldn't see her at first.

I knocked respectfully and waited impatiently, as I was ready to have this conversation over with and get back into the sunlight. Cardio apparently decided not to answer, but he wasn't as clever as he thought, as I'd detected movement from inside and a shadow darkening the peephole. I waved, letting him know I knew he was behind the door.

"Who's there?" a male voice called.

"Cardio Gates? I'm a friend of Patty Thorson."

A short, portly man opened the door, dark hair hanging in his face, a gun by his side. "Patty didn't have any friends."

"Put the gun away. A shootout would bring your neighbors charging into the hall, and the body count could be high. Besides, I'm not here for any trouble."

Fab stepped forward, pointing her gun at him. "You think about raising that gun of yours, and I'll shoot first and take my chances with the cops."

"Set it down on the floor and kick it away," I ordered.

With a brief glance down the hallway, Cardio stepped back and did as asked before crossing the sparsely furnished room, closing his laptop, and sitting in a rolling desk chair.

I shuddered, following him into the studio apartment. Strip kitchen along the far wall, and two doors — one I assumed led to the bathroom, the other open, a pile of clothes lying on the floor. The grey concrete walls and flooring made the space that much drearier, with only one small window that allowed in minimal light.

Fab flipped her private investigator badge out. At a quick glance, it would pass for a cop's badge. "Are you aware Miss Thorson is dead?"

"Murdered, I heard." He tilted his head, his gray eyes blank.

"You know anyone who would want her dead?" I asked.

"The Brad guy, the one they charged with the crime." Cardio laughed at us, conveying that we were dimwits. "Jealous sucker. Brad and Patty had a relationship, and when it ended, he left her with her emotions so scrambled, it drove her over the edge and she ended up in the hospital. Not a one of *my* girlfriends ever ended up in a mental institution."

Fab moved subtly, checking out the room, which was furnished only with a double bed, a desk, and a chair. Cardio wasn't a man for trinkets or even pictures. A pen and legal pad were the only items lying on the desk, aside from the laptop.

Brad and Patty had met a few months after he moved to South Florida, and that was a couple of years before I moved to the Sunshine State. "Were you in a relationship with Patty before she met Brad?"

Cardio rolled back in his chair, hands behind his head. "Patty and I were involved, but that was a long time ago. Got along good until she met Brad... some chance meeting. The dirty bastard convinced her they were soulmates, which is code for good sex, if any guy tries to sell you that line."

"Good advice," I said.

"Came home one day and she was gone. Left a note—adios!" He snapped his fingers. "Didn't hear a word until she ended up in the hospital again. She was never the same after the docs jolted her brain a few times—Zzzz!"

I flinched.

"Poor Patty. She's out, she's in, and out again." His eyes sparked more with annoyance than sympathy. "In between, she'd disappear without a hint as to where she'd gone, and then she'd turn up again. The longest she stayed out of touch was a year, and then another letter would arrive, the return address a hospital."

"That must have been hard on you." I did my best to sound understanding.

"If only she could've stayed away from that Brad character. I don't get the guy—it seemed like it was his mission in life to make sure she never recovered. After her last release, they hooked up again. This time the guy proposes; they even plan a big shindig wedding. Days away from the I do's, he turns on her with no warning, has her arrested on trumped-up kidnapping charges." Cardio clasped his chest.

Dramatic fellow. It was hard to figure out from his insincere act exactly how he felt about Patty.

"Broke my heart," he said with a sniff. "Didn't go back, and there were no more letters. Read in the news that she plea-bargained her way out of a prison sentence in favor of the hospital. Better the devil you know, I suppose."

Fab edged her way along the side of the room. Nervy girl wanted a peek at his laptop.

"Stay away from my computer unless you have a warrant," Cardio barked.

Fab shot him a weak smile.

"You know anyone else that might want Patty dead?" I asked.

Cardio stared down at the floor. "Patty was shy, a loner, but when she came out of her shell, people liked her—a real people person. The only person I ever heard about that had it in for her was that Brad guy."

Fab noticed two shelves built into the side of the desk that I'd missed. She bent down, saying,

"I love to read," and casually taking inventory.

When Fab stood, I said, "I realize we got off to a rocky start, but I want to thank you for your help on this case."

"Money would make it less traumatizing for me."

Cardio's request caught me off guard, but not Fab. She pulled some bills from her back pocket, along with a business card. I hoped it was the one with only the phone number on it.

Fab conducted business, giving a short speech about how to score more cash in exchange for information. I fidgeted, giving the place one last scan when what I wanted to do was grab her hand and race out of the building. I slid quietly to the door, cracking it open and turning my head to peer into the hallway. The last thing I wanted to do was turn my back on Cardio, so I backed out, Fab a step behind. Once we crossed the threshold, he shut the door in our faces. Neither of us felt like tempting fate and jumping down the stairs; instead we walked down. At the bottom, Fab looked up and waved. Cardio had come back out and now stood on the landing, his eyes burning a hole through us.

Fab started the engine and backed out, slowly heading to the exit. I kept my eyes glued to the rearview mirror that ran the length of the windshield, which I'd originally thought was ugly and excessive but now had no intentions of taking down. It proved to be useful, offering a wide view of everything behind and on each side of the truck. Once again, not a single person milling around.

"Did you find anything of note as you casually perused those shelves?" I asked. "I can't imagine he had a book in a genre you'd enjoy."

"Not a single book, but there was a picture that appeared to have been stashed last minute of him and Patty both staring like zombies at the camera. A handful of beta videos mired in the inch-thick dust—he didn't have a machine and they don't make them anymore, so I assume they have sentimental value." Fab wrinkled her nose. "Got the feeling that he was into Patty far more than any emotion he showed and that her obsession with Brad grated on him."

"I'd like to add him to my list of suspects, of which there are none, but if he did kill her, why not just shoot her?"

"Maybe because he didn't know how to handle that gun," Fab said in disgust.

"The only thing I got from Cardio was that the man is wound tight."

Chapter Thirteen

My phone pinged as we flew down Highway 1 not far from the cut-off to the Keys. I read the message out loud. "Miss January missing."

"How is that possible?" Fab snapped. "She's drunk most of the time, and she doesn't drive or walk around… much anyway."

"You're going to have to swing by The Cottages. If you're going to whine about it, I'll get Crum to drive you home." I turned away to keep from laughing, but when she didn't snap at me, I was afraid to turn and face her. Instead, I picked up my phone and called Mac.

"I quit," Mac said when she answered.

"We've had this conversation a dozen times already. Let me make this clear, you are not quitting unless I say you can, and I'm telling you now that you're going to have a long wait."

Mac blew a sigh through the phone so loud that Fab heard, judging by her upturned lips. "I don't know where Miss January went," she said. "Wandered off. She's been upset about Nestor's arrest and burst into tears when I had to tell her he wouldn't be back. At least, not for some years, judging by the charges they leveled against him."

"Fab and I are headed in that direction. Try to hold everything together."

Mac snorted. "Yeah, bye." She disconnected.

"Last time Miss January wandered off, we found her at a bus stop, so keep your eyes peeled," Fab reminded me.

* * *

Fab veered off the highway and took the route along the water as she rapidly approached The Cottages.

"There's Crum." Fab pointed to the sidewalk. "The one on the pink Barbie bicycle." She slowed at the next corner, turning into the gas station.

"There's Miss January and…" I pointed to a couple wrapped around one another. I'd recognize that flowery house dress anywhere, but… as Fab cruised past, I twisted in my seat. "Haven't seen him before." I craned to get a look at the older man. He had grey hair and dressed like a lot of locals, in shorts and a short-sleeve shirt.

"Since Miss January's got her hand fisted in the man's shirt and is attempting to drag him along with her, I'd say she knows him. Well… his name anyway."

Crum peddled in circles beside the station, not paying attention, and came close to a collision with the dumpster. He yelled and waved to get the attention of Miss January and her friend. When that had no effect, he rode alongside them, and whatever he said made them both jump. The man grabbed Miss January's elbow and kept her from ending up in a heap.

A menace on two wheels, Crum whirled around the twosome. A car flew into the driveway, having to jam on its brakes, and blasted its horn. Crum waved his middle finger.

"What's up with Crum? He doesn't have on his usual tighty-whities," Fab said. "One of these days, he's going to wander around naked and his excuse'll be, 'Oh look, I forgot my underwear.'"

"You're making me nauseous." I stared out the window. "I'm thinking this new getup might be worse—than the underwear, not the nakedness. Good grief." Did any of his fellow professors retire from that fancy college and prance around in a long-sleeve leotard, skirt, and a pair of mismatched tennis shoes? He raced around the back of the station, finding it a dead end and having to backtrack, dragging his foot on the pavement to come to a stop.

Fab pulled a half-block up and parked. "Not going to chance running over one of them." She powered down the window. "Don't want to miss anything," she said, just as I was about to remind her that she was breaking one of her own rules— no fresh air inside the car.

I was about to get out of the SUV and do... what, I hadn't decided yet. Mac saved me by running across the corner from the busy boulevard and skidding to a stop. She yelled at Crum, and he waved and rode into the street. He was lucky that the car that had just paused for the stop sign hadn't gotten there seconds earlier, as the man once again didn't look before riding into traffic.

Mac separated the kissing couple, linking their hands and directing them to walk single file across the street and back towards the property, reminiscent of a line of kindergartners. She whistled at Crum. "Get a move on." He caught up to the trio, bringing up the rear, paddling the ground with one foot and dragging the other.

"That was a long kiss." Fab started the engine and crept forward.

"My guess is they pressed their lips together and forgot what they were doing."

Fab followed at a snail's pace for two blocks. The Cottages in sight, she pulled around the walkers and backed into Mac's driveway.

"It's been a while since we've had a wager," Fab said. "I'm betting that the unidentified man has moved in already. I'd say he's doing it now except he doesn't have any plastic bags in his hands."

"No bets." I closed my eyes and took a deep breath. "How does the woman manage to attract men like flies? How long has Nestor been gone — two minutes?"

"Eww." Fab turned up her nose. "Rumor has

it she likes her... ah... hmm." She scissored her fingers together.

I laughed, and it felt good.

Mac led her charges into the driveway, ushering Miss January and her friend to her door. Crum raced away, attempted a wheelie, and came close to ending up on his butt.

"You're not waiting in the car," I said, getting out and waiting, tapping my foot, until Fab joined me. I latched onto her sleeve and tugged her to my side. "Don't disappear on me. That is, if you need a favor anytime soon."

"I never understood why you think it's a good idea to ask for my help with your tenants. Besides, you already told me I could get a ride home from Crum, but you're in luck there—the two of us won't fit on that bike, even if I got on, which I'm telling you now will never happen."

The image of the sexy French woman and... well... Crum made me laugh and Fab along with me.

Miss January plopped down on her bottom step, the man next to her, and put her head on his shoulder.

"Are you okay?" I took note of the man—sixties or better, tanned, character lines etched in his face... and sauced. "We worry when no one knows where you've gone."

"That's sweet," she cooed. "No need to worry. I've got Nedly here to look after me."

"Ned Bruberry." He held out his hand, which

Fab shook, casually wiping her hand on the back of her jeans afterwards. "Or Captain." He flashed a drunken smile. "I captain my own fishing boat out of Marathon."

Fab nudged me, and I glanced over my shoulder. Mac had an iron grip on the handlebars of Crum's bike. He hung over the side, perilously close to planting a facer.

"Enough," Mac scolded the man, helping him to stand. Once he was steady on his feet, she grasped his arm in one hand, the bike in the other, and walked him to his cottage.

"Where did you and Ned meet?" I asked Miss January.

"The Stop-N-Go. It was love at first sight." She threw out her arms, a big smile on her face, and planted a noisy, wet kiss on his cheek.

"She spit on him." Fab made a noise.

Both Ned and Miss January stared at me, hearing Fab's fake barfing.

I ignored their questioning stares, swatting the air behind me. As usual, the woman was prepared and stepped out of range. I'd known it was a long shot.

Ned grinned and swiped at the dribble on his chin.

"We're getting married once we get to know one another better. In the meantime, we're giving it a test run." Miss January smiled at her intended. "I'm tired."

Ned stood and helped her to her feet, then up

the stairs and into her cottage. "Nice meeting you all." He waved and banged the door shut.

Mac hustled up, and I turned on her. "What the heck is going on here?"

"The wedding is news to me." Mac sighed. "Miss January is the only one I know that can go to a convenience store and come back with a fiancé. I shouldn't be surprised, though; she bagged one of her men off the beach. Though there, at least, there was no mention of marriage. I didn't have the heart to tell Nedly that with her track record, he'll die or end up in jail."

"Keep an eye on those two," I said. "I didn't notice any belongings, so he might not stay long."

"I did find out that he owns a boat that he lives on, and when he's sober, which isn't often, he ventures out. Imagine sucking up fish smell all the time." Mac screwed up her nose.

I turned and snapped at Fab, "Would you stop with the noises."

"*Nooo*," she said, hands on her hips, and laughed at my burning glare.

"I don't want Miss January to get any wise ideas about boat living," Mac said. "I'd drown in guilt if she fell overboard and was eaten by fish."

I need aspirin. Forget that—tequila.

"Can we leave now that the lovebirds are doing…?" Fab completed the sentence with finger movements.

Mac giggled. "You can't leave until you say

hello to Joseph. He's been feeling down lately, complains that no one pays attention to him."

"What about Svetlana? The girlfriend," Fab reminded me, as though I'd forgotten.

"She's not very talkative," Mac chimed in, and the two laughed.

"If some manufacturer could make a blow-up woman that talked, it might make big money." Both women looked at me like it was the worst idea they'd heard in a while. "I know the man would get bored with the chatter, but that's why it would need an on/off switch."

I left them and practically ran to the opposite end of the driveway, knocking on Joseph's door. Not getting an answer or hearing any shuffling behind the door, I peeked in the window. He and Svetlana were sacked out on the couch, napping or passed out, beer bottles on the coffee table and the television on. I snuck away from the door, feeling bad, but only momentarily—I needed more energy to deal with him than I had.

"Joseph's asleep," I reported back to Fab and Mac. "Get Crum to take him for a man's night out. Make sure they take a cab, so they won't get arrested for being drunk in public."

"Crum's going to whine about that," Mac said, disgruntled.

"Throw in some incentive. Cash. If he still says no, then tell him to call me and tell *me* no." I edged my way towards the SUV. "Anything else I need to know?"

"Crum's starting an exercise class by the pool... for the tourists," she said to my raised brow. "You know he's a magnet for the ladies. Anything that keeps complaints about the lack of excitement down works for me."

"Crum's idea sounds kind of normal. Or am I missing something?"

"Normal and Crum in the same sentence is a stretch, no matter what we're talking about."

"The only ones that book cottages expecting 24/7 fun, legal or otherwise, are the relatives of your lawyer friend," I said. "Since he made his services unavailable to Brad, I couldn't care less where they stay."

"They're good for the bottom line," Mac reminded me.

"Your decision. Anytime you want to cut them off, you don't even have to ask. We'll just advertise more."

"There is one more thing," Mac hedged. "Corndog is moving in with his son, out Alley-way. The son just recently retired from the military and said he'd be bringing his dad around often—they're both excited to see the dock project finished.

"I'm sorry to see him go. He was never a problem, and the cops never showed up to execute a warrant for his arrest. He's welcome back anytime." I turned to Fab. "How does this affect the partnership with Didier?" The question was rhetorical—I'd get the answer from Didier.

"Corndog just informed Didier," Fab said. "Everything is staying on track, with Didier as head of the project. They've signed a new contract that spells out the new responsibilities moving forward."

"Happy to hear that, and also that there won't be any delays," I said.

"No more emergencies for today, but I can't promise about tomorrow," Mac shouted as we crossed the street.

Chapter Fourteen

Fab hopped down the stairs. Judging by the noise she was making, she had on tennis shoes. She also knew the guys hadn't returned from their run—if they had, she would've had to settle for a quieter way of getting down the stairs.

Leaning back against a pile of pillows on the daybed, I ran my eyes over her outfit as she jumped into the living room—ankle jeans and a sleeveless white top, Walther tucked into the front of her waistband.

"Ta da." She threw her arms out wide.

"Do you get that energy from coffee? I want some... maybe... or not. I'd have to hold my nose." I gave it some brief thought while conjuring up Fab and Didier's dark roast preference, which smelled like and had the consistency of mud.

"I'm trying something new—friendly, approachable, more like you."

Amused, I watched her performance, waiting to hear what she really wanted. "So I'm going to try on the surly role? For what?"

"I need you to lace up your tennis shoes and come with me." She sat on the arm of the couch, staring at my bare foot resting on a stack of files. "Give you a break from that pile of paperwork."

"I'll need more information to motivate me out of my office." I smiled at her annoyance.

After a long pause, she said, "Welfare check."

Mentally, I dug my toes into the cushion, but based on past experience, that would be futile — she'd get behind me and push me out the door. "Another couple without both oars in the water? What happened to the other two?"

"I had a short chat with Mr. Newton yesterday, which really annoyed him when he found out that the purpose of my call was to inquire about Carly and Globe." Fab grimaced, relating the conversation. "I thought he was going to tell me to mind my own business; instead, he answered in a ticked-off tone. Carly's got an attorney and is receiving outpatient mental care. Globe moved back home. I only called because I knew you'd ask. You're welcome."

"Today — more of the same?"

"We're checking on a property."

I held back a laugh. "Since when do properties qualify for a welfare check?"

"When you're rich. My client's words, not mine, and I wasn't about to correct him."

"You missed an opportunity to use the same snooty-ass tone you're using now."

"That good?" Fab patted her own shoulder.

"The job?"

"The neighbors who live to the right of my client, Mr. Knight, are having a weekend blowout of a party, and when they reached standing-room-only, the overflow took over his house. The neighbors on the other side went over and asked them to shut down the noise and got trash thrown at them. They weren't amused. They hot-footed it back to their mansion and got Knight on the phone, threatening him with the police if he doesn't get the party shut down and the miscreants sent on their way."

"Vacation home? Strangers invaded because... why the heck not? Maybe suggest to your client that he hire a caretaker. Cheaper than a new... mansion, but I'm only guessing."

Fab tapped her watch. "You going to change or what?"

"I'm not wearing jeans," I grouched and stood up, going upstairs.

"It's easier to climb a tree in jeans than a skirt," she called after me.

It took less than five minutes for me to pull on my favorite pair of crop pants and a top, corral my wild red mane into a hairclip, and get back downstairs. Fab lounged on the couch, Jazz and Snow by her side, each vying for her attention.

"Got a great idea while dressing for our outing." I spun around.

Fab did her best to suppress a smile.

"Let's take Creole. We've got that standing offer of his services, and he's got brawn for crowd control. Sure, we could empty out the house on our own, but without shots fired? Fancy neighborhoods take a dim view of that kind of activity."

"What neighborhood doesn't?" Fab snorted.

Creole and Didier burst through the patio door, out of breath, stopping short when they saw us. Fab and I each got the once-over from our respective boyfriend.

"What are you two up to?" Creole demanded.

Who me? I loved it when he growled, but that wasn't the sexy one.

"Sit," Didier ordered. "Neither of you goes anywhere until we hear what you're up to. All of it, not some abbreviated version." He disappeared around the corner into the kitchen. "Water?" he yelled.

"Just you and me," Creole yelled back.

This might take a while. I sat back on the daybed, grabbed a couple of pillows and stuffed them behind my head. I wiggled my finger at Creole, who shook his head. His expression remaining sternly composed, he jerked the desk chair around and straddled it.

Didier handed off water to Creole and sat on the steps.

"No big deal," Fab blew it off. "Another drive-by. At least it's not as bad a neighborhood as the one Madison dragged me to a few days ago."

I didn't miss the amusement in Fab's eyes. *Payback!* she telegraphed.

"First I'm hearing of this." Creole crossed his arms.

So sexy!

"You're not the only one," Didier grumped.

"It's your fault." I gave Creole an exaggerated huff. "I planned to tell you last night. Then you enticed me with food, drink, and, well... other things." My cheeks burned. "It was a rundown neighborhood, but everything was quiet. Happy?"

Fab explained the Knight job, glossing over the details.

"Right before you got back, I suggested that we ask you to go along with us," I said to Creole. "Right, Fab?" I leveled a stare at her.

"What's in it for me?" Creole asked.

"That warm feeling you get when you do something nice for someone else."

The guys laughed.

"Good one. Give me ten to shower and change." He brushed a kiss over my cheek as he went by.

"Oh, what the heck—you've got another backup," Didier said and followed Creole up the stairs.

"I propose that we take them to lunch when we're done cleaning house for your client," I said.

* * *

Fab behind the wheel, Didier in the passenger seat, we turned south on the Overseas. Creole and I were in the back, and as usual, I was stretched out, head in his lap.

"We're headed to Islamorada; the house is off the Old Highway." Fab adjusted the GPS screen.

"Gated?" Creole asked. Fab murmured in the affirmative. "You better have a key or security code or something. None of us is climbing over a fence."

"Mr. Knight messengered a gate card," Fab said.

Sure he did. Neither Creole nor Didier knew that not one delivery person had shown up that morning. Avoiding eye contact, I sat up and nestled into his side, head on his shoulder. He wasn't aware, and I'm certain neither was Didier, that Fab, Mother, and I had universal cards that opened most of the gates in South Florida. So far, we'd had a ninety-five percent success rate, and on the rare occasion it didn't work, Fab requested they be updated. The cards had been supplied by one of Fab's questionable connections, and she had yet to divulge the person's name.

"We're getting off at the next exit— Islamorada," Fab announced. It wasn't that far from Tarpon Cove, and the traffic had been light. Instead of cutting across the lanes at the last second, she signaled and pulled off the highway, then made her way to the Old Highway, which was mainly residential—one large lot after another, the houses barely visible from the street thanks to trees and lush, green surroundings.

Fab slowed at the address, how to get through the security gate was a moot point. Somehow, the unwanted guests had managed to roll it back and park more than a dozen pricey cars in a haphazard fashion, as though each driver had swung in, hit the brakes, cut the engine, and got out.

"Got a plan?" Creole tapped Fab on the shoulder and met her stare in the rearview mirror.

Since there was a "no parking" sign on the street, she backed the Hummer in, squeezing perilously close to the gate.

"Grab everyone's attention and invite them to leave?" Fab said.

"That's your plan?" Didier raised a brow. "You planning on leaving behind a few bullets in the walls and ceilings?"

Creole covered his face, rubbing his eyes. "I didn't volunteer for this good deed with the intention of getting arrested."

"Me neither," Didier grumbled.

"My client specifically stated that he wanted the eviction done in a civilized fashion," Fab said, and it was hard to miss the annoyance in her voice. "He doesn't want to make the nightly news."

"Let the calm one speak." I raised my hand in case there was any doubt as to who that was.

"Partiers are unlikely to be armed. If the intent was a gun battle, it would've happened by now. We pass ourselves off as private security, not *law enforcement,* and tell them that it would be in their best interests to hit the road in an orderly fashion. Let them know the alternative is calling in the police and having them hauled off in a police van."

"Since it's my client..." Fab said. "Instead of announcing who we are, hold up your badges." She opened the console, handing a black leather badge holder to Didier and tossing another over the back seat. "Hold it up." She demonstrated. "A person would need to look close to see that it's not a cop badge. Worked for us the other day."

"You're in trouble." Creole swiveled his head to glare at me.

I winked, unperturbed. "It's not illegal."

His eyes narrowed and, at the same time, his lips twitched.

"Where did you get these?" Didier flipped the cover open, flashing the badge around.

"Online. Mother has one too."

"Of course she does." Creole snorted. "Probably uses it on Spoon."

"Stop." I groaned.

"Here's my helpful tidbit." Didier laughed at himself. "I'd like to point out that this isn't my first job... assignment... sting... shakedown. I'll pair with Madison, and we'll be backup to you two."

"I kinda like 'shakedown.'" I winked at him. "I'm the mingler. You can be the man candy — attract the chicks and break their hearts by telling them to beat it."

Fab's blue eyes sparked with annoyance. "You two done?"

"Not quite." I raised up on my knees and reached into the far back, hauling a duffle bag forward and unzipping it. "This might be useful... once again." I whipped out a megaphone.

Chapter Fifteen

Quiet reigned across the front exterior of the pink, two-story mansion. It was already late morning, and with any luck, it would be a couple of hours before the hardcore drunks were awake enough to continue the party.

Fab and Creole agreed that Didier's plan was a good one. Creole flourished his hand, and stepped back, the signal for Fab to kick the door open.

"Try the knob first," I said, failing to keep the sarcasm out of my voice.

Fab took my suggestion and reached for the knob. When it turned in her hand, she was clearly disappointed. She shoved the door open. Next job she went on, maybe she could beat the door down. The entry was clear as the four of us stepped over the threshold. The same couldn't be said for the mammoth living and dining rooms. Surrounded by overturned furniture and the bomb of trash that had gone off, young people littered the rest of the furniture. Having run out of room, pillows had been snagged and the guys were passed out on the floor in various stages of undress, the girls in the skimpiest of bathing suits. None appeared dead, as demonstrated by the loud snoring.

One shirtless guy staggered in from the kitchen, sloshing coffee over the sides of his cup. "Come on in," he yelled and waved. "Party will start in a few."

How was it that so many kids didn't have anywhere to be on a weekday? The local college on some kind of break?

The sliding doors stood open, and checking out the backyard from this distance, I saw that more kids were asleep on furniture and pool floaters.

Fab bowed to Didier. "You're the one with the megaphone. Go for it."

Standing next to him, I laughed and smiled before moving over to the window for a head count.

"Wake the hell up," Didier yelled into the megaphone, his words echoing out to the patio. "Get your stuff together and get out."

"Not so loud, dude," a guy who'd snagged part of the sectional said. He struggled to sit up, but first had to relocate the female that straddled his body. "Who the heck are you, anyway?"

Didier flipped open his newly acquired badge and waved it around the room. "You're trespassing, and it's a felony," he ground out. His smirk let us all know he was enjoying himself.

A few hadn't moved an inch, not even to crack

an eyelid. Several sat up, groaning from aches and pains from sleeping on the hardwood floors. Most were too blurry-eyed to know what was going on.

Creole snagged the megaphone from Didier. He walked around to those that had plans to sleep in and had ignored the warning. Pausing, he directed the megaphone at the first sleeping body he came to, yelling, "Rise and shine," and not moving on until the person stirred, showing signs of life. After he'd snapped everyone into consciousness, he stood in the center of the room. "Two choices." He held up his fingers. "Get out *now* or go to jail."

Three guys punched each another in the ribs, stumbling to their feet, and made their getaway through the patio doors, heading in the direction of the beach.

A woman's squeals reverberated from the kitchen, catching our attention. Behind the island, she was staring down at the floor. So that was where the overturned stools scattered around the living room had come from.

Being the closest, I hurried over. The contents of a large silver serving platter sitting on the countertop caught my attention. It held an array of what I assumed to be recreational drugs. I wasn't familiar with the pills poured into small serving dishes, but I recognized the weed and the diminishing lines of white powder.

The girl noticed my approach and jumped.

Fear in her eyes, she ran in the opposite direction and out the patio door, another one making their escape via the beach. Feet stuck out from behind the cupboard where a young guy lay on the floor. Teenager? Certainly looked younger than college age, but it was hard to tell sometimes. Nudging his backside with my toe didn't get a response, so I tried again, stopping just short of kicking him. A chill ran up my spine when he still didn't move, and I stepped back. Glancing around the room, I caught Creole's attention and motioned him over.

"You okay?" he asked, a worried look on his face.

"I tried to rouse him, but he didn't move." I pointed behind the counter.

Creole kneeled down and checked his pulse. "He's alive, but barely." He stood, took his phone out of his pocket, and called 911. His eyes narrowed at the sight of the tray and its contents. He flagged Fab over. "I know your client doesn't want law enforcement involved, but I'm not letting this kid die. An ambulance is on the way."

Fab spotted the tray, and Creole must've read her intentions. He waved her hand away. "You're not destroying evidence. If this guy overdosed, these might be helpful to the doctor in figuring it out which drugs he took."

Fab turned away. Her phone out, she skirted around Didier, who'd come to see what happened, and had it to her ear as she stepped outside.

"Is there anything we should be doing?" I asked.

Creole shook his head. "Don't touch him."

In less than five minutes, sirens could be heard outside, and judging by how close they sounded, they had to be at the end of the driveway.

One of the partiers crawled up off the floor and made his way to the front door. About to cross the threshold, he skidded to a stop and stepped back inside, slamming the door. "Cops are here," he yelled and raced around the couch, slowing to kick a couple of bodies that had gone back to sleep. Another one made an exit out the back, yelling at stragglers as he went.

Slowly, the rest of the partygoers got to their feet, stumbling out to the patio, and the room cleared, with the exception of two guys who tried to stand and couldn't manage to get one foot in front of the other. They both collapsed back down on the closest piece of furniture, one in a chair and the other on a side table that he slid off, hitting the floor.

Fab strode in from the patio, shoving her phone in her pocket. A mutinous glare on her face, she stopped in front of Creole. "If this were *your* case, I'd have let you make the decision about what to do next."

"Fab…" Didier whispered.

"I'll handle it from here," Fab said. "The rest of you wait out on the patio in case the cops have any questions." She marched towards the incoming stretcher and directed them into the kitchen. One of the paramedics asked a couple of questions, which she answered.

Creole went out the front door, Didier and I to the patio. The pool area had a large grassy area that turned into white sand as it went down to the waterfront. It was in the same shape as the inside—trash everywhere, beer cans tossed around the pavement, drug paraphernalia scattered about. The patio and outdoor kitchen had been richly furnished, with high-end chaises, tables and chairs, and top-of-the-line appliances. The furniture had been overturned, and some of it had ended up in the water.

The two dawdlers finally dragged themselves outside, both stopping to barf in the bushes. One fell between two banana trees, passing out. The other continued to be sick but made progress in his getaway.

At first glance, it appeared that Mr. Knight enjoyed the luxury of a private beach. So where had the runners disappeared to? A private path? None of them were in any shape to swim and no one was in the water screaming for help, so I voted for a path that must lead into the neighbor's yard. If that turned out to be the case, Fab needed to suggest to her client that he put up a gate—one with spikes to discourage climbers.

"Let's track the runners," I said to Didier. "That should keep us out of trouble."

"Does it work for you and Fab?" He grinned.

"We're actually rather good at dragging each other back from the edge." Sort of, anyway, but that didn't sound as good. "We need to do a bushes check for anyone else that's passed out. If they haven't come to, including the puker over there, we need to let the paramedics know. Maybe we'll get lucky and find one somewhat lucid. Then we'll shout, 'Run for your life,' and follow casually to see where he goes."

"Mean." He nudged me with a laugh. "Except for the bushes that are currently occupied, the rest of the landscape consists of palm trees."

"Did you know a person can crouch behind one if it's mature with a nice big trunk?"

"I'm not even going to ask." He grabbed my hand. "It was short-sighted of the ones that left their cars behind. Is there a trick to getting them out unnoticed?"

"It's better if they wait until the police leave. They'll probably take down the license numbers and leave it at that. Even if Fab requested that the cars be towed, and I doubt she would, they'd tell her to call for a flatbed. Private property and all. It's a good lesson to learn early — careful where you park," I said.

"Does Fab always make sure she has a getaway route?"

I groaned. "No way am I going to be part of corrupting you."

"This job is better than the last one, where we

were running from flying bullets." Didier grimaced. "I'm proud of Fab—she's a tough cookie. I just want to protect her from all the bad stuff." As we got closer to the beach, he craned his neck in each direction. "This isn't a private beach—the way they constructed the houses, it gives that illusion. I'd never have guessed." He let out a low whistle, clearly impressed. "The homes along this road all share the beach. Hard to tell how long it is. There's an outcropping of rocks down there, but it wouldn't surprise me if they were easy to get around."

"Makes it hard to know which house the kids ended up at." I nudged Didier's arm and indicated that we should go right, since that property was the one the neighbor had complained was having the party. Before we went any farther, I looked back to see if we were needed back inside the house. Neither Fab nor Creole were standing outside, so now was a good time for me and Didier to check out the neighbors.

We'd chosen the right direction. When we stepped around the hedge that separated the two properties, it became clear that the kids didn't have far to go. An easy dozen lounged around the pool in chairs and chaises. Others snagged inflatables and were floating in the water.

I hoped that none of them were drunk, as most were asleep.

"This side has someone directing the action." Didier nodded to a woman who was ordering another woman around, pointing to areas she wanted cleaned. Hands on her hips and with a finger shake, she said something to the kids closest to her. Not a one of them acknowledged her presence. The one lying the closest, on a rubber raft on the ground, rolled over and closed his eyes.

"Since you're not only a looker but charming, I vote that you suggest she put an end to the party." I smiled at him, tapping my cheek. "My talent lies in making up plausible stories."

"Lies." He smirked.

"Inform her a guard will be posted next door to discourage trespassers. It's such a good idea, I'm going to suggest it to Fab. If that doesn't get her moving, remind her the cops are a phone call away.

"You really think it'll work?" Didier asked.

"Of course. Handsome, charming French guy? Why wouldn't it?"

"Charming, huh?"

"Toss in a couple of French words. They're a favorite with me." My eyes got big. "I know. Flirt with her."

"Did you forget who my fiancée is?"

"Oh yeah. You'd probably survive, but I wouldn't since it's my suggestion."

"You're not to leave my side," Didier warned.

The woman turned as we approached. After a

quick glance in my direction, she dismissed me entirely and shifted her attention to focus on Didier. She leisurely ran her eyes over him from head to toe. Twice.

Didier flashed his biggest smile and waved.

The woman smiled back, standing straighter, pushing back her shoulders and running her hand over her blond chignon and down the front of her sundress, smoothing the wrinkles.

One of the boys sat up, waving his arm to get her attention. She turned her back and edged her way around the side of the pool.

"Marjorie Ross." She preened, her hand outstretched.

Didier went into full charm mode. Taking her hand in his, he kissed the back, introducing the two of us. He didn't say a word about private investigators or security—in fact, he led her to the conclusion that we were friends of Fab's client, Scott Knight.

Marjorie completely ignored me, for which I was thankful. The whole handshaking ritual, envisioning the swapping of germs, made my hands fly behind my back. Some folks thought me ill-mannered, the others crazy, and some of them ought to talk. But I suppose people recognize kindred souls.

"Mr. Knight's house was broken into and trashed by an overflow of partiers." Didier went on to explain the chaos we had walked into. Also mentioned the "unfortunate" man on his way to the hospital.

"How I can help?" Mrs. Ross asked breathlessly.

"How long is the party supposed to last?" He cast a disapproving eye around her backyard.

"The kids have a long weekend from school." Marjorie sighed. "Today's the last day; they go back tomorrow."

"Your house fared better than Scott's."

"My son is well known for his parties, which makes him very popular. That will serve him well in life," Marjorie said, proud of her progeny.

Mother would have laughed in my face if I'd pitched that I needed to let my friends trash the house so I could be popular. Truth was, when she'd gone out of town, we'd thrown parties, but we cleaned up the evidence. Probably too well, which should've been a red flag, but she never said anything.

Marjorie hung on Didier's every word. The knock-your-eye-out diamond on her finger didn't inhibit her in any way.

Didier warned her about the police and that she should keep the partying and trespassing to a minimum. He even went so far as to suggest she send everyone home. "I wouldn't want you to get into any trouble."

Marjorie gushed and cooed. So sickening. One kid moved behind her, out of her line of sight, and unabashedly listened in, a huge grin on his face. Her popular son perhaps?

Didier brought up her status in the neighborhood. "You wouldn't want anything to blemish your reputation."

"You're so right."

Enough now. I knocked him in the back. To his credit and my admiration, he didn't so much as twitch.

"So very nice to meet you, Marjorie. We need to get back to the house." Didier kissed her hand again. "I'm sure we'll run into each other again."

"That would be lovely." She fluttered her lashes.

Didier looped his arm in mine, and we headed back toward the water.

"You were so sickly sweet, it made my teeth hurt," I said.

"Got her to promise to keep those unruly kids on her property and not let them stray over to my friend Scott's." He smirked. "I deserve a back pat for throwing in how bad an arrest for trespassing would look on their records."

I patted his shoulder. "Remind me to clap for your performance later. You rocked it."

When we came up the beach, a cop stood on the patio with Creole, who pointed to us.

"Wonder where Fab is?" I asked.

"Let's hope she didn't shoot anyone." Didier laughed, and I joined in.

As we got closer, I waved to the cop, recognizing him as Officer Jackson, a patron of Jake's. "Is the kid going to be okay?"

"He's lucky that someone called for medical help. Paramedics didn't think it was life-threatening, but it could have been," Officer Jackson said. "College kids don't always think— sometimes when a situation turns serious, they compound it by not calling for help." He looked down the beach. "Where did the rest of them sneak off to?"

Didier nodded to the right. "The house next door is party central, and there's parental supervision over there. Her son invited a few friends, word got out, and a hundred showed up. One of them got the bright idea to expand the party over here. Which one is unclear. Mrs. Ross is in the process of sending everyone home. It appeared she still had a couple dozen hangers-on."

Officer Jackson motioned me over to one side. "I want to hear your version of what happened."

Over my shoulder, I noticed that another cop had stepped forward to ask Didier questions. I told Jackson what had happened from the moment we walked in the front door. This was one of those times that I didn't exaggerate to make events sound more exciting.

Fab appeared at my side.

"Make sure you get the place secured," Officer Jackson said. "With any luck, the party is over and they won't be back until the next invite goes out."

"I overheard Marjorie tell Didier that the kids

were on some kind of four-day break from school and would be going back tomorrow."

"That's good to know. If I have any more questions, I know how to contact you." Officer Jackson crossed the patio to talk to his partner, who'd finished talking to Didier.

"You might want to suggest to your client that he get a caretaker," I said to Fab. "And not one of us. The mess? We better not be expected to clean it up."

The dirty look Fab gave me told me the answer was no. "I called Cook, and he's sending a cleaning crew. My client had the nerve to say that the cops descending on his property was my fault. Before I could stop myself, I told him off. Suggested that he be grateful I didn't have to call the coroner and let him know that it wasn't easy getting rid of dead-person stink."

"You're usually so kiss-assy with these entitled clients of yours."

"Do you have to put it that way? I half-expected him to threaten not to pay." She blew out a frustrated sigh. "I'd send Toady to collect. And the bill would be triple. It wouldn't be a civilized office call either — I'd suggest that Toady catch Knight off guard someplace and scare the you-know-what out of him."

"I love it when steam comes out your ears."

"As long as it doesn't dry out my hair." She flicked her fingers through her long mane.

I laughed. "Where did Creole go?"

"He went next door and gave the owners of the cars parked out front five minutes to move them or else they can cough up the three-hundred-dollar fee to reclaim them from the impound lot. I told him I'd move them myself and got an evil glare. Said I was going to tell on him to you."

"Bet that scared him." I tugged on her, steering her away from beer cans and around some empty liquor bottles. "What happened to the guy who passed out in the bushes?" I looked over to where we'd left him.

"Why are you asking me?" she huffed. "He's not there now." She scanned the entire yard. "Seems like a happy outcome to me."

"Now what?"

"We check on Creole's progress in emptying the driveway. Wait for Cook and crew, and then we can leave." Fab snapped her fingers for me to keep up as we headed back into the house, mindful of where we stepped.

Creole stood in the driveway, directing a driver so he wouldn't sideswipe the car next to him. Several guys walked up the driveway from the street, not making eye contact as they got behind the wheels of their respective cars and maneuvered their way out.

"Is there something we should be doing?" I asked Didier.

"We'll supervise, which means we can stand right here."

The last of the cars was just pulling out of the driveway when Cook's wife showed in a minivan with three college-age kids in tow. Everyone piled out, hands filled with cleaning supplies. Fab intercepted them, engaging in a short chat with the missus before handing her the key.

"Ready?" Fab asked over her shoulder as she headed to the SUV. She paused and turned. "Madison's buying lunch—where should we go?"

"That's low of you. I suggest you bill it to your client, along with charges for all our services."

Chapter Sixteen

Fab left the choice of where to eat to the guys. The vote was unanimous for Jake's. Didier wanted to shoot pool. Creole mentioned dancing, and I rolled my eyes. I laughed, imagining that his toes winced when he threw out the suggestion, picturing the quarter-size dance floor, me standing on Creole's feet as we maneuvered around the basketball arcade machine.

Fab flew into the driveway and around the back, honking at Junker, who was bent over, digging through watering cans in the back of a pickup and squeezing the woman standing next to him down to her best and final price. He waved his fist.

As we trooped through the back door, Cook was nowhere in sight. His stand-in had donned headphones and was dancing around as he put up one plate of food after another. The stools at the bar were filled—two-deep, in fact. Doodad had his back turned, restocking inventory, while Kelpie entertained the regulars, pouring beer from the tap and sailing it down the countertop. One tipped over the edge. The man caught the glass before it hit the floor, but he ended up wearing the contents down the front of his pants.

"Sorry Gip, this one's on me." Kelpie shook her assets, an ear-splitting grin on her face. The regulars laughed, clapping Gip on the back.

Two burly men sitting at the reserved table out on the deck caught my attention. The sign on the table said, "Don't sit here." Not sure how much clearer it could be. I'd deal with them once I put in our food order. I turned and followed Fab back into the kitchen.

On my way out to the deck to evict the poachers, I stopped at the bar and waved at Kelpie. "Margarita." I mimed tipping back a drink.

"Hey, boss." Kelpie picked up a drink off the back counter, handing it to me. "Doodad needs to speak to you before you leave. He's checking on the men in the conference room."

Gamblers in the house. The rules were play all the cards you want but no money on the table, which would keep us from being shut down. It was an exclusive, invitation-only bunch, and thus there'd never been any trouble.

I stepped out on the deck, picking up the sign and rubbing it on the side of my pants, then making a show of reading it and dropping it back in the middle of the table.

The two burly bookends stared at me, *What the...* glares on their faces. Both were muscled, with black hair slicked back, chains hanging out of their jeans pockets and decorating the sides of their motorcycle boots. I'd guess they came with the two spit-shined, gleaming Harleys parked out front.

Most people would step back, stuttering an apology, but I'd developed an immunity to glares and over-sized men who growled.

"We're waiting on the boss," one said, flashing a smile that would make most people flinch. "Doodad — yeah, that's his name — told us to wait out here." His friend's blue eyes bored into me.

"Are you now?" I grinned, certain that would annoy them, and it worked. "Perhaps I can help you."

"We'll wait," the same man said with disdain.

Fab came up behind me, poking her head over my shoulder. "What's going on?"

"These two are waiting for the boss *man*. I'm going to go find him. Please don't shoot either of them while I'm gone." I winked at Fab.

Doodad rushed though the doorway before I could take a step. "Drink refills anyone?" he asked, slightly out of breath.

"Yes, and get rid of these two," the man who'd done most of talking said. "This one is abnormally attached to this table." He pointed to me.

"You can't read." I flicked my finger toward the sign.

"This is Wolf and Blade," Doodad cut in. "We're winding up negotiations on an event

153

they're planning." He turned, stuck his head through the doorway, and whistled, holding up his fingers in a code only Kelpie could decipher.

"Why are you sharing details with her?" Wolf barked, crossing his arms, his biceps completely covering his chest.

"I'm the owner, Madison." I squeezed behind the table, sitting on the bench and patting the seat beside me. "This is my bodyguard, Fab."

Blade, the quiet one, eyed Fab up and down and, based on the twitch of his lips, liked what he saw.

Fab glared, and Blade grinned.

Wolf stuck out his hand. Noticing my lack of response, he stuck out his knuckles instead, and I reciprocated.

Kelpie twirled her way out to the deck, leaning over as she set the beers down, not the least bit reticent about offering a close-up of what she had stashed in that tight top of hers. Neither man looked away until she stood up.

"No wonder this place is full of men," Fab mumbled.

I craned my head for a better view of the interior of the bar, not having previously taken a head count based on gender, but now that she mentioned it, only a couple of the hardcore female regulars were sitting at the bar. Anna and her friend had staked out stools in front of the game machines at the far end of bar, trying to maneuver a drink in one hand and a controller in the other and losing.

Doodad cleared his throat. "Wolf's club is renting the entire place to hold their semi-annual meeting. It will be on a Saturday, and we'll open to the public by mid-afternoon." At my raised brow, he added, "There's a room rental fee, in addition to the food and bar bill. It's another way Jake's can branch out."

"I like the words 'money-making opportunity,'" I said.

"What kind of..." Fab started. She hadn't taken a seat and had chosen instead to lean against the wall.

"Wolf," Creole hailed from the doorway and nodded to Blade. He introduced Didier, and they pushed a couple of tables together to make room for all of us.

Creole slid in next to me and hooked his arm around my neck, pulling me close and kissing the top of my head.

Wolf raised his eyebrow. "You've got a handful there."

"And I'm loving every minute of it." He kissed me again.

Didier pulled Fab into a chair beside him. She resisted at first because it wasn't the prime seat for a quick exit.

"You three know one another?" I asked. "That's a good recommendation. He's holding a meeting here for his..." I realized I hadn't asked and Fab had gotten cut off.

"Motorcycle club," Wolf responded.

"Club." Fab snickered. "Should have known that pitch sounded too good to come without complications."

"We're not some thug group. We've got a good rep and raise a lot of money for charity," Wolf answered.

Whistles, cat calls, and shouts of "hit her" drifted through the patio doors. Heads turned to see what was happening inside—two women fighting on the dance floor. They had their arms wrapped around each other's torsos and were turning in circles, sumo style.

I pressed my fingers over my eyes and exhaled. Then tried to make eye contact with Doodad, whose face became a blank mask before he turned away, hands shoved in his pockets.

"Would you like me to break it up?" Fab drew her Walther. "I didn't get to shoot anything this morning." At my incredulous look, she added, "I'll put the bullets in the ceiling. It's calmed the crowds before."

I shrugged and shook my head—might as well let it play out. My first clue that some ruckus had been planned ought to have been a full bar on a weekday. Damn the little hairs on my neck for not giving me a warning.

The fight lasted for several minutes, during which all the men had their eyes glued on the women, thoroughly entertained. Finally, one collapsed on her back, and the other swooned across her. After a moment, the top woman got up, extending a hand and helping the other woman to her feet.

The room erupted in clapping, wolf whistles, and shouts of "kiss and make up." Even the guys on the deck clapped.

The winner shot her fist in the air, curtseying awkwardly to the crowd, then turned to the other woman. They shook hands and hugged.

"I probably should've offered to break up the melee, but it was kind of hot," Wolf said.

The guys nodded in agreement.

"Humph," Didier grunted after getting an elbow in his side.

"Kelpie is not fired but close," I said to Doodad.

"But, boss..." Doodad's eyes implored. *Was he whining?* "No one got hurt, and it's a money maker." He flourished his hand. "Look around, standing room only."

"How did you get the word out?" Didier asked, clearly intrigued.

"A few phone calls, 'fight' whispered in hushed tones, and phones are ringing off the hook." Doodad's cheeks flushed.

It sounded unbelievable, but I knew it was true.

"Even the old guys came out of their den. I bet they took wagers." Doodad pointed to the opposite side of the bar, where the poker boys were lined up.

"You're leaving out the best part—the cops show up." I nodded toward the front door.

Kevin, in his work uniform, strode over the threshold and straight out to the deck. He dragged a chair across the concrete, sitting next to Wolf and acknowledging him and Blade with a nod.

I guess I didn't know everyone in town.

"Heard there was another fight," Kevin said. "Sorry I missed it." He wiped away a non-existent tear.

"If you hadn't taken the long way when you got the call, you might have someone to arrest," I said.

The guys laughed.

"No one got hurt," Wolf informed him. "The entertainment was enjoyed by all. Maybe not those two." He pointed to me and Fab.

"Would you like a drink?" I asked Kevin.

"Are you bribing a uniformed officer?"

"Not this time." I motioned to Doodad. "Signal Kelpie for a Coke. I haven't learned the finger sign language yet. I only know one, and that won't get me anything."

Fab was the only one to laugh.

I smiled at her.

The busboy rolled a cart of food up to the door, and Kelpie handed her bar tray to Doodad, who set Kevin's soda in front of him.

"What are you eating?" Kelpie nudged Kevin and got back a grunt. "Either you're hungry or not," she huffed. I didn't hear what he ordered, but she took off in the direction of the kitchen.

Business talk was tabled while the guys exchanged stories about what they'd been doing since they last ran into one another.

Fab reached across the table and clinked the rim of her glass against mine. "Thank you for shaking down the neighbor."

"It wasn't me. It was Didier, and he rocked it." I picked up a spoon and banged it on the table. "Almost forgot. Round of applause for hottie of the day." I pointed to Didier. "He handled that snooty Marjorie Ross like a pro."

Didier's cheeks heated up, and his lips twitched despite his glare.

Everyone clapped, including Wolf and Blade, both questioning what happened.

Creole hit the highlights of the morning, filling them in on the drunken college partiers and how one ended up going to the hospital. "Got a text that he's going to be okay."

"You should text your client," I told Fab. "That should calm his shorts."

Fab laughed. "If only I could say it that way. You could call as my assistant, but then he'd probably never hire me again."

My attention switched to Creole when I overheard Blade asking him what he was up to these days. It surprised me that he knew Creole had retired from the police force.

"I'm in hot demand." Creole grinned,

satisfaction with life showing in his eyes. "You know that section of the docks that burned down? Well, Didier here pressured me to sign on as General Contractor, since the man who filled the role moved north to live with his son."

"I consider myself lucky to have a man I trust on the project." Didier clapped Creole on the shoulder.

Creole and I exchanged glances, and he telegraphed that there was more on the subject that we'd be talking about later.

"Got a friend that's interested in space for an arcade down there," Blade said. "He talked to someone, must have been you," he said to Didier.

"Thought it was a great idea," Didier acknowledged. "Once we get final approvals, the spaces will be ready to move in. I'm striving to make the area a go-to fun place to bring family and friends. With any luck, it will also entice tourists to stop on their way to Key West."

Cook's nephew set down Kevin's taco plate, along with another Coke.

"Great job," I mouthed to him.

"You arrest anyone lately?" Fab asked Kevin.

"It's been quiet here and at The Cottages." Kevin laughed, a huge fan of his own humor, toasting the two of us with his soda.

Chapter Seventeen

Today was a first. Fab and I both had appointments, and we each wanted the other's company, but neither meeting could be rescheduled. I flipped out. I pointed out that, since her meeting was with Brick Famosa — her oldest and most problematic client, and that was putting it kindly — it could be rescheduled. And also asked why she cared if Brick was irked with waiting since she was giving him the boot. Wait until he found out that tidbit. There was no way she was going by herself. But she didn't want to change the appointment, so I tipped off Didier.

Unfortunately, he also had a meeting, and when he arrived home last night, he told her in no uncertain terms that she wasn't to go by herself. Either move the appointment time or cancel. Then he dragged her up the stairs as though she were a naughty child, lecturing her about her safety. I'd wondered at what point she'd erase the big grin off her face that I noticed as they reached the top.

That morning, as I got to the bottom of the stairs, Fab came out of the kitchen dressed in a black sheath dress that showed off a tummy bump. If you didn't know better, you would think she was several months pregnant. When she'd called to reschedule, Brick agreed to move up the time, leaving off any snide comments.

"One of these months, you're going to have to produce a baby," I said, twirling around. "How do I look? Casual yet business is what I'm going for." I'd chosen a black sleeveless dress with low heels, wanting to make a good impression in my lunch meeting with a social worker friend of GC's to discuss how to maneuver through the system.

She gave me a thumbs up. "Thank you for calling Didier. I appreciate it. I should have just asked him, but I know he hates everything Brick."

"Didier's probably at least partially disappointed he can't go. He had fun on your last job."

Fab sighed. "It was stupid to even entertain the idea of going by myself. I've had plenty of time to think, and when your client scares the heck out of you, it's time to put an end to the relationship. There were a couple of times on my last job for the man that I thought he might actually kill me."

"Promise you this—if he was that stupid, his death would be hideously slow and excruciatingly painful." I gave her my best deranged smile.

"I'd expect nothing less from you. And so you

know, you've got the same promise from me." Fab opened the door. "I'm going to be late if we don't hurry up."

I closed the door behind us, following Fab to the SUV. "I'm hoping we both have successful meetings. I'd like to get all my questions concerning Brad's possible custody case answered today. He deserves an answer, one way or the other." I had fully intended to keep Brad's secret, but Fab overheard when I was setting up the meeting with the social worker.

"It would be fun to be aunties," she'd said.

It had surprised me that she skipped shock and went straight to enthusiasm, embracing the idea.

"Knowing you, whether she's related or not, you're not going to want to leave her behind."

Impulsively, I hugged her.

"What are you doing?"

"It's just a hug; you'll recover."

Fab roared out of the driveway and down the street in typical style.

* * *

Fab and I had been both lost in thought on the drive to Famosa Motors, and at some point, she'd turned on music, filling the silence. It had been a while since we'd set foot on the car lot, and I, for one, hadn't missed it at all. At the time, Brick had been up to his eyeballs in a murder, and his true role in the whole thing had never come to light. Then he'd left the country on an extended vacation with the wife, which was suspicious on its own for a workaholic, and stayed gone for a couple of months. Blowing up Fab's phone signaled his return and that he had one job after another for her, mostly repo stuff, which both of us turned up our noses at and refused to do. Just because a person stopped paying for their car didn't mean they had any intention of letting it go without gunfire. We'd yet to meet a person that said, "Here, take it." That had a lot to do with said *persons* being criminals to begin with and stupidly thinking they had nothing to lose.

Fab swung into her favorite parking spot between the two exit doors.

"Am I waiting in the car or coming with you?" I asked.

"Not to hurt your feelings, but you're not high on Brick's list of favorites."

"It would surprise me if I even had a mention at the bottom under 'used to tolerate.'"

Brick had made it clear he found it offensive that I even sucked air. He blamed me for the fact that Fab's wild side had calmed down significantly since we met. I was happy to take credit, but it had more to do with Didier, who wanted to marry the love of his life, not visit her in prison or, worse, have to say good-bye at a cemetery.

"The thought of being alone with him for very long makes me edgy."

I knew what she wanted, so I said it for her. "I'll wait for a few and then come up. I'll enjoy ramping up the annoying. I haven't come up with anything yet, but last-second inspiration has worked for me in the past."

"I don't think a missing cat story would work in this situation."

We both laughed.

"I apologize in advance for his rudeness." Fab opened the door and slid out from behind the wheel. "How do I look?" She ran her hands over her baby bump.

"Yes, you look pregnant." I smiled at her attack of nerves. "One of these days, that's going to be a real bump."

"Didier told me the other night he wants eleven kids."

I gasped.

"That's how many it takes to field a soccer team."

"He needs to calm down." I frowned. "So, eleven for one side?" Fab nodded. "What about the opposing side? Are you going to procreate them too?"

"I thought you could pump that side out."

I threw my head back and laughed. "Wait until I tell Creole. The teams need to be coed, and just so you know, our side will run over your side."

"Our daughters are going to kick serious butt." Fab winked and, before closing the door, reminded me, "Don't wait too long."

Change of plans. Forget waiting. Once Fab disappeared from sight, I planned to sneak in the side door and bypass the Amazon at the front desk. Last time, Everly pulled a gun, and I wasn't looking for another confrontation. I smoothed my dress down. "Nope, not getting this dress dirty," I said to myself.

Getting out of the SUV, I patted the Glock holstered to my thigh. I pushed open the door used mainly by sales personnel and checked out the reception area. Not seeing a single person milling around, I headed for the stairs that led to Brick's office. Two steps later, a shot rang out and glass exploded somewhere behind me. My hands flew over my head, I sent my heels flying, and drew my gun, hiding behind a snack machine.

"What in the hell?" Brick roared from the top of the stairs, his cannon in his hand. He caught sight of me below and bellowed, "What the f—did you do to my front window? I'm calling the cops."

I was of a mind to yell back, "Dare you," but thought better of it, instead yelling, "I didn't do it."

"I thought she was an intruder sneaking in the door," Everly said, sidling around the elevator. "You want me to call the police? The bitch didn't bother to come in the front door and check in, instead sneaking in through the side door. That makes it criminal trespassing."

"You're dumber than a stump, Florescent," I said, tossing in a dig at her dyed red hair. "This is a business, and you're freakin' *open*," I ended on a shout.

Brick continued to glare at the shattered floor-to-ceiling window.

Fab popped her head around his shoulder. "You're a terrible shot," she said to Everly, a sneer in her voice.

"Is that what you do all day?" I asked Everly, itching to shoot her. "Lie in wait and shoot customers who use the wrong door?"

"Not once have you ever bought anything." Everly sniffed.

Good thing most businesses don't have a "don't buy, get shot" policy. "I suggest you turn around and look out what's left of the window. The Hummer parked in the front was purchased here for a hefty amount of cash."

"Everly," Brick snapped. "Get on the phone. The window needs to be boarded over until the glass can be replaced." He turned to me. "You're paying the bill."

"Over your dead body."

Fab stepped forward and gave Brick a slight shove. "Enough you two. I want to know why Everly would shoot at Madison. Did you tell her it was okay?"

"Of course not," he said and stomped back inside his office.

I collected my shoes and didn't waste time getting up the stairs. Instead of sinking into a chair in front of Brick's desk, per my usual, I hung back and leaned against the wall. Standing on the other side of the office was close enough for me.

"As I was saying," Fab took control of the conversation. "I've got a really good guy that can handle all your collection problems. He has a near-perfect record of getting what he goes after."

That has to be Toady. When Brick met the man, it would annoy him endlessly that Toady couldn't be pushed around.

"I've got a couple of guys on call now." Brick sniffed, unhappy with the suggestion.

"I won't be hands-on on any jobs for the foreseeable future, but that doesn't mean I can't get your jobs done. The one stipulation is that they'll have to be mostly legal." Fab flashed a smile, which he answered with a growl.

"Sounds like I'm going to have find me a new crew."

Brick wasn't happy with how the meeting had gone thus far, but what did he expect—Fab to jump up and run out on his every job? After all, she was pregnant... or so he thought.

Brick would soon figure out for himself that the "snapping of his fingers" days were over. Now, though, it was time to get out of there before things deteriorated further. I contemplated fainting but couldn't remember if I'd pulled that one before or not.

Fab to the rescue. She rubbed her stomach and stood. "I can't believe I'm not embarrassed that my stomach growled. Guess who's hungry?"

I practically leapt through the doorway, waiting in the hallway.

Brick came around his desk and hugged Fab, who stiffened. "If you ever need anything," he said.

"This isn't the end unless you decide not to use my people. I'm always a phone call away. We've been friends a long time, and that doesn't have to change." Fab smiled.

We got to the bottom of the stairs, and I tugged Fab toward auto repair. "Coast is clear this way." The other two exits were blocked by glass and Everly.

Fab nodded. "Let's get out of here as fast as we can."

"Can't say I'll miss this place."

"I'll be hearing from Brick again." Fab shuddered. "He doesn't have anyone decent to do his jobs, or he wouldn't have called me. I think what annoyed him most was that I have people to get the jobs done. Thanks to you. I hope I was appropriately appreciative that you nagged me about getting contractors."

"You weren't. So let's remember this moment, and maybe you'll listen to my next suggestion."

Outside at last. I took a breath of fresh air as

we cut around the corner to the front lot. Before getting in, I walked around the Hummer and inspected the exterior. Not a single scratch.

"If there was so much as a nick in the paint, I'd be on the phone to the cops," I threatened.

Fab absently patted my hand. "How about a lemonade to calm your nerves?"

"If it has strawberries in it." I licked my lips, certain it would have a calming effect.

"Let's hope our next appointment is less hair-raising."

"There won't be any brandishing of weapons," I said. "I'm leaving mine in the car. I don't want anything to go wrong. If the social worker were to see it, she might end the meeting and I'd never get my questions answered."

Chapter Eighteen

The location was kind of dicey, but anything with tacos in the name and I was in. El Patron Tacos was located on a side street off a busy highway in a run-down commercial area. The mobile home-turned-restaurant sat nestled under a grove of trees. Picnic tables dotted the gravel lot, and it also offered a covered patio for seating.

"Since the parking lot's almost full and it's not even noon, the food must be good or cheap or both," Fab said, pulling into a space.

"I'm thinking there's no bar. But I suppose sucking down a tequila midday wouldn't make a good impression anyway."

"We need a girl lunch. Pick up your mother, find a new restaurant to check out, and get sloshed."

I groaned, images of my last drunk-on coming to mind. "Last girl-outing, my hangover was brutal. Besides, then we have to call the guys for a ride home. Spoon is the worst, accusing us of corrupting Mother."

Fab pointed over the steering wheel. "That woman is sitting all by herself; wonder if that's your appointment."

"Celia Yaley. Remember, she's a friend of Alex's, so no referring to him as GC and having to come up with some lame lie."

"Got it." Fab saluted. "What's my story?"

"Sister. Maybe half. Different set of parents. We're so alike—you're Euro chic and I could easily pass for a wild-haired local."

Fab reached over and fluffed my hair. "You've got it under control most of the time, unless it's near a hundred-percent humidity. No Carrot Top moments in all the time I've known you."

I laughed. "Thanks for that. I think."

"Ready?" Fab pushed the door open.

"Pinch me hard if I get off track. Making a good impression is paramount here."

"Breathe," Fab ordered. "You get an attack of nerves, picture her in granny underwear sitting next to a blowup dude and you'll do fine."

"You think—"

"Absolutely no to whatever you're thinking." Fab groaned.

"If it would keep Miss January from trolling the streets…"

"Out." Fab pointed. "The woman just looked over here."

El Patron had no walkway, so Fab and I trudged over the pea gravel. How the woman next to me did it so gracefully in high heels was a mystery to me.

"Celia Yaley?" I asked the woman nursing a lemonade.

"Madison?"

I nodded.

"Have a seat. Nice to meet a friend of Alex's."

"This is my sister, well, step-sister, Fab Merceau."

We slid onto the bench across from the woman.

"This is going to have to be a quick meeting. I just got a call about a last-minute meeting that requires my attendance." Celia reached into her bag, pulling out several sheets of paper and a booklet.

I took them and quickly scanned the first one, which was a list of guidelines. The booklet had to do with how Social Services operated. "Thank you, this will be quite helpful."

"Follow the instructions, and you'll be ahead of the game. Most try to deal with the system without knowing how it works and get frustrated when the process doesn't go smoothly. The first thing Mr. Westin needs to do is contact Mila Thorson's caseworker and request a paternity test. We do our best to place children with family. The fact that she's languished in the system without anyone expressing an interest will make it easier for your family." She stood. "I hate to be rude, I really do, but I can't miss this meeting. If you have any questions, call me. I don't have access to Mila's files, as she's not one of my cases, but if I can be of any help, I'll be happy to get you any answers you need."

"I appreciate your meeting with me," I said. "Are you sure I can't buy you lunch?"

"I got here early and ate. I recommend the taco platter. My card is stapled to the second sheet, along with several useful numbers." And with a wave, she made her way across the gravel.

"That didn't go quite the way I thought," I said to Fab, who watched Celia pull out onto the street. "Five minutes?"

"Barely," Fab said. "I'm guessing this quick meet-and-greet pays back a favor owed to GC."

I stood. "Two taco platters coming up."

Chapter Nineteen

After our meeting, Fab had dropped me off at Creole's, since we planned a quiet night together — dinner and a walk on the beach. I told her I wouldn't need a ride the next morning, as Creole would take me home.

Surprised would be an understatement when, the next morning, I walked out of the bathroom and found Fab standing in the living room, pink bakery box in hand. Didier stood behind her, looking ready to wring her neck. Thankfully, when I got out of bed, I'd grabbed up one of Creole's t-shirts and pulled it on.

"Bonjour," Fab said in a cheerful tone.

Creole rolled over, caught sight of the duo, and jerked the sheet up under his chin. Thankfully, nothing more had showed than his bare back. "What the...?" He jerked into an upright position. "I'm certain you didn't knock."

"The door was open." Fab pointed to the patio doors.

Creole's eyes shot to me.

"I opened them earlier," I said. I should've added *not because I was expecting Fab* but wasn't in the mood to ratchet up the awkwardness.

"Sorry." Didier held up his hands. "I thought we were invited—or at least that you were expecting us to show up—not barging in like burglars. What a good way to get shot." He nudged Fab.

"You got decent coffee?" Fab ignored Creole's and Didier's growls and headed into the kitchen, setting the box down on the counter. Making herself at home, she opened the cupboard and pulled down mugs.

"What are you doing?" I asked, following her. "Besides annoying my boyfriend?" I'd almost said fiancé but caught myself in time. "And yours."

From the corner of my eye, I saw Didier pick up Creole's sweatpants off the floor and toss them at him with a laugh. Creole gave him the finger.

"Just be patient. I have some news, but it's better with a little show and tell," Fab said.

"Did it ever occur to you to knock and wait for one of us to answer?" Creole grouched. "No, of course not," he answered for her in disgust and disappeared into the bathroom, slamming the door.

When I heard the shower start, I went into the closet and grabbed Creole a change of clothes, setting them on the bathroom counter. Disappearing back inside the closet, I pulled on a pair of his sweat shorts before joining Fab and Didier in the kitchen.

Fab was rooting through the cupboards, looking for coffee. I got it out of the refrigerator and set it in front of the coffee maker, which I pulled away from the wall.

"You can't do this again," I told her. "There's no privacy as it is. You could've walked in while we were in the middle of... you know."

"That would've been icky." Fab scrunched up her nose.

"I promise you, she won't be doing it again." Didier leveled a glare at her.

"Thanks for not shooting," Fab said with a cheeky smile. "From the look on Creole's face, I'm lucky he didn't shoot anyway."

As much as Creole might want to, he'd never hurt her on purpose.

"You make the coffee." I handed her the bag. "It's not your Turkish blend, but you pour enough grounds in the machine, you can make it taste like sludge anyway." I lifted the lid on the bakery box, looked inside and licked my lips. "I call dibs on the pecan roll."

By the time Fab had the coffee ready and the pastries arranged on a platter she found, Creole had finished his shower. She'd even boiled water for my brew.

The smell of coffee lured Creole into the kitchen. "This better be good," he said to Fab.

She pointed to the platter. "I got your favorite—cinnamon rolls." She handed Didier and him a mug.

Creole groaned. "You must be in really big trouble."

Didier laughed. "Oh yes, she is."

Fab shot Creole an icy stare. "Let's sit." She picked up my mug and hers, walked out on the deck, and set the coffee on the table. Creole and Didier followed with the tray and a handful of napkins.

"Since Didier and I are getting married, we're talking about buying a house." Fab flashed a smile around the table. "The plan is for us to be neighbors."

"Moving?" As hard as I tried, my eyes filled with tears anyway. I didn't want them to move.

"I knew this would happen," Fab crabbed. "Fix it," she ordered Creole.

"Why? It's your fault." He pulled me to his side, giving me his best sideways hug.

"It was inevitable," I said, swiping at my face. "When's the moving date?"

"We haven't found anything yet," Fab assured me. "The reason we came over this morning was because I wanted to show you that if we were neighbors or lived close by, nothing would change. We could still have morning coffee — my house, your house."

"Another possibility is for the four of us to build a couple of houses to our liking... Fab would want an access tunnel between the houses," Didier said.

"Great idea." Creole rolled his eyes.

"I'm not suggesting you sell your Aunt Elizabeth's house, since I know you inherited it and it's a tie to a woman you loved. Renting could be an option to check out. Go through an agency that attracts a different kind of renter than The Cottages."

Aunt Elizabeth's house had run out of room a long time ago, and yet we'd made it work. I'd never thought to move, and the idea brought on a wave of sadness. Creole and I hadn't discussed moving, and I imagined he had a few of his own ideas on the subject.

Fab pulled her phone out of her pocket. "Found this house at the end of the street, down from Creole's, and arranged to check it out." She handed it over for Creole and me to see. I was surprised to realize the house was one of the four on Creole's secluded street. "The current owners are selling because they're getting a divorce. We'd be a short beach walk away. Or we could meet in the middle."

"Another option is adding onto my house," I said. "Not sure it would get approval for building permits though. The cats will miss you. Especially you, Didier. I'll need a treat list from you to keep the howling to a minimum." Sounding enthusiastic wasn't easy. "You promise you aren't moving next week?"

"This isn't good-bye. Before you ask, neither Didier nor I entertained purchasing an all-glass condo in Miami."

Creole put his finger under my chin. "We'll talk later and make whatever we decide to do work."

"What would be fun is to have our own little compound."

I smiled at Fab's enthusiasm.

"Nothing has to change—coffee, meetings, barbeques," Fab said adamantly. "Maybe a third and fourth house for your mother, Spoon, and Brad. Getting your brother to leave his penthouse might require kidnapping."

"Show of hands." I held mine up. "Who thinks this project should be put in Fab's capable hands?"

Creole's and Didier's hands shot in the air.

Chapter Twenty

After finishing up my morning coffee, I leaned over the sink to pluck a couple of dead leaves from an orchid and decided today would be perfect for dropping in on Brad. I didn't call and ask how he felt about it, instead opting to surprise him. Depending on how that went, it might be a short visit.

I was the first to use the electronic notepad Fab had installed on the refrigerator, scribbling a message for her. Her early-morning work hours were ridiculous, but they worked for her, and most mornings, she left the house with Didier and was back home by noon.

On the way, I swung by the Bakery Café, ordering Brad breakfast to go. In the Westin family, food tamed the surliest of attitudes. While waiting, I called Cara, who answered quickly, excited to hear from me.

"What are you up to?" She giggled into the phone. "I only have a minute; the school bell is about to ring."

"I'm here at the bakery and want to get something for Alex—what does he like?"

"He loves those sink cookies."

"Those are delicious. But at a thousand calories a cookie, it makes them a once-a-year treat... for me anyway."

"How are you going to get it to him?" Her voice turned serious.

"No worries. I won't be doing anything underhanded."

"I've got to go." She hurried and hung up as a bell blared in the background.

At some point, GC would have to accept that anonymity was over between us and him. I'd have to reassure him that neither of us would out him, even if we went our separate ways.

Between the food and cookie orders, I filled up two shopping bags. I ordered a fun breakfast for Brad and satisfied both men's sweet tooth.

Turning into the underground garage, I pulled in next to Brad's loaner Escalade, backing into the space. Then sat there for a second, scanning the different spaces, trying to figure out which two had been assigned to GC. The numbering was no help, as it didn't correspond to unit numbers, making it impossible to figure out.

I had a couple of "none of my business" questions for the man, such as: did he have an office? Work out of his penthouse? I'd have to figure it out myself, since I lacked the nerve to outright ask.

When the elevator arrived on Brad's floor, I set his bag in front of his door before backtracking to

GC's. In mid-knock, I changed my mind and rang the doorbell. I'd give it to the man—he was quiet; it took me a minute to realize that he was looking out the peephole. At least, I hoped it was him and not a scantily clad guest. I'd suggest (or not) that he upgrade and get one that didn't give away a person's presence by the change of lighting. I needed to check with Fab and make sure that, if she hadn't upgraded at our house, she would put it on her list.

I held up the bag, showing off the label as incentive to open up. Nothing. What the heck? Stubborn man wasn't going for bribery. It took about a second to dismiss the idea of making a scene in the hallway. Instead, I opted to pull out my phone and call the man. The call went straight to voicemail, and I called again.

"I'm not going anywhere," I said to the door.

Still nothing.

Last resort—a threat I'd never actually carry out, but GC didn't know that—was pulling my lockpick out of my purse and waving it back and forth in front of the hole.

I wanted to do a fist pump when I heard the lock turn and the door cracked open.

"What the hell do you want?" GC barked through the opening, keeping his face out of sight.

"You're beyond ridiculous." I snorted. "You've apparently forgotten I can now pick you out of a lineup."

"Five seconds and I'm shutting the door," he barked.

"I came by to say thank you in a way that men love—cookies. All you have to do is crack the door open a little wider, and I'll shove this bag through. You don't even have to say, 'Thank you, what a sweet thing to do.'"

He shoved his hand out the opening, and I hooked the bag over his wrist. "I better not get sick."

"You're welcome."

Surprisingly, he didn't shut the door with a resounding bang, instead waiting until I'd taken several steps back towards Brad's before closing it with barely a sound. Once again, I rang the bell, this time at the other penthouse condo. I'd promised my brother long ago not to just barge in. To be annoying, I stuck my finger over the peephole.

I lurched forward when Brad jerked open the door. "I knew it was you. Your juvenile tricks sometimes amuse me," he said with a smile. He looked down and grabbed the bag, then stuck his face inside, sniffing. "Smells good. You came at the right time. I'm starving and have no food."

"You never have food. You should drop a hint to Mother—she'd have your cupboards and refrigerator stocked in a blink." I followed him into the kitchen.

"There are times when she drops by with leftovers... or so she says. But they're always complete meals that have never been touched. The best part is she remembers the sides I like, the sauces, and there's always dessert. Plus, she hasn't yet shown up with some kind of 'What is this?' that makes your nose curl up in disgust."

"Mother spoils us. I miss her showing up in the morning with something yummy for breakfast. Now that she's married, she's doing naughty things with her husband instead."

Brad groaned. "Please, not on an empty stomach." He set the bag on the kitchen counter, grabbed a fork, and popped the lid off the container. "Beer or water, help yourself." He motioned for me to follow as he ate.

I grabbed a water and crossed into the living room, sitting next to him on the couch.

"The kid mine or not?" Brad asked between bites.

"Her name is Mila." I pulled one of my cards out of my pocket — I'd written the information on the back. "You'll need to take a DNA test."

"I'll call today and make an appointment," he said. "If she's mine, I'm going to get a lawyer and get custody. They probably won't give it to me, but they will to you."

I ruffled his hair. "I'll do whatever it takes. We both know that Social Services favors family members. I'm thinking I have a good chance."

"Even if I were to get custody, the two of us would have to move in with you. I don't know anything about kids. You have some experience—you have cats."

I laughed. "You'll figure it out as you go along, just like every other first-time father. Look at Liam—he loves you."

"He was a pre-teen when we met. I treated him like a guy friend, which would probably have been looked down on if I'd been his father. But look at us now. He's such a great kid." Brad drifted off. "One thing I'm certain of—I don't want my kid in foster care. Guess I'll have to grow up."

"Don't be so hard on yourself. It's not for sure, and whatever happens, it would be nice if Mila got placed permanently. Just remember that you have family that will do whatever you ask. And Mother, how excited is she going to be?"

"Not a word until we know for sure."

"I'll let you break the news." I zipped my lips. "You working from home these days?" I glanced over at his desk, which he'd moved in front of the window. It was piled with paperwork, the monitor glowing.

"Might as well—Bordello and Phil went to Chicago for some kind of family get-together. I wasn't invited, and I suspect I wouldn't have been even if I could leave the county."

"How are things with Phil?"

"We're both ignoring the fact that we can barely stand to be around one another." Brad blew out a long sigh. "Too many secrets. Every time I see her, I wonder what else she's hiding.

Phil wants us to live in ignorant bliss, and Bordello is mad because I didn't take it well when I found out all the secrets that Phil had been keeping. I wanted to tell him to shove his 'get over it' attitude. He wouldn't tolerate that from one of his multitude of women."

"Where does the condo project stand?" Bordello and he had signed the partnership agreement before the truth came out about Bordello having a sister. That wasn't the problem. It was that Phil didn't think Brad needed to know she was related to his partner until after they were married that Brad hadn't gotten over.

"We're ahead of schedule." Brad smiled at his accomplishment. "I'm surprised that Bordello hasn't made an offer to buy out my interest. I truly have expected that shoe to drop."

"Would you take the offer?" I didn't like the man, and the feeling was mutual. He had, after all, schemed to put Fab and me behind bars.

"I wouldn't want to but probably would. After that kind of offer was extended, it would be hard to work together. One thing's for certain — there won't be another partnership. After this, I'm going to take some time off, and my next venture will be solo. Having control over your own business is everything."

"I'm sorry."

"Oh, stop feeling guilty for blurting out the whole sordid mess." He practically licked the inside of the container and tossed it back in the bag. "If not for you, I would've married a woman I didn't know." He rubbed his stomach. "Goood. You got any good news?"

I told him about Fab's moving idea, not bothering to mention that I hadn't come around to the idea yet.

"The idea of a waterfront family compound sounds way damn cool."

"Waterfront?" I laughed. "That just upped the price tag."

"I suppose, since I haven't received an invite or anything, that I'm the last to know where Creole lives, after even Mother?"

"Mother doesn't know the location. The only reason Fab and Didier know is that we needed their help on a case." I told him about Fab barging in for coffee, and that had him laughing.

"Fab's so damn nervy. One thing's for sure — you can depend on her. She's called a couple of times, checking on me. Asks prying questions, most of which I avoid."

"She's full of surprises, all right." I stood and grabbed the shopping bag, putting it by the door.

"What are you doing with that?"

"Dumping it in the trash for you."

"You know I've got a dude for that. You hired him. He's good at cleaning but damn unfriendly."

I sat back down next to him. "I can get you someone different."

"We don't need to be pals for him to do his job and me to stay out of his way."

"Let me know when you take the DNA test. Mila's caseworker said she'd stay on top of it. I think she'd like to see a match." I stood. "I should let you get back to work."

Brad grabbed me in a bear hug. I nudged him lightly in the ribs, and he loosened his grip. "Come on." He hooked his arm around my shoulders and walked me to the elevator.

Next time, I'd kick GC's door on the way out.

Chapter Twenty-One

Fab had been very secretive about her plans for the all-girl dinner, which she'd thus far not shared one detail about, except that Mother and I were the only guests. I demanded the name of the restaurant, and that got me nowhere. Even Mother expressed complete ignorance. Fab *did* say casual attire, about which I was happy, as I'd expected black tie, which I wasn't going to do, no matter how long she went on about the fun I'd miss. Fab full of secrets should've been a red flag.

Before I got in the shower, she'd even gone so far as to lay out an outfit on the bed, which I planned to ignore just like she did me, walking out of my bedroom while I was in the middle of telling her, "I'm not six. I don't need you picking out my clothes." The only problem was the white bohemian skirt and hot-pink top were favorites. To my shock, she'd even chosen a pair of ankle-strap sandals.

The first stop was Mother's. I offered to run upstairs and get her, but Fab insisted on parking and both of us going up.

Fab announced us over the security system,

which was a first. The woman preferred her lockpick. When we got to Mother's floor, Spoon stood in the doorway. He kissed our cheeks, ushering us inside. Mother met us, handing me a margarita and Fab a martini. Brad, Liam, and Didier waved from the living room. Fab walked into Didier's arms. I crossed the room and stood next to Brad and Liam, holding up my glass in a toast.

The patio doors were open, and it was easy to see that the table had been set. I mentally counted the place settings. There hadn't been a mention that the guys were having a dinner and expecting guests. I turned to catch Fab's eye, but she ignored me.

"How much time do we have before our reservation?" I asked.

"There's been a change of plans," Mother said, a bit too cheerfully. "No worries—Fab and I have this all planned."

Judging by everyone's expressions, they were waiting for me to figure something out, but what? Maybe I was overreacting. I downed the rest of my margarita and handed the glass to Spoon. "I'll take another."

"I've got a pitcher made." He smirked, amusement in his eyes.

"So the all-girl outing was ditched in favor of coed? Or was that always the plan?" I leveled a look at Didier, who nudged Fab and motioned for her to stop ignoring me.

"Just the family," she said with too much sweetness.

"Works for me. When will Creole be here?"

The doorbell rang. Spoon handed me my refreshed drink, but instead of heading to the front door, he gave Mother a slight shove in that direction.

"It's probably Creole." I stood. "I'll get it."

Liam, who had changed chairs and was now standing next to me, tugged on my arm. "Let Grandmother get it."

My first or third clue should've been that all eyes were focused on me, waiting for... what?

I'd never seen the man coming through the door before. Brad's age and height, reasonably good-looking, he was dressed in beach casual, like the rest of the guys. Mother looped her arm in his. "This is Greg Reed." She introduced him around the room before turning to me. "This is my daughter, Madison."

I smiled, wondering how this stranger fit into a family dinner. Salesman? I managed to contain a laugh at the thought.

Mother asked the man something I couldn't hear, but I had my answer when she signaled Spoon to get him a glass of wine.

Liam stood, offering Greg a seat next to me, which he took, sitting too close, which had me squirming away, only to find I was out of room. I tossed Liam an annoyed look, which he answered with a wink.

"Your mother's told me a lot about you." Greg took his glass from Spoon and clinked it against mine.

"I wish I could say the same." Okay, that didn't sound friendly. "You'll have to catch me up." Where was my phone? I had a one-word text for Creole: "Hustle." Come to think of it, he hadn't said a word about coming to dinner, only that he had a stack of paperwork to wade through.

So far, no one had said a word after the "nice to meet you," comments each person uttered as Mother introduced him around the room.

"I met Greg through my friend Jean," Mother said. "We hit it off so well, I thought it would be a great idea to invite him to dinner, so we could all get to know him."

Spoon openly glared at Mother and motioned her to his side, which she ignored. Didier whispered to Fab, who stepped away, or tried to anyway—he tightened his hold. Money exchanged hands between Brad and Liam. I'd find out what the bet was later.

"How many others are coming?" I asked Mother.

She bustled around the room, all nervous energy, offering to refill already full glasses. "Everyone's here, dear." She smiled.

"Except Creole." Did he get sick? I couldn't imagine any other reason for him not showing up.

She ignored my question. "Get to know Greg better while I check on dinner."

It would be rude to laugh, but everyone in the room knew that Mother didn't cook anything. Spoon did. My eyes landed on the big man—he still wasn't happy with his wife. He wasn't a man used to being ignored, and instead of requesting her presence again, he cornered her as she attempted to slide by him into the kitchen.

It finally clicked. This scene was familiar, bringing back memories of Mother setting me up with the man who ran the retirement home— whatever his name was.

Greg laughed, amused by Mother and her antics. "She's not very subtle, is she?" He patted my hand. "You first—tell me all about yourself."

"If you'll excuse me for just a moment..." I stood and gulped the rest of my margarita, setting the glass on the table. I went back into the entry and, once out of Greg's line of sight, turned to Fab and motioned her to *get over here.* She shook her head.

Didier was watching the two of us. Leaning down, he whispered something in Fab's ear. She flinched.

Okay, time to confront the deceiver face-to-face—one of them anyway. I practically stomped across the room. "What the hell's going on?" I hissed in Fab's face.

"Ask your mother."

I gave her a scorching look.

Brad, who'd claimed a stool less than a foot away, spoke up. "I'll tell you. Before you go ballistic, I only found out after I got here."

"Well...?" I tapped my foot.

"The friendship ring isn't enough of a commitment for Mother, and she got the bright idea to introduce you to other men. There sits candidate number one." He nodded toward Greg. "Just in case."

"Has she lost her mind?" I asked as the fact that he was supposed to be my date sank in.

"You know Mother." He held out his arms. "Hug?"

"No. Thank. You."

Brad grinned. "Sis, don't toss a drink or challenge Mother to a brawl. Greg has no clue that he's an unwitting pawn. You'll feel bad later if you're not your usual charming self to the man."

"Just a little brawl." I held out my thumb and forefinger, a tiny distance apart. "Thanks for the laugh." I patted my cheeks and forced a smile. "Charming, huh?"

Brad gave me a thumbs up.

I detoured to hug Liam and whispered in his ear, "Call Creole. Tell him what's going on and to get here *now*." I stepped back. "Don't give me that lame look. Mother won't find out unless you tell her."

He nodded and looked around. No one was paying him any attention, so he slipped out on the patio.

I reluctantly returned to the sofa. Brad was right—it wasn't Greg's fault Mother got him here under false pretenses. "You first." I sat down, this time leaving space between us.

He appeared confused but smiled. He had to have noticed the weirdness in the room. "Your mother was so hot on us getting together, convincing me that we'd make a good match. Normally—" He let out a nervous laugh. "—I'd never say yes, but she's quite a convincer."

"Mother can be very persuasive."

"I agreed that getting to know one another in a casual setting to see if we're interested was a good idea. It's my good fortune that Didier's here—we were introduced once before, but he probably doesn't remember. I've been wanting to set up an appointment about renting space down at the docks."

Before I could respond, Liam came up, another margarita in hand. I refrained from gulping it down and yelling, *Refill*. "Thanks." I smiled up at him. After taking a long sip, I said to Greg, "I'll introduce you to Didier." I left unsaid *so that tonight won't be a complete waste of your time*. I led him over to where Didier and Brad stood and made the introductions, telling him Greg was interested in retail space.

"I'll never speak to you again," I whispered to Fab as I walked past her and retrieved my drink. No more alcohol after this, I admonished myself, promising to stick to water for the rest of the evening. I'd walk out right then, but I didn't have a ride, it was dark, and my feet would fall off. I'd left my car keys on the counter at home, and that would never happen again. Just in case, tomorrow I'd be getting a hide-a-key that only I knew the location of.

"Hold on." Fab jerked my arm. "Look at that rock on your finger. It's a *friendship* ring, which is nothing in the way of commitment. You're not in high school."

"In case you haven't noticed, Creole and I are in love," I said in the snottiest tone I could muster. "We'll get married when we're damn good and ready. And you and Mother will be lucky to get an invitation." Eloping was sounding better and better.

"Marriage." She sniffed. "I think he's commitment phobic."

"Take a long look at this ring." I held up my finger. "It belonged to his mother. He's not going to give it to someone who's nothing more than a friend or just a —"

"I apologize." That wasn't a word Fab said often. "It seemed like a good idea and a shove in the butt to Creole. I cringed when I saw your disgust and then the hurt on your face. I promise it won't happen again.

"Did Didier know?"

"Heck no, and I'm going to pay for this one. The only reason Didier's still standing by my side is so that I can't get away and deprive him of the pleasure of killing me. Your mother and I thought that the fewer people that knew the real plan, the better, hence getting everyone here under false pretenses. Both of us thought it was the best way to go." She squeezed her eyes shut. "Not so much."

"If it were Mother or you standing in my position, you'd be livid. As for you—" I pointed my finger at her. "This means no sex. I'm going to suggest in a nosey, unladylike fashion that he really hold out on you."

"You wouldn't."

My eyes narrowed. "I believe I will."

Brad came up just then and led me away from Fab. "I'm doing my brotherly duty, preventing a chick fight."

"If I thought I had a chance of winning… it would be on, right here in the middle of the living room."

"Thinking strictly about myself, I need you whole and in one piece." Brad hugged me hard. "You've been a rock throughout this Patty mess. I need you to remind me that everything is going to work out." He looped his arm around my shoulders. "By the way, no way do you tell Mother that Phil and I are hanging on by a thread. Next dinner, it will be me in the hot seat, with some woman sitting there, looking at a book of wedding dresses with Mother." He shuddered.

"Your secrets are safe with me—all of them."

"I'm certain Tarpon doesn't have a dating service," Brad mused. "We should start one and put Mother in charge of other people's love lives."

"That's actually a good idea. I wonder if there'd be any interest. She could start with The Cottages, and if she can get those crazies fixed up, the normal ones should be easy."

Brad roared with laughter.

All eyes turned our way. To my surprise, no one asked what was so funny. Probably afraid of the answer.

The doorbell rang.

"That's Creole." Brad hip-bumped me. "Liam was unaware that he had one set of eyes on him when he escaped out to the patio, and I cornered him when he attempted to sneak back in via his bedroom."

Spoon caught my eye and pointed to the door.

I shook my head. "Mother can answer it." She hadn't heard Brad's comment because she had her head turned.

Spoon interrupted the conversation Mother was having with Didier and Greg, and whatever she said, he responded to with a shrug.

She shot him a dirty look and headed to the door. When she opened it, Creole leaned down, kissed her cheek, and boomed out for everyone to hear, "My invitation must've gotten lost." He hooked his arm around her shoulders and led her back into the living room. "Hey, everyone," he said. His eyes zeroed in on Greg. "We haven't met." He looked down at Mother, waiting for her to make the introductions. For once, she couldn't come up with anything to say.

Greg ended up introducing himself, covering an awkward moment.

Spoon handed Creole a beer. He took a long drink. "Madeline, why don't you tell Greg here how I fit into the family picture?"

Mother appeared completely chagrined, doing her best to melt into her husband's side. "Spoon, you tell him."

"I wouldn't want to deprive you, sweetheart." He crossed his arms across his chest. "If, for whatever reason, you can't quite spit out the words, I suggest your cohort, Fab, fill the man in. Everyone knows she's never short of something to say."

It amused me to recognize Fab's look as total disgruntlement. She really wanted to shoot Spoon.

No one said anything, and an awkward silence ensued.

"I'm sorry for the misunderstanding, Greg." I stepped forward, reaching out and entwining my hand in Creole's. "Mother was under the impression that I was available, and I'm not. But if you're interested in meeting someone, I'm sure she'd love to help. Wouldn't you?"

Mother's cheeks bloomed bright red. "I'm

sorry about the confusion."

"No worries," Greg said. "This has been fun. I've enjoyed myself." He got extra credit for being a good sport when he was clearly confused as to what was going on. After a moment, he continued his conversation with Didier.

Creole set down his beer, crossed to Mother, put his arm around her shoulders, and ushered her over to just outside the patio doors. He bent his head to hers, and they engaged in conversation. Brad and Liam tossed glances their way, unlike Spoon and I, who openly stared.

"He won't kill her, will he?" Spoon said, half-joking.

"I think he's having a conversation with her that he should have had a while back, and afterwards, everything will be fine." I crossed my fingers behind my back, hoping that was what was happening. "Mother can move on to meddling in someone else's life. She's running out of candidates. Brad and I just tossed around the idea of her starting a dating service."

"If either of you mentions that to her, you're both dead." Spoon cracked his knuckles with exaggerated menace.

"Ouchie." I shook my finger at him. "You take your scary stare and unleash it on someone who'll give you the satisfaction of running. You're not getting that here."

"I think my only regret is that I didn't have children." Spoon smiled. "Too old now."

"One day, there will be grandchildren, and I suspect you'll be good at it," I said, giving him my vote of confidence.

"Grandchildren are a way better idea than some damn dating service," Spoon grumbled and winked.

"They're finished." I pointed. Creole was kissing Mother's cheek. "That's a good sign."

The two of them came back to where Spoon and I stood. Mother hugged me and said, her voice low, "I'm going to make this up to you with a legitimate girl outing. Creole thinks it's weird for the boyfriend and the potential date to be in the same room." She sighed in my ear. "So he's sneaking you out."

"What was your conversation about?"

"He told me about the proposal." Mother sighed again. "So romantic."

"It had a couple of stumbles, but I wouldn't change a minute of it." I hugged her. "Fab doesn't know, and when you tell her, you should lord it over her that you knew first. Behave yourself. But not totally, so we can have fun."

Creole had come to stand next to me, and I heard his stomach grumble. I grinned at him. "Hungry? How about we go get something to eat?"

"You sure?"

I nodded. "It would be weird to stay here with Greg, and he'd like to talk business with Didier anyway, so it will be a good night for him."

Chapter Twenty-Two

The next morning, Fab insisted on meeting at her office. Halfway there, I realized I'd left my purse sitting on a chair at Creole's and had to turn around. When I turned onto his private road, it surprised me to see a white Lexus slowly cruising the street. I eased off the gas, coasting until the car made the curve out of sight.

That was a first. There were only four houses on the street, including the home at the opposite end that had caught Fab's interest. I suspected all were second homes, as I'd never seen another car on the road or anyone using the beach. Oftentimes, Creole and I had joked about having our own private beach. The "no parking" signs discouraged anyone who detoured off the highway wanting an isolated place to swim.

All the houses had garages, and Creole had paved parking for two in the front. I pulled in haphazardly, knowing I'd be right back out, and had barely gotten inside the house when my phone rang, Mac's smiling face popping up.

"What's up?" I asked, sitting down on the couch.

"You know how you're always grouching

about wanting to be the first to know when stuff happens?"

"I object to grouching."

Mac snorted. "Here's your headline for the day — Crum's first exercise class is today. All the female guests signed up, and a couple of women from the neighborhood wandered in."

Exercise class? All women? How many of those so-called exercisers turned out to be ex-lovers would be the determiner for whether the cops got called. "Anything you're forgetting?" I leaned my head back against the couch.

"Damn it. Miss January is out cruising the driveway, bottle in hand. Last time she fell. Nobody around here listens. Heeey," she yelled and disconnected.

"Just great," I said to no one. Today was turning out to be a twofer for trouble — both Miss January and Crum running amuck. Change of plans. I'd need to stop by The Cottages and... do what? Be the mean one. Order the two back inside their cottages and tell them to stay there until tomorrow under threat of eviction? My luck, Miss January would burst into tears, and Crum would favor me with one of his patented condescending stares.

The doorbell rang, which snapped my attention to the door. It wasn't Fab — she'd have picked the gate lock and kicked the bottom of the door to announce her arrival. That had been her compromise for not picking the entry lock and announcing herself as she walked in. "At least you'll know it's me," she told Creole. Knowing he wanted to strangle her, I had looked down at the floor to mask my laugh.

My hand sought out the remote, and I flicked on the television, bringing up the security screen. The Lexus was back—parked in the middle of the street. A fiftyish fellow stood out front in dress pants and a shirt. He rang again.

I got up and crossed to the security pad, hitting the speaker button. "Can I help you?"

"You the owner?"

"What do you want?"

Although the speaker sound was excellent, he grumbled something I couldn't quite make out. "I have a client who's interested in your house, and I'm here to make an offer," he said in an insincere cheerful tone.

"Not interested." I expected him to turn and leave, but instead, he stepped back, appraising the exterior of the property.

"It's a solid offer that's worth considering instead of rejecting out of hand."

I didn't offer a response and watched as he snapped a couple of photos with his phone. I briefly entertained the idea of going out and shooting the phone out of his hand. Creole had made privacy a high priority when he remodeled the place. The man's pictures would consist only of the ten-foot high fence that surrounded the property—he couldn't get a glimpse of the house.

The side fence opened to a path that led to the pool area and was only accessible with a security code.

The bell rang again.

"What?" I asked.

"I'm certain if we could speak face-to-face, we could come up with a mutually agreeable offer."

"Like I said before, I'm not interested." I took a calming breath. "Don't come back."

"I'll stick my card in the fence."

This was a man who didn't take "not interested" for an answer. I sat back on the couch and watched. He walked the street from one end of the property line to the other, his phone out in front of him. Then he attempted to get the side fence open, and when that didn't work, he slipped off his shoes and stood on the back of his car. No respect for the pricey car, and as far as I was concerned, I'd had enough.

I unholstered my Glock and was already out the gate when he jumped down. There was more than one way to encourage the man to not come back.

Making eye contact, I leveled my gun at him. "I told you nicely that we weren't interested in your offer. Get in your car and don't come back."

"You can't shoot me," he said in full indignation. "I'm on public property."

"Then I guess I'll have to drag your body back over the property line." I'd morphed into Fab, and it was fun. "My accuracy is spot on. I can just as easily nick you as send you to the afterlife—my choice, which I'll make a split second before pulling the trigger."

"All I want—"

I interrupted him. "I know what you want, and you've been told multiple times that we're not interested. Now I'm out of patience. Hit the road. If you ignore my warning and come back, you're gambling with your life." I sounded so badass, I wanted to clap myself on the back.

The man had the sense to hustle to his car. Opening the door, he said over the roof, "I'll be back, and it will be with the cops." He threw himself behind the wheel and gunned it down the street.

I waved and watched as he disappeared between the trees that dotted the side road before going back inside.

Back in the kitchen, I grabbed a sticky note and scribbled down "security fencing." I wasn't sure what it would take to enclose the entire street, or if the neighbors would go for it, but it was worth looking into. Grabbing the remote, I reversed the security tape, freeze framing on the Lexus, and copied down the license plate number.

I grabbed my purse, slinging it over my shoulder. All my annoyance at having to circle back was forgotten. I was happy I'd been there to catch the man and all the picture taking. On the way out, I bent down to retrieve his business card, which lay on the ground. It listed Rodney Naple as a realtor, along with a phone number. Flipping it over, I saw that nothing had been scribbled on the back.

After backing out, instead of heading directly back to the main road, I detoured down the block, checking out the neighborhood, which I'd only done once before. Three of the four houses were barely visible from the street, thanks to fencing, trees, and foliage. The house on the end, gauging from the roofline, was in the process of being remodeled and had doubled or even tripled the square footage in comparison to the others. What were Fab and Didier going to do with all the room, if that was the one they decided on?

One thing the houses all had in common was business cards stuck in the fencing that ran along the front of their driveways. There were no mailboxes — out here, you rented a box at the post office and picked your mail up there. I predicted the cards would blow away in the wind and hoped they did, as interest in the entire street smelled of development.

Driving back to the highway, I kept one eye peeled for places someone could park unnoticed, and there were none. Once on the Overseas, I stepped on the gas — one minute late, and Fab would be tapping her watch — and swung off at the next exit, a little-known curve in the road down to the docks. Speeding by Spoon's Auto

Body, I waved, certain it would go unnoticed, though if he was watching the security monitor, he'd certainly notice my Hummer. Half a block farther was Fab and Didier's sign-less business. The only identifier was a large brass address plate to the left of the security pedestal. As if on command, the fence rolled back.

Toady. I made a face when I spotted his red truck parked in front. This should be interesting. I knew that Fab had been using him more and more of late, and in her typical style, she'd been vague about the jobs she sent him out on. The man had such a huge crush on her, I felt certain he would agree to do almost anything she requested.

I parked in the garage of the warehouse, which was reserved for employees — technically there were none, only the two owners — and walked up the million and a half steps. My exercise for the day. That made me smile. Earlier, I had watched an exercise video about people contorting their bodies, standing on one foot and picking up pieces of paper with their mouths, which of course I had to try. Thankfully, I'd hung onto the handle on the stove or I'd have hit my head.

The doorknob turned under my hand, which surprised me. Fab must've seen me pull in and had Toady unlock the door. Or it amused her to think someone might have the not-very-bright idea of breaking into her business. If she caught sight of that in action, she'd lounge back in her chair, waiting patiently, one of her long legs across the corner of desk, for the person to enter; then, with a smile, she'd shoot. With any luck, the perp would stumble backwards out the door, making the cleanup easier.

"Toady." I waved. The old alligator was dressed up more than usual, in blue jeans, a wife beater, and a suit jacket. He wasn't actually a reptile but did have the same texture skin—some would say dried out—and beady eyes. Instead of a mouth full of teeth, he only had one, but it was gold and front and center.

"Madison." He stood and bowed.

Fab smirked in greeting from behind her desk.

Unlike the exterior of the building, which looked like the other warehouses that dotted the street, Didier and Fab had gone all out on the interior, ripping out the walls and making it one large space, each claiming a side. Both were shiny and modern, Fab's pristine and white, Didier's side chrome and infused with color—navy, black, and grey.

I headed straight for the kitchen, a strip along the wall with a curvy island that seated four separating it from the rest of the room, and helped myself to a bottled water. I'd turned down office space of my own and opted for a corner of Fab's desk on the rare occasions that I made an appearance.

"What are you working on?" I asked Toady,

dropping my bag next to the chair I'd dragged over from the corner. Asking Fab wouldn't necessarily result in a straightforward answer.

"Found the *gold* digger woman." He laughed at his own joke.

"She still alive?"

"Of course." He snorted and wiped his nose on his shirt.

Just breathe.

"It took work to track Reva Lee down, but she's not as smart as she thinks. Found her at a beachfront hotel in Daytona. Once Frenchie passed on the information to her client, she gave me the heads up to hang out and wait for him to show. No way to know what went down between the two of them—if only I coulda got a bug planted, but no opp for that. Dude stayed about an hour and left. I knocked on her door with a cockamamie excuse, saw that she was still breathing, and headed south." Toady beamed at Fab. "Frenchie's got me a new client. I want her to be the go-between. Keeps us close. Know what I mean?"

I figured the client was Brick. About the latter point, I had no clue and wasn't about to ask. Instead, I quirked my head to the side. Then, realizing it wasn't an appropriate response, I nodded. It must have satisfied him, because after picking his thumbnail, he asked, "You need anything else?"

"I appreciate your help and your discretion in

keeping secrets." Fab bestowed a huge smile on the man.

Toady stood and blew her a kiss. "Anything, you call." The door slammed behind him, and less than a minute later, the sound of his engine roared.

"Does Didier know he has competition?" I asked.

"Didier and Toady got reacquainted after I decided to avail myself of his kick-butt services." Fab grimaced. "Toady again declared his intention of scooping me up, his words, if the two of us were to go kaput. Didier told him that, if that happened, he'd give him a call. I told Didier no sex for a week, and he laughed. Told me not to lead the man on. I really wanted to throw something at him."

"Where's your snack bowl?" I banged her desk with my foot, jerking it out of reach before she could kick me. "I could use a cookie or a shot of tequila."

"Beer or water." She pointed to the fridge.

I turned up my nose. "Why am I here anyway? I forgot to ask before you hung up on me."

"It's time we acted more professional and started having meetings," she said in her snooty tone.

I sighed loudly and said, with all the drama I could muster, "Once we get in the car, you can start by explaining why we need meetings. In the meantime, we're missing Crum's exercise class and probably other things."

"Take me home first. Spoon's got my car for a checkup, and it won't be ready until late this afternoon."

"Meeting." I rolled my eyes. "More like limo driver. I can't imagine you setting your stiletto in the back of a cab."

"You have to go with what sounds good."

"Here's my compromise. You come with me to The Cottages and you can drive. If not, I'll drive and you're still coming with me." Without waiting for a response, I stood and practically ran to the door.

"Hold on a second." Fab sniffed. "I've got to change."

She went into the bathroom, which was the size of a small bedroom, and came out in record time in jeans and tennis shoes. I held out the keys, which she grabbed, then wiggled out the door ahead of me.

"There's a drive-thru liquor store a couple of blocks over—let's stop for a bottle," Fab suggested, gunning the engine as she pulled out of the driveway.

"It's bad enough dealing with the crazies at The Cottages—doing it liquored up will end in a certain felony."

"Want another good idea?" Fab squealed around the corner. "Once a week, circle the driveway and shoot the place up. They wouldn't hang around outside so much."

"Let's set aside the fact that what you suggest is illegal." I grabbed the sissy bar, surprised that the tires didn't lift off the road. "There would be some that would sit out on their porch waiting for the action to begin. I intend to change the criteria for future tenants to ones that are sedate and enjoy walking the beach, in bed by six."

"You know what they say about the quiet ones?" Fab cleared the yellow light and resumed driving like a crazy woman, which I suspected was an attempt to scare me to death.

Chapter Twenty-Three

Parking in Mac's driveway had become the norm. Halfway across the street, I rested my head on Fab's shoulder and made a barfing noise.

Fab jumped a foot.

I laughed at her look of horror as she brushed at her top. "That's payback for the hair-raising car ride."

"You're so mean."

Hearing music coming from the pool area, I said, "Let's dance," and grabbed Fab's hand.

She jerked her arm back with a growl.

Mac whistled, motioning for us to get a move on.

We rounded the corner and saw Mac leaned against the gate. I stared open-mouthed, estimating that there were twenty women, close in age to Crum, in various stages of undress, or so some would say — technically, they had on bathing suits made of string and patches of material, inviting a wardrobe malfunction. Arms over their heads, they swung their hips side to side in an exaggerated fashion; they swayed and twirled, prancing around the pool, bending over in lewd positions.

Where was Crum? I spotted his white hair standing on end where he was leading the parade. Instead of the forbidden tighty-whities, he'd opted for a g-string. His white cheeks shook and sagged as he shouted encouragement to the women.

I covered my eyes with my hands, took a breath and told myself not to look below his chest.

"Happy I didn't miss this." Fab pulled up a chair, taking her phone out of her pocket before sitting.

Turning to Mac, I noticed several men on the far side of the pool, sitting under the tiki umbrella drinking beer. "This is porn," I said to her. "Inform Crum that his bathing suit is also banned. He's not covered front or back. It's too small."

"I suppose putting a stop to the class is next," Mac fumed. "Every single tourist guest is out here, and you have to concede that everyone is having a good time. What's better than flesh and beer?"

"Yeah." Fab toasted, nothing in her hand, and laughed her head off.

"There's more nudity here than on the beach," I said. "All it takes is one nosey neighbor and the cops will be sailing in the driveway. The lot of them will be hauled off in cuffs, having to register as sex offenders."

"You need a chill pill." Mac put her hands on my shoulders and turned me toward the gate. "No looking. While you're at it—breathe."

I caught sight of Kevin headed in my direction and closed my eyes, wishing it wasn't too late to hightail it to the beach, the escape route for criminals wanting to evade the law. Peeking out from under my lashes and noting his shorts and t-shirt, I blew out a mental sigh. His day off!

"Someone call?" He laughed. He stopped short of the gate and stared, open-mouthed. "I'd better be able to scrub this spectacle from my brain, lest it ruin my sex life for forever, and then I'll sue."

"If your case made it before a judge—and even if it didn't—you'd make headlines and would be hot gossip until long after your demise." I made a face. "Make yourself useful—discharge a couple of bullets and send them home."

"I'm happy to break it to you that they're not doing anything illegal." Kevin grinned. "Displaying an obscene amount of flesh isn't breaking any laws. You're lucky I don't have this pool unit." He pointed to Joseph's cottage. "I'd be sitting in your office non-stop, complaining and eating you out of snacks."

"You have nothing better to do on your day off then hang out here? No girlfriend?" Like half the men in town, Kevin liked his women cray-

cray. Maybe he was in rest-up mode.

"Heard the music and saw your car and, psychic that I am, knew there'd be some sort of exhibition going on. Firsthand news is always better than second." He winked at Mac, who preened and giggled. "And I wanted to do my duty as a friend. Besides, I have news."

Fab snorted and made a puking sound.

"You want to know or not?" Kevin snapped.

"Ignore Fab, like you usually do," I said.

"Thought you should know that Miss January and her squeeze dragged a card table out to the curb and are selling coffee." He was definitely pleased to be the bearer of bad news. "Which is illegal, as they need permits and Health Department clearance. You're in the biz—you know what's required. Sooo, you best hustle out there and put Grandma out of business. I'm not doing it. She likes me."

"Grandma." I humphed. "She's young enough for you to date." Sort of, if he liked them older, and he didn't, as far as I'd seen. "Tell her about your penchant for strippers—all she needs is a pole, and she might get lucky with you."

Kevin glared.

Mac put her hands on her hips. "I hope you at least bought a cup to support her venture."

"Oh, hell no," he said. "Heed my warning: Do not drink any of it."

"Why don't you just blurt out whatever is going on? You know you want to," Fab said.

"This is my day off. And I've hit my nice quota."

"You're the PI." I pointed at Fab. "I'm hiring you to investigate. And in case you've forgotten, I'm one of your freebie clients."

Fab rolled her eyes. "Only because my curiosity needs to be satisfied." She grabbed my shirt. "You're coming along."

Miss January and her recent find, whose name would come to me... hopefully... had set up a table on the sidewalk beside the driveway. The table sagged to one side, and the chairs had once served as a feast for vermin. My guess was the set was a dumpster find, courtesy of Crum. All the ways the two could hurt themselves flashed through my mind.

I smiled at the duo, patting Miss January on the top of her head. "What are you two doing?" I included the man in my smile, then turned to Fab and mouthed "name?"

"You're asking me?" she said with disbelief. "I'll have to teach you how to get through a conversation without needing to use a name."

Turning back to the enterprising couple, I noticed that Nedly — that was his name — had an iron grip on a yellowed plastic pitcher, a relic from the sixties, and hoped it wasn't another trash find.

"We've opened a coffee business." Miss January giggled. "Ten cents a cup. Got the idea when Nedly said my coffee was the best he'd ever had."

Ten cents reminded me of a lemonade stand I'd had. Apparently Miss January hadn't heard that prices had gone up and kids now demanded a dollar for flavored water with too much sugar.

Nedly pulled a stack of plastic cups off the ground and put them between his legs.

Fab poked me in the back. Ms. PI was enjoying the show and had forgotten she was here to be helpful. Mac and Kevin had trailed behind us from the pool, and both leaned against a palm tree nearby.

"Good news, bad news," I informed Miss January.

Nedly's eyes narrowed and zeroed in on me.

"In order to sell anything, you have to apply for certain permits," I explained to Nedly. Miss January had zoned out. "How many cups do you have left?"

"Twenty." Nedly glanced at the stack. "We only have enough coffee to fill about six."

"Tell them your idea, Fab."

Death stare. "You do it."

"If you insist." I smiled. "Fab's having a client meeting and wants to serve your coffee. She'll buy all the cups and even the pitcher, since she's terrible about returning things." I flashed Mac the hand signal for money, then removed the pitcher from the table and set it on the ground next to the cups.

Mac glared and pulled a twenty out of her pocket, sidestepping me and handing it to Miss January. "No change necessary."

"Thank you, dearie." She smiled at Fab. "I'm happy to make more coffee for you anytime. Mornings are my best time."

Most afternoons, she was drunk and passed out in a chair on the porch. No one was mean enough to point that out.

"No need to worry about the table and chairs. Kevin will haul them to the office, and we'll store them in a cupboard." I glanced over my shoulder, making eye contact with him. "Won't you?"

"I got a deal on the set from Crum—five dollars." Miss January beamed. "Since we're out of business, let's tape a 'for sale' sign on the set, and I can get my money back."

"That's a great idea," I said with a little too much enthusiasm. "I know just the buyer."

"I already have a set," Fab said.

"I'm sorry, I didn't think about you. I have another buyer in mind. Thinking a fair price would be ten dollars."

Miss January clapped.

"We'll pay you now." I held out my hand to Mac, who, knowing me well, had the money in hand.

"What if you're not able to sell it?" Miss January worked her lower lip.

"No worries. I'm certain this is a sure deal." I

patted her shoulder. "This way, I won't forget to give you your money."

"You're the sweetest."

"I had you pegged all wrong." Nedly took Miss January's hand and helped her to her feet. "You're getting her a good deal."

I pasted on a weak smile and gave a short wave as the two trudged back to her cottage. Miss January could be heard squealing over their earnings.

Once the couple was out of hearing distance, I turned to Kevin. "Throw the table and chairs in the back of Mac's truck. Please."

"I have a better idea than paying someone to haul it to the dump," Mac said. "Next trash day, make Crum haul it out to the curb and force him to watch as it's crushed in the back of the truck."

"Great idea. Don't forget to reimburse yourself with interest and bill Crum. Due immediately. If he balks, call me."

Kevin eyed the table. "This is nasty. I need gloves."

"Oh, brother." Mac stomped over.

I put my hand in the center of her chest, and she came to a halt. "Kevin can be chivalrous, even if it's forced on him."

Fab pulled a pair of latex gloves from her back pocket and handed them to Kevin. "You owe me."

"You plan ahead in case something illegal comes your way last minute?" Kevin snarked.

"In exchange for one of the many favors you owe me, one day I'd like to inventory your pockets," Mac said to Fab. "The most interesting stuff comes out of them."

"Don't go taking after Fab; you'll end up in jail." Kevin snapped the gloves on. "Before I go and do yet another good deed, pour yourself a cup of coffee."

Picking up the pitcher, wishing I had a pair of gloves, I stared down into it—it looked like coffee. Took a sniff—it smelled like coffee.

"Let me be a gentleman." He took the pitcher from my hand and picked up a cup, filling it halfway. He glanced down, a devilish smile on his face. "Here you go."

I reached for the coffee and, at the same time, noticed something floating on top. It looked all too familiar—a cockroach, the flying kind. I yelped, and the cup flew in the air, landing in the bushes. "What the…" Okay, I knew they were the baby variety, but still.

"It gets better." Kevin slowly poured the contents of the pitcher into the bushes. When it was almost empty, he tipped it toward me, and I saw there were six more of the cockroach's siblings or friends. "Miss January shared with me that one morning, she made coffee for Nedly… must be a family name."

"The rest of the story." Fab snapped her fingers.

"When they finished the last drop, that's when

they noticed the dead roaches languishing in the bottom. Both of those nitwits thought it tasted better than plain."

"I'll get the bug dude out here tomorrow," Mac said.

"Happened after old Nedly moved in—his idea of a housewarming gift?" Kevin dropped the pitcher.

"I was here when he moved in; he didn't have any personal belongings," I said.

"You need to stay informed." Kevin smirked. "Nedly found himself a cubby hole in an abandoned gas station restroom and figured it would make good closet space. How do I know? Caught the twosome lurking around one night and offered them a ride home. Told them, in exchange for not taking them to jail, they'd have to give me the straight scoop."

"That wasn't a crime," I said. "But I'm surprised you didn't haul them off to jail anyway."

"I have my moments of being a nice guy."

"I thought Nedly owned a boat," I said.

"That dry-rotted shell had about half sunk when it got pulled out of the water and hauled to impound. At some point, it will end up at the dump. Even if Nedly had the money, why would he bail it out? It'll never be seaworthy."

"You need to get moving," Fab directed. "We've got another appointment."

Kevin folded up the table, piled the chairs on

top, and carried them to Mac's truck.

I picked up the pitcher, flung out the rest of the bugs floating in the bottom, and handed it to Mac as she followed Kevin. "Make sure this never turns up again. This wasn't fit for use when the previous owner tossed it."

"Not sure how helpful you were, but thank you anyway," I said to Fab.

"Cockroaches." Fab shuddered. "Let's go to the beach and get tacos, my treat."

"I should probably check on everything before I leave."

"That's a bad idea." Fab pushed me in the direction of the SUV and shouted to Mac, "Call if you can't handle it yourself."

Mac stuck out her tongue and waved.

Chapter Twenty-Four

When Fab and I got back to the house, we found Brad sitting by the pool, soaking up the sun, beer bottle by his foot, clicking away on his phone.

He stood and hugged me. "It's not often, like never, that I get to break into *your* house."

"It's not illegal, since you have a key. I'm loving this impromptu visit." I returned his hard hug. "You should drop by more often. I liked seeing your car parked out front."

Fab waved from the doorway and disappeared back inside.

"Depending on what this says, you might get your wish." He handed me an envelope as we sat in the chairs under the umbrella.

The return address was that of the lab where he went to get the DNA test. "That was fast."

"I paid for expedited — seventy-two hours — or I'd have to wait for who knows how long. The waiting was getting to me as it was, and I couldn't think about anything other than 'is she or isn't she my daughter?' I think I'll be a bit disappointed if I'm not the father."

"I'll be disappointed too." I handed him back the envelope.

"I didn't want to open it by myself." He fingered the envelope. Flipping it over, he ripped it open and removed the paper. "I'm a father," he said, a shimmer of tears in his eyes.

"Congrats, Dad," I said, teary-eyed.

"A little girl." He fingered the report. "I perused parenting books online and made a list—guess I'll be ordering as soon as I get home."

"You were a great big brother, and our parents were excellent role models." Happy memories brought a smile to my face. "If Mila is like either of us, you're going to have your hands full."

"The report your guy sent over about Mila being quiet and introverted made me sad. I'm hoping, with our outgoing family, that we'll have her yelling and running around in no time." Brad squeezed my hand. "I'm holding you to your promise to become her guardian until my legal mess is settled… and beyond, if necessary."

"I'll call the lawyer you chose right away. Emerson Grace, huh?" I raised an eyebrow. "Interesting that your criminal lawyer's daughter followed in Mom's footsteps, except in family law."

"Met her at Ruthie's office. I think Emerson only gave me her business card to annoy her mother."

"Or maybe she'd like to get to know you better. Duh!"

"Probably not." Brad laughed. "I'm thinking

your sex appeal dims when you've been charged with murder."

"There are women out there that marry inmates."

"I wish you didn't know this stuff."

"Just be happy that it's not firsthand experience and I'm not married to Bubba the knitter," I teased. "Back to business. I'm going to tell Emerson that I don't want any delays in getting the process going to get Mila out of foster care. To that end, I'll be available whenever my presence is needed."

"Pretty sure Emerson was surprised to hear from me, but she took the time to answer all my questions. She also thought your chances of getting custody were good, especially if I stay out of it." His smile was tinged with sadness. "You're going to like her—she has a great sense of humor. I also want to be a part of every meeting with Emerson."

"I'll keep you in the loop every step of the way, so expect lots of email. No ignoring my calls." I held up my right hand in an "I swear" gesture. "I've been doing some research, and the sooner the first home visit happens, the better. It's my hope that if I take advantage of every visiting opportunity offered, not only will we get to know one another quicker, but the transition of moving here will be easier. I have to calm my own enthusiasm and take a breath, knowing I can't make the process happen any faster."

"Whirlwind Madison." Brad laughed.

"If it's allowed, I'll get a load of pictures. If not, maybe Fab can sneak a pic or a dozen."

"When do I tell Mother?"

"Anytime, now that you know for sure. Social Services might want to interview her, though it might not be as intensive for her, since she's not applying to have Mila live with her. I'm only guessing. Either way, I don't have any doubt that we Westins will pass muster." Mother wouldn't like that Brad had waited to tell her but would understand his not wanting to get her hopes up. "Make it a special mother-son moment. Once the shock wears off, she's going to be ecstatic."

"What about Patty being the mother?" Brad frowned.

"It wouldn't be Mother's first choice, but that won't be an issue. It's rude to say, but the process will be a lot easier now that Patty can't interfere; she'd have blocked it any way she could. What surprises me is that no one from Patty's family was interested in taking Mila."

"Do they even know? Patty probably kept it a secret from them, like she did me. It's hard to believe that she wouldn't make the well-being of her daughter a priority; there wasn't a single reason for Mila to end up in foster care," Brad seethed. "I'm going to get this father thing down and make up for her first three years."

"Don't be so hard on yourself. It's not like you knew." I side-hugged him. "Just know that you and Mila will have family at your beck and call."

"We'll have to introduce Mila to the family slowly, so we don't overwhelm her. Ixnay on a family party where a fight breaks out."

We laughed.

"In fact, no more fights of any kind at family affairs," he said sternly. "We're going to have to discuss our problems like other people. Use our quiet voices."

"I love you in Dad mode." I smiled. "One thing's for certain: Mother *will* throw a party."

We sat in amiable silence for a few minutes.

"Any idea how long the process takes?" Brad asked.

"Depends on a lot of factors, the biggest being the case worker assigned to the file and how many other files she has sitting on her desk. We have several factors in our favor, one being biological ties. Plus, they've yet to find a permanent home for Mila—the current family is only interested in a temporary placement."

"I'll personally remind everyone to be on their best behavior when talking to the social worker." Brad checked his watch. "Let's take this inside. I'll call Emerson and see if she's still in her office so we can get the ball rolling."

"Great idea, and perfect time for a conference call."

It surprised me to see Fab sitting at the island. I was also surprised that she hadn't joined us out on the patio. She'd made a pitcher of iced tea and another of flavored water and set out glasses.

Brad and I each claimed a stool. Brad pointed to the water, and I held up two fingers. Fab filled the glasses.

"I can leave," Fab said.

"Pull up a seat." Brad motioned to one, phone in hand. He scrolled through it, finding the number he was looking for, and waited while it rang. "Brad Westin for Ms. Grace."

It was the first time I'd heard Brad's business voice, and it made me smile.

"Good news." He smiled at the phone and, after a pause, said, "I'm a dad."

Whatever her response was, it had him laughing. It was nice to see the stress drain from my brother's face.

"I was listening when you underscored patience, but the sooner we get things moving, the better, and my sister is on board and excited about getting started." Another pause. Then he asked me, "Do you have time now to run over to Ms. Grace's office?"

"Absolutely." I nodded and motioned for Fab to follow me into the living room so Brad could finish his call in private. "I didn't ask what you thought, taking it for granted that it would be okay to add one more to the family. We'll be aunties."

"Space is an issue, but I drew up a couple of living arrangement designs for how we could make it work. I have the file upstairs."

"I don't suppose there's a second set of plans for Creole's?"

"Got it covered. And on the nights that you and Creole want alone time, just wait until Mila is asleep and be back before she wakes up. Didier and I will take our little-girl-sitting responsibilities seriously."

"You're amazing." I smiled. "Mila's going to be spoiled by all the people who'll love her."

"There is one thing. I get first dibs on taking Mila shopping. Every little girl needs a cute dress and shoes."

"No stilettos." I shook my finger at her.

"I'm thinking she'll have to wait for those until high school."

"You've put a lot of thought into bringing Mila into our lives."

"You're crying," Fab said in exasperation and slugged me in the arm.

"Ouch," I said pitifully. "What are you going to do when Mila cries?"

"Scoop her into my arms, find out what the heck is going on, and if it's because of someone else, that person is toast."

Fab's fierceness made me laugh. "You can't scare little kids."

"No, but I can pay a visit to their fathers and discuss the situation rationally."

"Does your idea of rational include nicking him with a bullet?"

"Maybe."

Brad crossed over to the two of us, putting his arms around us. "You might as well come along. You can drive," he said to Fab, then looked at me. "I assume you've filled her in on everything."

She beamed at him. "You're the best faux-bro ever."

"The faux siblings." I tried for a group hug and instead got the crazy look from both of them as we headed for the door.

Chapter Twenty-Five

Emerson Grace's office was located on the opposite end of the same building as her mother's, "Family Law" painted on the picture window. Made sense, since per the property tax office, Ruthie Grace owned the whole building.

"I'm staying here," Fab said. "I'll check out who comes and goes. Maybe pay a visit to Counselor Grace, give her another business card." She smiled secretively.

The attorney was tough, demanding, and used to getting her way, but she'd met her match in Fab. I expected the phone to ring one of these days with a case. Hopefully, she wouldn't expect anything that brought up grey-line issues… or as Creole called them, illegal ones.

The yellow-and-white reception area had a cheerful ambience, with comfortable seating and a play area in the corner filled with toys. At the sound of the bell, Emerson came out of her office in a flattering red business suit, her brown hair pulled into a bun. She welcomed Brad and me, pointing us to chairs in front of her desk.

Emerson removed her jacket and settled behind her desk. "I'm happy for you; I can see your excitement." She smiled at Brad. "Once Mother clears you of the pending charges, we'll go to court, get you full custody of Mila, and you can take your little girl home. In the meantime, your sister is the next best thing."

"When do we get started?" I asked, noting her framed credentials and awards. She'd had a first-class education.

"I'm filing the paperwork tomorrow." Emerson patted a file on her desk. "The first thing is to get visits for you and Mila. They'll start out supervised, and if those go well, then you'll get to meet with Mila alone. I have no doubt her case worker will move the process along to reunite Mila with her family. You can expect some home visits. The first will be scheduled, but just know that Social Services can drop in at any time. I've got a couple of contacts in the department and will call on them. Hopefully, they can speed things along."

"I wish I could contribute more to the process," Brad said.

Emerson noted the look of concern on his face. "That's why you hired me." She pushed a notepad in my direction. "Phone number. You'll need to stop by first thing in the morning and sign documents."

"This is top priority for me, and with a little notice, I'm available anytime and will rearrange my schedule for anything you need," I assured her. "When you set up the visit with Mila, I'll take whatever time is convenient."

"I know it can seem like a nerve-wracking experience, but it can go smoothly, as long as you stick to the rules." Emerson smiled reassuringly at Brad. "You both should read up on the visiting process and know what's allowed and what isn't." She opened her drawer, removing two files and handing them across her desk.

"Since I'm a newbie at this and children, I'm thinking about taking a picture book for the first visit." I waited nervously for her response, half-expecting an eyeroll. "Beats staring at one another."

"That's perfect." Emerson clapped. "If you have any questions, anything at all that comes up that you're unsure of, call me."

Brad murmured his agreement.

I took that as "meeting over" and stood, but Brad didn't move.

"Meet you at the car," he said to me.

"Nice meeting you." I smiled at Emerson. "See you tomorrow." I showed myself out and was a bit surprised to see Fab sitting behind the wheel. I slid into the passenger seat.

"We're missing one," Fab said.

"Brad wanted to speak to his attorney alone. Like you, I'd like to eavesdrop, but sometimes I have to know when not to, and this was one of those times. I'm happy that Brad got over his anxiety about my helping." I went on to summarize the meeting.

"Your brother is protective, not stupid." Fab made a face. "I told him he'd be a fool to turn down our help. I reassured him that I was your official hand-holder, if you did that sort of thing."

"We could hug." I held out my arms, which she ignored. "Did you manage to barge into Counselor Grace's office?"

"Nooo." Fab blew out an exasperated breath. "Got no response, even after kicking the door. You'll be proud of me—I didn't pick the lock to see if she was just being obstinate."

"Thank goodness. Now is not a good time for you to go to jail."

"I was thinking that 'best behavior' doesn't apply to me until Mila comes to live with us."

"You're going to need to set a good example, be someone Mila aspires to be."

"Forget the latter. I want Mila and our kids to know they're loved and chase what makes them happy in life."

I beamed at her. "Speaking of children, you haven't mentioned your father of late."

"Caspian's in DC on business. I got him to agree to a dinner with my Florida family when he gets back, helicoptering everyone to the island."

"Finding out your father had moved to the Keys only after he almost ran you off the road wasn't the way I imagined meeting him. Now that I have, I'm eager to get to know him and watch how the two of you interact." I wanted to genuinely like the man.

"I'm surprised you haven't done a background check."

I felt my cheeks heat up. Oh, I wanted to.

Fab smirked, as though reading my mind. "It would tell you that he's a respected businessman and philanthropist, with no criminal record and a yacht full of money."

"And if his daughter were writing the report, what would it say?"

"There's no mistaking that we're father and daughter. We share similar features, and basically, I'm his mini-me in guts, tenacity, and never backing down from a tough situation." Fab smiled throughout her description. "He'd like to have more influence in my life — it grates on him when my life goes awry — but instead of harping on my mistakes, he discusses with me how it could've been handled better. He's supportive, even when what he wants to do is strangle me." She half-laughed. "Caspian had the nerve to tell me that I don't listen. Can you imagine?"

"Does he know about your penchant for eavesdropping?"

"I'm certain that he knows everything about me — good and bad." Fab blushed. "He's never expressed disappointment or implied in any way that I don't measure up."

"I'm predicting now that the dinner will be the hottest invite in the family. Also, I'm already

RSVPing for me and Creole."

"Here comes Brad." Fab pointed over the steering wheel. "He looks a lot more relaxed than when we got here."

Brad got in the back. "How about ordering takeout? We'll eat dinner by the pool. I'll pay—I figure you don't invite yourself unless you're the one with the food."

"I almost forgot," Fab said. "Dinner by the pool all right, but Didier's got that covered. First on the agenda is getting your lazy butt out for a run."

"As of today, I'm picking myself up out of the doldrums," Brad said. "Mila will give me something positive to think about."

"That calls for a toast," I said. "We'll do it when you guys get back." I turned, looking over the seat. "Did I sense a little sizzle between you and your lawyer?"

"What's not to like? I'd have to be dense not to notice she's smart, funny, and oh yeah, hot. But I'm no catch. Apparently you've forgotten I already have a so-called girlfriend, who rarely speaks to me anymore. Forget messages, she doesn't answer most of them."

"Is she the one you want to spend the rest of your life with? Make Mila's stepmother?" I shuddered at that thought.

No answer. Instead, he stared out the side window.

"Don't stress about it," I said. "I know that the

thought of a drama-filled breakup gives you hives. Let it play out; let her end it."

"I just might take your advice."

Chapter Twenty-Six

It had been a couple of days since the meeting at Emerson's office, and more often than not, I caught myself staring at my phone, willing it to ring. I'd just finished my second coffee to quell my annoyance over my inability to snap my fingers and speed the process along, and the four of us were sitting outside on the patio, talking about our plans for the day. At least, they were— I'd zoned out. I was brought back to the conversation when Creole asked what I had planned.

"Going by Jake's to check out the biker meeting." I turned to Fab. "Coming?"

Creole and Didier hid their smirks behind their coffee cups but weren't quick enough—I still saw them.

"I'm sure I have something better to do." In response to Didier's frown, Fab stomped her foot.

Most mornings, her antics would amuse me, especially if they annoyed Didier. Not today.

I leaned over and kissed Creole's cheek. "Later. Your house." Without saying good-bye, I crossed the entry, grabbing my car keys, and went out the door, banging it behind me. I squealed out of the driveway in true Fab style but slowed as I turned the corner. Unleashing my frustration had relieved some of my stress, but not much.

When I'd first heard about closing Jake's for a private party, I hadn't wanted to admit to having a bad feeling about the idea. But I had and still did, and it intensified when I pulled into the driveway and spotted the ambulance parked at the front door. I shook my head. Only one ambulance this time. Where were the cop cars?

I zipped around to the back, jumped out of the SUV, and flew through the kitchen into the bar area. A woman lay on a stretcher, oxygen mask on her face, paramedics working on her.

"What in the hell?" I snapped at Doodad, who was leaning over the bar top, resting on his elbows.

He held his hands up. "Granted, it looks bad, but it's not what you think. Medical emergency."

Kelpie sidled up next to me. "No fights. No guns." She sounded disappointed. "Doesn't matter. Gossip will fly, the death count will be in the hundreds, and people will flock in to get the scoop. My plan is to be vague." The woman's smile let me know she was proud of her idea.

"Your sympathy overwhelms me."

Kelpie gave me a cross-eyed stare.

If Fab were here, she'd be impressed.

Doodad set a drink down in front of me.

"What's this?" I picked it up and sniffed—not tequila on the rocks.

Kelpie snatched it out of my hand and loaded it with cherries and an orange slice, frowning at Doodad as she set it back down. "This is the way Boss Lady likes her soda."

I toasted Kelpie, who grinned in response. "Is the woman going to be okay?" My attention turned to the door, where the paramedics were in the process of rolling the woman outside, a couple dressed like a bride and groom by her side. I was astounded I hadn't noticed them before. The bride had opted for a short version of a wedding dress, accessorizing with a long train that dragged on the floor. "You two need close supervision. What the heck have you cooked up now?" I demanded.

"Refill?" Doodad held up the soda gun. I held my glass out. "The only two that knew a wedding was happening here today were the bride and groom. Surprise!" He waved his hands. "They thought it was a great idea to spring the nuptials on their biker group. Even showed with the preacher, along with the bride's mother. I need a beer." He grunted and poured himself a soda. "Dearly beloved…"

I rolled my eyes at him. What would it take to get a complete explanation of what went down? "Hurry it along."

"Anyway. Where was I?" Doodad scratched his chin.

"The attack," Kelpie whispered hoarsely.

"Oh yeah. The preacher didn't make it past the first line before the mother had an asthma attack and lurched into the bathroom. The father of her future grandchildren got her inhaler out of her purse, and she half-assed got her breathing under control. Not enough for me. I called 911. Sadly, the preacher had another wedding—"

"Funeral," Kelpie interrupted.

"Not wasting a minute, the couple asked that the service be performed in the bathroom. The club members were in unanimous support and lined the walls. So moving." He wiped away a non-existent tear.

"I liked when the bikers cheered—all the happiness shook the beams." Kelpie scanned the ceiling.

I looked up, holding my breath in anticipation of what I'd find. "Are we going to have to close for repairs?"

From the way Kelpie stared at me, I'd have to check later to see if I'd grown an extra head. "Where's your sense of romance?"

I let out a snort-laugh that made me cough. "Bathroom weddings. Let's put that in our marketing brochure." Not that we had one, but maybe we should.

Kelpie raised her hand. "It's got my vote. We advertise weddings and let the couple choose their own special spot—bathroom, of course, kitchen, deck."

"Parking lot," Doodad managed to say straight-faced.

I frowned at my soda, wishing it had alcohol in it, or better yet, was my favorite straight up.

Wolf, the president of the group, ambled over. "This wasn't what we had planned, but everyone's had a great time. We'll be booking the bar again."

The look on his face didn't match his words, so I didn't expect to see him again. "The woman?"

"The paramedics are transporting Mrs. Frost to the hospital at her daughter's insistence. They seemed to think she'd be fine."

"Happy to hear that."

But Wolf's attention had been diverted to the other side of the room. He turned and made his way over to where a group of members were waiting.

Raul and Dickie peeked their heads inside the front door, looking surprised that we had a full house so early. Doodad whistled and flagged them over. Raul, the approachable one, had a huge smile on his face, acknowledging all of us. Dickie looked his usual self—uncomfortable in his own body.

"We're here for our appointment. Is this a bad time?" Raul asked. "Excellent turnout for this event, whatever it is. Not that I had any doubt that this will be the perfect venue for our party."

"Let's move this into the private room. It's the

only place that isn't standing room only." Kelpie picked up the tray of drinks that Doodad had poured.

It surprised me that he knew what the funeral duo enjoyed drinking. Maybe they were regulars.

"I'll have another of these." I pushed my glass across the bar.

"Two drink limit unless you have a ride home." Kelpie let loose a guttural laugh.

Not about to miss a minute of this meeting, I led the way down the hall. Once inside the room, I opened the doors that led out to the deck, letting fresh salty air whip through, and flipped on the ceiling fans.

"You two doing okay?" I asked.

"Left a message for Fab that we need a meeting," Raul said.

"A situation we need to discuss," Dickie said, moving the salt and pepper shakers around in a dance.

"We'll handle that in private," Raul said. "Did Doodad tell you that we're here to rent Jake's for a party—a get-together for our fellow directors?"

I was about to reply when Kelpie started serving the drinks, bending down and shaking her assets nearly under the noses of Raul and Dickie. I had seen her do that before but didn't think it part of her everyday routine. Raul took full advantage of the view while Dickie's cheeks burned, the most color I'd ever seen in his pale face. Kelpie tucked her tray under her arm and hustled back to the bar.

Doodad entered the room, slapping a notepad on the table. "How many people?"

"We've had twenty-five responses plus their significant others, so fifty," Raul answered. "We're thinking dinner, drinks, and dancing."

I stayed silent, not wanting to point out the obvious—that Jake's was a dive bar and what they were planning sounded fancy.

"Band?" Doodad asked.

"Jukebox."

"One question before I leave." I pushed up my sleeve, checking my watch, giving the impression that I had somewhere to be—no one needed to know I never set the time. "Are there going to be any dead bodies in attendance?"

Raul shook his head, squinting, clearly giving the idea thought. He looked at Dickie, who shrugged. "Some would get a good laugh out of that, but probably not all. That's something we'd have to do at Tropical Slumber—there'd be permits to pull if we wanted to do that here, and you know how the county can be. Not to mention the families would need to give permission to use their loved ones."

That sounded like "no" to me, but just in case… "I hate to be a theme-killer, but I'd prefer not."

"I'll make note of the idea for the next party, with a few changes, such as mannequins. We'll have an even bigger turnout," Raul said.

I planned to beg off sick if any party invitation arrived from them. "It's good to see you both. I'll remind Fab to call." I went back to the bar, setting my glass down. "Do you shake your assets in all our customers' faces?"

"Only those that tip extra."

"I'm afraid to ask, but what do you have up your sleeve that I haven't seen?"

"Nothing yet. I'll think of something." Kelpie winked.

"That scares me."

Kelpie laughed and turned her outgoing personality on the burly man at the end of the bar, who'd just shouted, "Bartender."

On the way out, I paused to text Fab. "I'm taking the funeral job and billing them this time." That would get Raul and Dickie a response before I got to the car.

Chapter Twenty-Seven

On the drive home, I got a text from GC that a girlfriend of Patty's had been located. He included her home and business addresses. Kelly worked at a Waffle House, and her shift would be ending in a couple of hours.

My plan once I hit the house was to shove Fab into the car, no matter how much she protested. I wasn't going by myself to meet anyone connected with Patty. But it didn't quite work out the way I planned. When I entered the house, the sound of splashing could be heard through the patio doors. I bent down to scratch the cats, who were sacked out in one of their prime places, which afforded them a view of the pool. It amazed me that they had little interest in exploring the backyard, about which I was happy. Occasionally, they ventured to a chaise and took a nap in the sun, but that was the extent of it.

Didier and Fab were on floaters, playing tag, splashing water everywhere, and I didn't want to intrude on their fun. There had been no sign of Creole's truck when I pulled into the driveway, and I didn't want to take the time to track him down. Instead of making my presence known, I ran upstairs to change. I'd left the house earlier in a skirt and low heels. The only change I planned to make was kicking off my less-than-comfortable shoes and replacing them with flip-flops.

On the way to the car, I pulled my phone out and called Liam on the off chance that he had some free time. "I've got a job opportunity. It involves waffles and cash," I said when he answered, then went on to explain about GC's message.

"This is so cool," he said. "You shouldn't go by yourself, since unstable people usually attract like-minded friends. And just so you know, the waffles were the seller." Liam's enthusiasm came through the line, making me felt less guilty, knowing he wasn't doing it just for me.

"I'll text you the address. If you get there ahead of me, grab us a table and scope out the place."

* * *

Traffic was light all the way to Miami, and I made it in record time, but still arrived at the restaurant after Liam. I parked next to his truck and headed in. Walking by the windows, I spotted him at a corner table and waved.

"This is one of Kelly's tables," Liam said as I sat down. "You timed this right—just finished my classes for the day."

"Thank you for meeting me."

"Are you kidding? I'm always up for a little excitement." He passed me a menu. "No hurry. I told Kelly that I'd flag her down when we were ready to order. Charmed the heck out of her and laid the groundwork for a private chat when she gets off work. Told her that I was interning in the district attorney's office for college credit, and when my supervisor got here, we'd have a few questions."

I groaned. "DA? I'm a horrible influence."

"Not entirely sure she bought my story — she asked how much cash was involved."

"Informants always want money, which is why I don't meet these people without cash in my pocket." I put the menu back behind the napkin holder. "How's your other job?"

"Giving eulogies isn't a job I admit to having." He laughed. "Can't beat the pay for a college kid. For anyone really. The kids at school think I'm getting an allowance."

"Mother says she attended a couple of the funerals and that you do a really good job."

"The last one, she brought her friend Jean. They ran into a couple of women Jean knew and ended up going out to lunch."

"Wonder what story she came up with for Spoon." I laughed.

"Her modus operandi is to weasel around her husband with some made-up story, which he always sees through. When she's done and looking quite pleased with herself, he crosses his arms, glares, and says, 'Now how about the truth?' She pouts a little and then spills all." Liam waved over the waitress. "Kelly, this is my supervisor, Madeline." I almost laughed when he introduced me using Mother's name. "We're ready to order now, and we'll wait right here for you to get off."

Kelly took our order, flirting with Liam the whole time.

When she left the table, Liam said defensively, "Madeline was a good name choice. Kelly's chances of meeting her are zero, and if she did, Grandmother would play along. Give Kelly your business card, the one that doesn't have your name on it. I'm surprised those cards haven't raised an eyebrow and more questions than you want to answer. Let's face it, they're shifty."

"I'm thinking that you, Mr. Charmer, should lead the conversation. Kelly's eyes never left your face; she barely gave me a glance."

"This is going to be fun." Liam grinned. "Waiting for you to get here, I made a few notes." He pushed a napkin that he'd scribbled on across the table. "We want the deets on her friendship with Patty — the good stuff, if she wants any cash. Other friends of Patty's? Men in particular."

"Great questions for your first time." I grimaced. "Mother and Brad won't be happy when they find out I involved you."

"We don't volunteer any information. We wait for them to ask and then, of course, tell a tamed-down version of the truth. Besides…" He waved his arm. "We're in a restaurant, what could happen?"

"Don't ask that." I shuddered and pulled out my wallet. "Did you agree on a price?"

"I told her that depended on the quality of the information."

My eyebrow shot up, and I raised my fist. We knuckle-bumped, and I handed him cash. "Your decision."

"Already got a little out of her. They were friends in the hospital but only talked once after Patty got out. Patty called to tell her that she was getting back with the man she'd been in love with for forever."

"I'm impressed."

Kelly came back with our order. We'd both ordered waffles, plus orange juice for me and Coke for Liam. Once again, she made eye contact with Liam and gave him a flirty smile.

When she was out of earshot, I said, "She's too old for you, and a stay in a mental hospital disqualifies her completely."

"You know it's against policy to date informants." He shook his finger at me, amusement in his eyes. "If not, it should be." Between bites, he said, "Kelly's willing to talk about life inside the hospital—that's when the money issue came up. Not sure how important this is, but to get in and out of a ward, you have to go through three sets of locked doors. Kelly said if you were burly enough and had the necessary strength, you could kick or shove open the last door that opens to freedom."

"Wow, you covered a lot of ground before I arrived. The security of the hospital was laid out in a report I got from GC. Kelly gave you the straight scoop on it, which hopefully means all her information-sharing will be truthful."

"Do you need anything else?" Kelly interrupted us.

"Food's great. We're good," Liam said.

After she left, I said, keeping my voice down, "Patty didn't escape from the ward, but from the emergency room of a local hospital she'd been transferred to following a diabetic episode. I'd like to know if she planned her escape or had an actual medical emergency that she took advantage of."

Kelly cleared away the dishes and cleaned off the table. "Since it's quiet, I've got permission from the boss to use this table, as long as we don't get busy. Told him Leo here is an old friend and you're his sister—almost said mother, but you don't look old enough. You'll need to leave a tip for squatting."

Leo, I mouthed at Liam.

"Don't worry." Liam oozed charm. "We'll take care of the boss and even better care of you."

"I'll go get my stuff and be back." Kelly beamed at him and left.

"You won't be so amused when she asks for your number."

"I'll apologize and tell her that I didn't mean to lead her on, but I have a girlfriend."

"You've been hanging around Brad and his silver-tongued ways too much."

"Brad likes being in a relationship, as opposed to dating; he just needs to be in the right one," Liam said.

I agreed with him—the right one indeed.

Kelly came back, cloth bag slung over her shoulder, and slid into a chair next to Liam.

"Would you like something to drink?" Liam offered.

"That's sweet of you, but I'm good."

"How did you meet Patty?" he asked.

"We met at the hospital and became fast friends. We're both bi-polar. I had run out of medication and had an episode. My parents lost patience and Baker-acted me—means committed." A wave of sadness rushed over her face. "Patty stopped taking her pills deliberately—she loved the highs and lows and didn't want to give them up. She was adamant that, if left alone, she could handle her life and refused to admit that she couldn't, even though she ended up staring at a long prison sentence. She was offered a plea bargain, which she wisely accepted."

"But you're doing better." Liam patted her hand.

"I was fortunate, and my counselor, Mary White, was a blessing. I followed all the rules and did everything that was required. Ms. White encouraged me to sign up for a program that helped me get this job and another that pays for my meds, so I don't have to stress about how to pay for refills."

"Did Patty have any other friends?"

"Patty was pretty much a loner." Kelly paused. "We hung out with a couple of other patients on occasion, but they're still in the hospital."

"Do you know how Patty managed to get out of the hospital?" I asked.

Kelly gave her answer to Liam. "Doctors, nurses, everyone actually, underestimated how smart and conniving Patty was. She was diabetic, and like other patients on meds, she had to line up every morning for her insulin. Cool as a cucumber, she went into the dining room for breakfast afterwards, but she didn't eat anything and managed to hide it from the monitors. She passed out and was transported to the hospital. From there, she snuck out."

"I'm surprised the hospital didn't post a guard at the door," Liam said.

"Don't know anything about that." Kelly shrugged. "Maybe they were busy that day. Patty was a smart cookie and didn't give away that she planned to escape. I could never do anything like that. I admired her guts, but look at all the trouble it got her into. Since we were friends, the hospital questioned me, and I told the truth—I didn't know anything."

"Did Patty have any male friends?" I asked.

Once again, Kelly directed her response to Liam. "There was one guy that she hung out with in the lounge; the two of them played cards." She took a bottled water out of her bag, taking a long drink. "There was another guy that visited a couple of times, but when I asked Patty about it, she clammed up. The first guy is still in the hospital. Patty made it clear that she didn't want to be bothered when she had visitors, so I didn't get the opportunity to meet the other one."

Damn, I wished I had the names. Maybe GC could get the info.

"Two weeks after Patty escaped, I got released. Before Patty made her getaway, she gave me a number where I could contact her—should have been my first clue she was up to something. Called the number, and I could've sworn Patty said hello, but then the line went dead. Called back, and it went to voicemail. A couple weeks later, I tried again, and the number had been disconnected."

"Do you still have the number?" Liam asked.

"I never erase anything." She pulled her phone out of her pocket and scrolled through it. "Here it is." She held the screen out, and Liam entered the number in his phone.

He shot me a glance, and I pointed to the door, certain she's given us all the information she had.

"You were very helpful," he told Kelly. "We appreciate all the information." He reached into his pocket, pulled out the cash, and handed it to her, then threw a tip on the table.

She counted the money. "Thank you." She glowed. "You know where to find me if I can be of any more help."

Liam stood and extended a hand, helping her to her feet. "Nice to meet you."

It surprised me when she left without any conversation about hooking up in the future.

"You were excellent," I said.

"Seriously, this was fun. You get another job, I'm in."

Liam walked me to my SUV, we hugged, and I slid behind the wheel. I waited until he got in his truck, then waved as I drove out of the parking lot.

Chapter Twenty-Eight

The next afternoon, my phone rang with the call from Emerson Grace that I'd been waiting impatiently for — a home visit with Mila had been scheduled for the next day. It would be for one hour and supervised. The short amount of time disappointed me, but I eagerly accepted.

"It pays to have friends," Emerson said, her smile audible through the phone.

Hanging up, I called Brad and found that his lawyer had called him first. "Get a picture," he reminded me. "There's one in the legal file, but it's all grainy. I wanted to go, but Emerson said absolutely not, that it could stall the process, a murderer trying to visit his daughter."

"You're not going to get convicted," I said adamantly. "Fab doesn't know it yet, but she's coming along, and with her penchant for picture-taking, she'll get a file full. I promise to relay everything that happens word for word."

"Call me as soon as the visit is over."

I tossed my phone on the nearest pillow and maneuvered myself around the sleeping cats and off the daybed. That they barely budged was a good indication they had no intention of moving out of the way. At the bottom of the steps, I cupped my hands around my mouth and yelled, "Fab, get down here. Now." My throat felt scratchy. Not so loud next time.

"You'll be lucky if I don't tell Didier about your insufferable manners, subjecting you to a lecture," Fab sniffed from the top of the stairs.

"My meeting with Mila is tomorrow, and I'll need your help. Brad wants pictures, and I suspect that's probably breaking the rules, which is where you come in."

"I've been thinking about this." Fab flung her leg over the banister, riding it to the bottom and sliding off, then sitting on the bottom step. "If you're agreeable, I'll mic you up and put a camera on you. You'd be my test run, which would qualify you for a discounted rate. I'll take a raftload of pictures too, and no worries about catching me either."

"I'll let Brad know so he can check your invoice to make sure you didn't forget the discount." I backed up and sat on the arm of the couch. "You won't be obvious, will you?" I interpreted Fab's glare as a *no*. "Fingers crossed for no rain. I'm going to suggest that we sit outside. I'm hoping Mila will think it's fun."

"Let's hope the foster mom is agreeable and they have a yard or porch."

"They have both. I researched the address. There's nothing private anymore."

"That really bugs me."

"Another of the multitude of things we agree on." My phone rang, Creole's picture popping up. On my way to the patio, I said, "Be ready to go in the morning. We can't be tardy."

"We're never late," Fab yelled at my back as I crossed the threshold.

* * *

The next morning, Fab was waiting for me downstairs. She quirked her finger, motioning for me to stand in front of her. "Hold up your hair." She tied a pendant necklace around my neck, adjusting it to hang in the middle of my chest. I marveled at how small the camera was.

Since this wasn't a job where a quick getaway needed to be factored in, I'd chosen flats over tennis shoes to go with my skirt. Fab had opted for workout gear.

"A jogger isn't going to garner attention." Fab held out an earbud. "Stick this in your ear, and we'll do a sound check. We'll be able to stay in touch if needed. The guy I got all this from promised no glitches, and I'll be able to pick up the conversation, video, everything."

* * *

Fab flew down the Overseas Highway and into Miami. The day had dawned warm but not hot, baby blue skies filled with white fluffy clouds.

The foster home was located in a modest neighborhood. The homes were built in the 1940s, and some had been remodeled to be larger than the two-bedrooms of the time period. Most had fenced yards and were well-kept.

"It's that one." Fab pointed, driving slowly past it. "I wanted to bring a larger camera that would fit my monster lens but thought that would stick out. I'm using a little one that I've had for a while that's supposed to produce the same results." She pulled over at the corner. "When the visit is over, I'll be waiting here for you." She reached under the seat and pulled out a baseball cap and large, black-lensed sunglasses. "I'll be the one doing leg stretches."

I crawled over into the driver's seat and amused myself watching Fab, standing on the corner as she demonstrated her athletic ability. Butterflies filled my stomach as I drove around the block and parked in front of the blue one-story house. The porch was welcoming, with a pair of rocking chairs and a large birdhouse with several feeder slots.

It dawned on me that there wasn't another car parked nearby, which surprised me, as the visit was supposed to be supervised. I double-checked my watch, which I'd actually set—four minutes to spare. I got out and grabbed the blanket and book.

The waist-high chain-link fence was locked. Next to the fence was a pole, with a rope attached to a large bell. I tugged and glanced over my shoulder, checking to see if the neighbors had come out to check on the noise. The owners needed one that wired into the house. If Fab had been able to tag along, she'd have them talked into an upgrade before they realized they'd agreed.

The door opened, and a woman in her forties stepped out on the porch, her hair piled into a messy bun, wearing a long skirt and long-sleeved tee-shirt, a toddler hooked to her hip.

"Mila's aunt?" she called.

I nodded. "Madison Westin."

The woman reached into her pocket, taking out a key as she came down the walk. When she got close, she introduced herself. "Holly Redmond, and this little one is my son, Paul." She pushed the gate open, motioning for me to follow. "I'm surprised that you showed today, since the case worker called in sick."

"I didn't get a call."

"She probably forgot. You're here now — we might as well have that visit anyway."

The TV was blaring as we entered the house, two little faces glued to the screen, watching a cartoon. Mila wasn't one of them, and I wondered where she was.

"Mila is a quiet one," Holly whispered. "I told her about your visit, but I didn't get much of a response." She stared pointedly at my full arms.

"I thought it would be fun to sit on the lawn

and read to her. I wasn't sure what the protocol was, and a three-year-old probably wouldn't want to hear me talk non-stop." I let out a nervous laugh.

"It's a little chaotic today," Holly said wearily. "The kids are feeling rambunctious, and if I let Mila go outside, they're all going to want to play in the backyard. Do you mind three more little ones running around?"

Flustered by the question and unsure what to say, I said the first thing that came to mind. "Maybe they'd all enjoy the story."

"No offense, but running around trumps everything. The jungle gym's been a hot item ever since my husband put it up." Holly pointed out Mila, who was sitting on a booster chair at the kitchen table, a coloring book and crayons in front of her and a look of boredom on her face.

Mila looked up, her father's brown eyes staring back at me, half her shoulder-length sandy hair in a pigtail, the other side hanging down. It took everything in me not to scoop her into my arms for an enveloping hug. I furiously blinked away tears.

Low key, I reminded myself and scooted into a seat next to her, dropping my bag on the floor. "I'm your Aunt Madison." I left unsaid until she was older, *I'd have been here sooner, but I just found out about you.* "I'm hoping we're going to become good friends." I laid my hand, palm up, on the table.

There was no verbal response. Instead, she stared wide-eyed at my fingers, which I wiggled at her.

"I brought a book." I reached down and grabbed it from the top of my tote, holding it up to show the cover, which depicted a princess's crown. "I thought we could go outside and I'd read to you. Would you like to do that?"

It felt longer than a minute, but she finally nodded.

I held out my arms, and she held out hers. I lifted her off the booster seat and set her on the floor. "You get to choose the spot where you want to sit." I grabbed the blanket.

Mila led the way and stood back as Holly nodded her approval and opened the back door, which required unlocking three locks. Then Holly stood to one side, feeding her son from a bottle as the other children ran out of the house like they'd been shot out of a cannon, scurrying in circles and yelling.

Child safety. That was a task I'd immediately assign to Fab. It would be fun to see what she came up with. It wouldn't surprise me if it included a tracking device.

Mila held onto the railing and jumped down the three steps one at a time. She looked at me like, *Okay, now what?*

"How about over here?" I motioned to a spot.

She ran over and plunked down on the grass. I spread the blanket out next to her, and she crawled onto it.

I handed her the book, sitting down next to her when what I wanted to do was hold her in my lap. But I didn't want to risk scaring her — a stranger being so pushy — and it would make for terrible pictures for Brad. Opening the cover of the book she'd laid on her lap, I slowly flipped the pages, reading the story and making comments that I hoped a three-year-old found interesting. Mila traced every page with her little fingers. As Holly'd said, the other children had jetted over to the sand pit, and two were on their hands and knees, pushing trucks around. The third one stared around in wonder.

My allotted time flew by fast. It wasn't long before Holly called, "Nap time." The other kids groaned loudly but ran to the house. "Once I promised snacks for good behavior, it got easier to get them in the house without histrionics."

"Good idea." It didn't seem like I'd been there an hour, but glancing at my watch, I saw an hour and a half had passed. "Thank you for the extra time." I stood and lifted Mila to her feet, grabbing the book. "I'll get the blanket on the way out." Mila and I followed Holly to the back door. At the steps, I kneeled. "It was amazing to meet you," I told Mila with a smile. "I'm going to visit again soon. Can I hug you?"

Mila threw herself against my chest and hugged me. It was hard to let go, and I took an extra moment to brush at the corners of my eyes.

I handed her the book. "This is for you." She clasped it to her chest.

Holly held out her hand, which Mila took until the handrail was in reach. Then she climbed the steps, and at the top, she waved before going inside.

Holly turned to me. "I'm going to report back that the visit went well. It's been my experience that when family is involved, everything possible will be done to expedite the file. Mila needs stability and more attention than I can give her. I must say, I'm a little jealous — Mila was more responsive to you than she's ever been to me."

That made me happy. "I promise she won't be short of attention when she comes to live with me."

"That's good to hear." Holly waved and rushed inside, as the kids had begun to scream at the top of their lungs.

After triple checking to make sure the gate was secured behind me, I drove to the end of the block and picked up Fab. This time, I slid out and was about to round the front of the car when Fab pulled me into a hug. "Don't be sad. You'll have another visit soon." She tugged my hair. "I'm stopping for coffee."

"Did you get everything — pictures, audio, video?" I asked.

"Who do you think you're talking to?" she asked in faux annoyance. "Mila's adorable. I got great shots — Brad's going to be happy."

Chapter Twenty-Nine

On the way home, I called Brad and reported every detail about the visit. Fab snapped her fingers, wanting to speak to him. She assured him she'd have everything ready for him in the morning and told him he was invited for breakfast and needed to stop on the way and pick it up. I growled, which she rewarded with an eyeroll before ignoring me, finishing her conversation with Brad, and hanging up without asking if I wanted to talk to him again.

"Why did you pass the turn to the house?" I asked.

"Because we need to make a stop at the funeral home," Fab said, as though it were a no-brainer.

"You make it sound like a trip to the grocery store for bread."

Fab took her phone from the cup holder, handing it to me. "Call Raul, tell him to put Dickie on the other line, and *you* can tell them both they can go to… That we're not interested in helping them anymore, even after all they've done for us. For good measure, toss in, 'You're both weird.'"

I threw her phone on the floor and stomped on it.

Fab shrieked, pulled to the side of the road, and jumped out, running around and reaching for the door. I clicked the locks.

"Open the damn door." When I didn't respond, she drew her leg back, and I powered down the window about an inch, yelling through the crack, "You kick my car, and I'll sledgehammer your Porsche.

"You've lost your mind."

Probably, but I was certainly enjoying myself.

Fab went back around to the driver's side. She hadn't closed the door all the way and reached in to pull the keys from ignition, then went back around. When she was just about to insert the key in the lock, I unlocked the doors. Steam blowing out of both her ears, she jerked the door open, almost pulling it off the hinges, and snatched her phone off the floor.

I watched out the windshield as she paused in front of the car, running her finger over the screen. She shot me her "mean girl" glare times two and stomped back to the driver's side, sliding behind the wheel. "How old are you?" she snapped.

"Twelve. Maybe ten." I turned my head towards the side window and smiled at my reflection.

"Thank you for not ruining my phone." She hit the gas, sending the SUV jerking forward, and raced to the signal, and to my surprise, not ignoring the red light.

"Do you know what the funeral boys want?"

"A guy they just buried has somehow climbed out of his box and is wandering around again."

"Before or after he was buried? Probably before. He'd have a tough time digging his way to the top… unless he's a rodent of some sort."

Fab hit the steering wheel and, to her obvious disgust, laughed. "You're the planner—you've got time to come up with something."

"Sooo, you want me to put on my 'looking for a dead guy that's not really dead' hat? If it were cremation, that would make a bit more challenging." I let out a few spurts of laughter. "I don't want coffee. I'll take something sugary."

"I know just the place." She hooked a u-turn into the drive-through of our favorite coffee house and ordered a latte and lemonade. We didn't have to wait long since they weren't busy.

I sucked down most of mine before we got to Tropical Slumber Funeral Home, an old hot dog stand that had morphed into a business dedicated to meeting all your final needs, including a crematorium and pet cemetery.

Fab rolled up to the red carpet that ran from the parking lot to the front door and parked. "A classy touch, don't you think?" Didier had mumbled when he first saw it. I couldn't recall my response, so there probably wasn't one and

I'd instead opted to paste on an almost-sincere smile.

I got out, waving to Raul, who stood in the doorway. I stuck my head back in the car and said, "You better have come up with something because I sure as heck haven't." I shut the door without waiting for a response, betting that she didn't have a plan either.

Astro and Necco barreled out the door, skidding to a stop at my feet. "Hey guys." I scratched the necks of the two Dobermans. "The three of us—" I circled my finger around me and the two dogs. "—are hoping that there's some funeral eats in the lobby."

"You're in luck," Raul said. "We had a service this morning, and Dickie packed up the food and left it on a platter for you. You're spoiling the dogs."

"I'll only give them one. Or, since they're probably tea sandwiches, maybe two."

"No wonder the dogs adore you. You're synonymous with treats and head scratches." Raul smiled fondly.

"Won't kill them," Dickie grumped, motioning us inside.

I passed Dickie with a hello. "There's napkins on the table." He motioned to the large circular table that sat in the middle of the entry. I headed straight for the platter of sandwiches, the two dogs plastered to my leg, and snuck two off the plate, holding them down by my side... and when no one was looking, fed them two more. I ended up passing on the sandwiches and instead helped myself to a couple of cookies, then claimed my favorite plastic slip-covered chair next to the door. The dogs laid on my feet and went to sleep.

Fab circled the room, looking for intruders — dead people walking? Who knew with her. She stuck her head into the viewing rooms. I suspected they were empty, as she didn't linger.

I wanted to go home, and to that end, instead of whining, I said, "Fab gave me the short version. What is it you want us to do?"

Dickie, who'd been pacing, hands fidgeting, spoke up. "Raul and I were out for dinner. When we were standing under the restaurant portico, we caught sight of Dow Gibbons, whom we buried three weeks ago, meandering across the parking lot. Surprise! Shock! By the time the valet delivered our car, he'd disappeared."

"Was he buried locally?" Fab asked.

"Transported him to Homestead," Raul said. "Since we figured you'd ask... and, well, we wanted to know, as well, we drove to the cemetery and checked out the burial site. It hasn't been disturbed."

"Maybe a twin?" I suggested.

"Dow made arrangements for his own service ahead of time — there was no mention of any family members. And we would've noticed if someone showed up at the funeral looking like the deceased," Didier said.

"Could be a doppelganger thing," Fab said, pleased with her idea.

"Any friends show up at the funeral?" I asked. "Anyone inquire about Dow after the service?"

Dickie shook his head to both questions. "This could ignite a storm of bad publicity and ruin our business." He ran his hand through his shorn hair. "We don't want to get into any trouble, legal or otherwise. If word gets out that we buried the wrong person, it's bad for business, and we could get closed down pending an investigation."

"I've never had a request to find a dead person before," Fab said and turned to me.

I shrugged. *Don't look at me.* "We can run a couple of checks and see if anything comes back. This might be a case of letting sleeping ghosts lie."

"You need to work on your funeral humor." Raul's lips twitched.

I'll be sure and do that. I smiled weakly, since this was another time I had no clue how to respond.

"We'll do our best, but I don't want to give you false hope that we'll be able to come up with anything." Fab counseled Raul: "In the meantime, don't worry so much. The man you buried was dead?" Raul nodded. "I'm certain you followed all the rules, and that's all that can be expected."

Both Dickie and Raul nodded.

"On the upside, it hasn't made headlines." Heads turned in my direction. Apparently that wasn't helpful.

Raul handed Fab a piece of paper containing all the information they had for Dow Gibbons. My guess was that if Raul and Dickie had managed to track the man they'd seen down, up close, they'd see similarities but would know it wasn't Dow.

Raul and Fab hugged.

Dickie and I waved.

Back in the car, I powered down the window. Fab leaned across me and waved before shooting out of the parking lot.

"Those two need to chill," I said before Fab could ask. "If no one's asking questions, they should let the dog sleep."

"We'll have GC run a report—hopefully that will make them happy."

"Be sure you tell GC he's tracking a dead guy. That will move your request to the top of the pile." Fab better not be thinking that I was going to call and ask. "The boys are planning a party at Jake's—hopefully they'll get caught up in the details and forget about dead-or-alive Dow." I told her about them renting out Jake's for a funeral-givers get-together.

"I'd prefer one of those arranged fights of Kelpie's."

"Kelpie has to be threatened not to arrange

one of those every other night. She marches to whatever music's going on in her head." When Fab half-laughed, I said, "I thought it sounded better than demons. The regulars love her. She's good for the bottom line, and no one's ended up dead."

"If shootings are good for revenue, imagine how much a few dead people would bring in."

"Can you believe that people flock in at the mere mention of dead people, and blood spots attract even more of them? They take pictures to commemorate the special moment that they'd had no part of and would be disappointed to know that, most times, was highly exaggerated."

Traffic was light on the way back to the house. When we hit the corner, Fab complained that Didier wasn't home. I needed to check in with Creole, as his truck was nowhere in sight either.

Inserting the key in the lock, I asked, "When will the Mila footage be ready?"

"I'm going upstairs now to put it together. Don't worry, Brad's going to be happy."

"I'd like a peek, but I'm not asking, because Brad should be the first to see everything." I kicked my shoes into the boot tray.

"You're a good sister."

"He's damn lucky that he has both of us willing to turn over whatever rocks we come across. Thank goodness he got over himself and gave the thumbs up for our help. Probably because he knew I'd just do it anyway." I sat on the daybed, rearranged the cats, which garnered a meow, and propped a pillow behind my head. "While you're working, I'm going to text the guys and figure out dinner."

Fab made a face.

"It's not like I'm asking you to cook."

Fab laughed on her way up the stairs.

Chapter Thirty

Brad unlocked the door and walked in, loaded down with shopping bags from the Bakery Café, everyone's favorite for breakfast. He'd inherited the Westin gene for buying too much food and put everything on the countertop next to where Creole was making coffee.

"You think of this on your own?" Didier asked, sticking his nose in one of the bags.

"Heck, no. Your girlfriend said if I didn't bring food, no pictures."

Didier turned and growled, "What?" Fab sat at the island, an innocent look on her face, ignoring Didier and at the same time swaying out of his reach.

Brad grinned over Didier's shoulder.

"Did you leave anything for the Café's other customers?" I peered into a bag, then looped them over my arm and gave Brad a shove towards the patio.

"Warning: I'm taking home the leftovers," Brad said.

"That's fair." I set them on the outside counter. I'd set the table earlier so we could enjoy the sunny morning poolside.

Creole carried out a large pot of coffee, and Didier brought a tray with orange juice, flavored water, and a bowl of fresh fruit.

Brad lined up the boxes down the middle of the table and flipped up the lids, buffet-style. "I think I know what you like but ordered extra just in case."

I spotted the box with the soufflés that Fab and I liked and snapped my fingers, pointing it out to her.

There wasn't a lot of talking as we sat around the table eating.

"It's fun having you for breakfast." I side-hugged Brad.

"When you called yesterday, I wanted more details about your visit but was in an intense meeting with Bordello. Thought it would never end, and when it did, it was late."

"Partnership getting any better?" Didier asked.

"You know the old saying about it being a bad idea to mix business and pleasure? Sums up the situation. Since my relationship with Phil has deteriorated, so has the one with Bordello, and the criminal charges made it worse." Brad poured the last of the coffee in his cup and held the pot out to Fab.

Creole laughed and grabbed it. "Not a word until I grab the backup pot." He unplugged it from the counter and brought it back to the table.

"Bordello hasn't actually said he thinks I'm

guilty, but if I read into what he doesn't say, then he definitely thinks I murdered Patty. He certainly passed judgment on my choice of women." A deep rumbling sigh came from his chest. "What really annoyed me was that yesterday, he asked a couple of questions about the case that he clearly already knew the answers to. That can only be because he has someone checking up on me."

"I'd like to shoot him for you, but it's illegal, and so is feeding him to an alligator." Fab sighed.

The guys laughed.

"Since you've never asked for advice, I'm offering it for free now." Which garnered more laughs. Fab stuck her nose in the air. "Be the get-along guy until your problems are behind you. Then you can make decisions with a clear head. In no way do you *ass-kiss*."

"What do you know? Good advice." Creole winked at her.

"I'm certain I haven't said thank you enough for everything you've done since I got arrested." Brad reached over and patted Fab's hand. "I appreciate every single thing. Nothing has escaped my notice. One thing about being suspected of murder—it's made me more attentive than ever to the people in my life. Threw out the tinted glasses when it comes to assessing people and looked more at what they don't say."

Creole clapped him on the shoulder. "We're

all here for you. Don't hesitate to call, day or night. We're used to middle-of-the-night calls, aren't we?" He smirked at me.

"I learned the hard way, and I'm not taking anything at face value. Friendship like this—" Brad circled his finger. "—is rare. I don't have to worry about what any of you is going to do behind my back."

Fab lightened the mood by telling the guys about me pranking her by stomping on her phone and locking her out of the car. When she was done, the guys were laughing and giving me thumbs ups.

I smiled at her, wanting to hug her.

Eventually, Creole and I cleaned off the table and I repacked the food, of which there wasn't much left.

Fab disappeared upstairs and came back down with her laptop, setting it down in front of Brad. She slid into the chair next to him.

"Here are the pictures I promised from Madison's visit with Mila." She put a USB drive in his hand. "This is a surprise, which I didn't tell you about because I wasn't sure how the finished product would turn out."

Brad adjusted the screen so everyone could see and motioned for us to sit. "We can all watch this together." He patted the seat next to him for me.

"Even though I was there, I'd like to get a copy, if that's okay," I said to Fab and Brad.

"I'll need one of these for Mother." Brad pointed to his shirt pocket, where he'd put the drive. "Been dragging my feet long enough and finally called. Her suspicious nature went into overdrive when I suggested a mother/son lunch."

"What did you tell her?" I asked.

"What?" He threw up his hands. "I don't need an excuse to take my mother to lunch."

"Except in this case." I laughed. "If that's what you said, no wonder she went into alert mode."

"I sweetened the outing by telling her we could go looking for trouble, maybe find a police sting going down. At which she laughed and said she'd be carrying. What she doesn't know is that I'm taking her gun away before we get out of the car."

"When's your date?" I asked.

"She and Spoon are out on the boat and will be back late this afternoon, so we're on for tomorrow. Can you deliver before then?" he asked Fab.

"I can do better." Fab pulled another drive out of her pocket and handed it to him.

Brad clicked on the video. Not taking his eyes off the screen, he watched as Mila jumped down the steps at the back of the house where she lived. After a minute, he turned it off. "I'll watch the rest of this later. If that's okay." His voice was choked with emotion.

I stood and threw my arms around his neck

from behind. "Of course it is. Think about making a few selfie videos—something fun you can share with Mila. Show her how cool you can be. She'll adore it, especially as she gets older and wants to look back at how her dad acted when she was younger."

"I can't believe I had a part in creating such a cute little thing." Brad absently touched the laptop screen. "Thank you for finding her."

"You're going to be so good at this dad thing." I blinked back tears.

"Mila's the lucky one," Fab said. "She's going to have a large family that dotes on her."

Didier clapped Brad on the back. "How about a run?"

"I just want some alone time." Brad scooped Fab up in a bear hug, twirled her around and set her back on her feet. "Thank you for all your sneakiness. With the help of you and Madison, one day, I'll be able to take Mila home."

I walked Brad out to his car. "Call me for anything."

He wrapped his arms around me in a fierce hug.

Chapter Thirty-One

Fab gripped the steering wheel, blowing down the Overseas in a snit over my mention of getting hamburgers from Roscoe's. "That's a greasy pit, and we'd have to eat in the car." Indignation blanketed her face.

My phone rang, and GC popped up on the screen. I put my fingers to my lips and answered, hitting the speaker, not saying anything.

"Grow up," he barked. "I can hear you breathing, and it sounds like you're panting."

"What do you want? I'm taking a page from your phone manners booklet."

He snorted. "Got a case for you. Warning: It comes with a weirdo label."

"Family member? Friend?"

"Out-of-state client."

Fab and I exchanged shrugs.

"Does that mean we get paid?" Fab shouted.

"Something better than cash — my goodwill."

"Got a rule for you. We will never give up the right to tell you, 'Oh hell no.' We also reserve the right to add future rules that you'll agree to without any 'tudiness. Agreed? If not, you can hang up now."

"*My* attitude? What about yours, Pot?"

"I prefer Kettle."

Fab covered her mouth and laughed.

"Here are *my* rules: Your safety is foremost, and you're not to do anything to put yourselves in jeopardy. A 'yes, sir' from both of you will be sufficient."

Fab growled so loud that, instead of sounding like one annoyed dog, she sounded like a pack.

I laughed. "I'm sure you heard—Fab answered for both of us."

"The client is worried about her sister. Turns out she's been missing for two years. Somehow, the client managed to get an address for the sister's boyfriend at the time, and he's here in the Keys."

"Two years?" I said incredulously. "Has the client been looking this whole time or did it just dawn on her that she hadn't talked to her sis in a while?"

"The answer isn't relevant to the case. Anything else?" His tone told me he was tired of the conversation.

"You disconnect, and the answer is, 'Hell no, we won't work for you.' What is it that you want us to do—hold the man at gunpoint and question him until we know his sock size?" Fab smiled, so she liked the idea. "Or are you suggesting, in a not-very-direct way, that this case may involve murder?"

"I'm saying be prepared for anything. The

sister seems to think foul play is involved, but when I talked to her, she'd either been drinking or wasn't stable in general, and it zapped my patience trying to get details out of her."

"Text over the pertinent info," I said. "I'll discuss it with my partner and get back to you. When do you need this completed?"

GC grumbled something unintelligible. Then, "Today," he snapped. "Listen up, I've got the info for you. I'm about to impart everything you need to know to get the job done pronto."

I reached across the dashboard and grabbed the GPS. "What's the address? You can text me the rest."

GC rattled off the address as fast as he could, barely intelligible.

"I didn't get any of that," I grouched. "Text whatever you've got."

"Steven Smith is the man's name," he said. "I've also got a picture."

"If it's an alias, it's not very original," Fab said. "What do you know about Steve, so we know what we're getting into?"

"Name's legit. Checked him out, no criminal record. He's been employed at a local hospital for the last ten years, no blemishes on his file, exemplary employee. The house he lives in is in a good neighborhood and part of a family trust." He paused. "I just sent pictures of Steve and the missing woman, Merry Winters."

"We should have something for you in a

n of days," I said, knowing it would annoy
him since he expected service at the snap of his
fingers.

"This afternoon," he barked.

"I'll text if I learn anything. I'm surprised you
stayed on the phone this long, knowing how
much you hate talking."

"Sooner on this case would be better." He
disconnected.

"Put the home address in GPS," Fab said.
"Maybe it's close. Call the hospital and see if he's
working. No, that's not a good idea. Not sure
how they'd track down an orderly—it's not like
he's going to have his own office—and I don't
want to get him fired."

"Take the turn two exits past the city limits of
Tarpon Cove." I directed after looking at what
came up on the GPS. I didn't dare turn on the
sound—Fab found it so annoying, the GPS
would end up in the street. "It's an area of older,
well-kept homes that have survived more than a
few storms. Plus, I'm sure plenty of new
construction, as that seems to be the trend."

"First we knock, and if Stevie answers, we
inquire about our dear friend Madison."

I rolled my eyes. "A better name would be
Fab."

"If he doesn't answer, then we snoop around.
How close the neighbors are and whether
anyone's loitering about will determine whether
I use my lockpick." Fab eased off the highway

and made a hard right at the first signal.

"There's another possibility." I turned and scoped out the houses as Fab cruised past. "Merry answers the door. With our track record, though, that would be too easy."

"If it's a different woman, we stick to the same story. Except maybe she's got a forwarding for Merry or an idea where to start looking."

"If it's another woman, go into PI mode. Or do what comes naturally and scare the devil out her, and get the information that way."

"You're mean."

"It happens." I flashed her a cheeky smile.

Fab pulled into a four-block tract of homes and turned on the first street. There were few variations on the two-story houses, and all had open garage space underneath. Some were more weathered by nature than others.

Steven Smith lived in the middle of the block in a grey A-frame on stilts with a wraparound deck, a large grey shed was the only thing at ground level. No cars anywhere on the property made it an easy guess that no one was home.

We parked in the front and got out.

"Plan P: I pick the lock, you stall anyone who shows up," Fab said, thoroughly amusing herself.

"You're forgetting, in that plan of yours, that we first check out the perimeter before any picking. You need an exit that doesn't involve jumping out a second-floor window and hoping to land on a branch of one of the trees." Glancing around, I saw there was one tree and no shrubbery. "You'd be lucky if all you did was break a bone or six." I winced at my memory of tree climbing.

"If the worst happens, I'll fight my way out." Fab made a couple of air-chops.

"At least you didn't say shoot." I shot her an evil glare and followed her to the stairs. "If whoever interrupted you wasn't a complete nimrod, they'd get my license number. Next stop, a jail cell."

"Let's get this over with."

"Hold on." I grabbed at her shirt and came up empty. "I say we wait and see if Steven shows up. It's past shift-change for hospitals, and he could show up any minute. If not, we question the neighbors, starting with the old guy in the rocking chair across the street. Whip out your dude magnet, and he'll be putty in your hands, telling you everything you want to know."

Fab shook her head, barely halting on her way up the steps.

Hanging onto the railing, I ventured up a few steps, figuring I could be lookout from midway up.

Fab turned the knob on the front door, shaking it. She cupped her hands and peered in the small window. Seconds passed, then she circled the deck, peering in every window that didn't have coverings. "There's a back door," she called, coming around the corner. "Locked."

Bored, I walked back to the SUV, one eye on Fab and the other on the street. "Car coming," I yelled up to her. To my frustration, it passed the house and kept going. I eyed the man across the street, who hadn't moved—from my vantage point, it was hard to tell if he was awake. I'd hate to interrupt his snooze just to slow Fab down in breaking and entering.

Nothing ventured... Might as well try. Heading down the driveway, I paused to yell, "Hold up," to Fab, seeing her hand coming out of her back pocket. She'd be inside before I got to the middle of the street.

Weaseling information out of the neighbor could turn out to be helpful or make him suspicious. Too late. She'd disappeared inside. I looked back at the guy across the street—he was slumped over in his chair and hadn't woken up. I leaned against the car door, hoping Steven didn't come home until Fab came back out.

To my surprise, Fab shot back out the door and down the steps in under a minute. Even though she had experience, I suspected that was the fastest housebreaking ever, unless she found something. "Did you go through all the drawers and closets?"

Fab bent over, hands on her knees, and took a deep breath.

Dread washed over me. "Please tell me Steven isn't dead."

"If he is, he didn't croak inside the house. But…"

An electric car motored quietly into the driveway, parking next to us. "Hi, ladies," the good-sized fellow said as he got out. He bore a resemblance to the photo GC'd sent over, the blue scrubs and flattop another clue. "You waiting on me?"

"If you're Steven Smith," Fab said.

His easygoing stance changed to fidgety. "That depends on who wants to know."

"We're here about Merry Winters. Do you mind answering a few questions?" Fab asked politely, a tone she didn't often use.

He motioned for us to follow him upstairs.

"Have a seat over there." He pointed to the front deck, opened the door just enough to squeeze through, and slammed it shut, the lock turning with a click.

"Do you think he'll come back out?" Fab asked. "Or just call the police?"

"Depends on what he's got to hide."

"You're not going to believe—"

The door opened, and Steven came out. He double-checked to make sure it locked behind him, then walked around to the front of the deck, sliding onto the bench at the picnic table. We sat in chairs on the opposite side, facing him.

"Merry, huh?" Steven shifted his stare between us. "Haven't heard that name in a while. Not sure how much help I can be."

"Merry Winter's family is trying to find her, and someone we spoke to mentioned you as a friend," Fab said.

"Family? Now there's a surprise. You probably don't know this, but Merry and I met while she was a patient at University Hospital and became good friends. To my knowledge, Merry never had a single visitor, and she was there two months. After she was discharged, I never saw her again. That was a year ago."

Even though the man wasn't being obvious about it, it was clear he was describing a painful time. I heard him faintly whisper, "I loved her."

"Any idea where she might have gone?" Fab asked.

Steven shook his head and stood. "If that's all?"

"Sit back down," Fab ordered.

I'd wondered how long it would take for "nice girl" to hit the road. I was about to find out what Fab had found in that house.

"You don't get to tell me what to do." Steven puffed out his chest and slid off the bench. "I can pick up your scrawny butt and pitch you over the railing in a flash."

"Don't be stupid." Fab jumped up and whipped out her gun, pointing it at him. "I know what you've got in the princess bedroom."

He wisely held up his hands, stepping back. The fear on his face was replaced by outrage. "You're not taking her from me. I love her."

"Murdering a woman is a felony and carries a life sentence, and that's if you're lucky." Fab gestured with her gun. "Sit."

"Murder?" he shrieked, backing up towards the house. "No. Oh, hell no. I've never hurt anyone in my life, nor have I done anything illegal."

I raised my hand. "Odd woman out here would like someone to fill her in." They both ignored me.

"Is the dead woman in the bedroom Merry? It's hard to make an ID on a mummy."

Steven continued to back up until he hit the sliding glass door. "How much for the two of you to go away and forget you were ever here? I don't have a lot of money, but I can make payments."

"Like that's even possible," Fab yelled.

"Is the body inside Merry or not?" I asked.

"Yes," he snapped. "Satisfied? Merry wasn't murdered, and I can prove it. Pull a copy of her death certificate, and you'll find out she died of a massive heart attack while in the hospital." He swiped at his eyes.

"Sorry." It was the best I could come up with while wondering how long Merry had been dead and whether it was the year ago he'd mentioned. "Merry's sister claims she been trying to find her for two years and must have had a pretty poor PI for that death certificate to go unnoticed."

"That's bull," Steven blurted. "Where was this

so-called sister when Merry was in the hospital dying? There were no attempts to claim the body. If we hadn't married hours before she died, she'd have been given an indigent burial. Thrown in a hole somewhere."

"It's very sweet of you to give Merry a funeral service."

Fab coughed. Her look left no doubt I'd lost my mind.

"I promised Merry that I would take care of her, and I have." A low rumble came from his chest. "Now what? You take her and do what? She didn't want to be buried, and she likes it right where she is—her spirit told me so."

"Tell us about your love story." Okay, lame question, but it seemed to calm him down and earn me some indignation from Fab.

"Merry and I knew it wouldn't be long. I did some research, and found Preacher Pink online to perform the ceremony."

"Marvin Pink?" I gulped back my gasp. There was a name I'd hoped to never hear again.

"Very nice man. He rushed right over."

I bet he did. Now wasn't a good time to tell him the marriage probably wasn't legal.

"Merry passed away later that night. Preacher Pink hung around, and we were able to have a short funeral service. Thankfully, instead of her being shipped off to the county, I was able to intervene and call my friend, who works as a driver at a local funeral home. He got the night crew to clean her up and transported her here. The bedroom wasn't decorated as it is now, but Merry didn't seem to mind."

"That's quite the love story." I squirmed, unable to make eye contact with the man.

"Merry's the center of my world. She waits for me to get home, eager to hear about my day."

"Where else would she go?" Fab snapped.

In Florida, it was lawful to bury your loved one in the yard, providing you got the appropriate permit. Keep them in the house? He wouldn't be the first person I'd known to do that, but that person had had their loved one embalmed before the body snatch.

"How did you stave off deterioration?" I wrinkled my nose. "The smell must've been overwhelming."

"He did something to her," Fab accused.

"I preserved her." *Duh* in Steven's tone.

Fab leaned forward. "How?"

Of course she'd be interested in that!

"As her skin deteriorated, I replaced it with silk, stuffed the body to retain her shape, and used perfume to disguise the smell." He smiled, as though reliving those moments.

Looking down, I squeezed my eyes closed, not wanting that image burned in my mind as it was Fab's.

"You did a decent job," Fab said. "Merry looks mummified."

High praise from Fab.

"What are you going to do?" Steven jabbed his finger at us. "Take her from me? You'll have to call the police, and you broke into my house — I'll press charges. I'll be in trouble, but I don't care. You're not putting her in any hole."

I looked at Fab, silently asking her the same question.

The silence stretched out.

"Nothing," Fab said. "You said there's a death certificate?"

He nodded. "Filed in Miami-Dade. I have one in the house, if you want to see it."

"That's not necessary. If your story checks out, you can forget today ever happened. If you're full of it, I won't be back, but the police will."

"We'll let the sister know that she passed — that should satisfy her. It would be up to her to pursue it after that, and that would be costly."

Steven leaped on Fab, engulfing her in a bear hug.

Fab growled and shoved him on his butt.

I bit my lower lip. No one would believe what had just happened without pictures.

"You made the right decision." Steven's face glowed. "I'll continue to take good care of Merry. Would you like to say your good-byes to her in person?"

"No, thank you," I said over my shoulder as I struggled not to run to the steps.

"Your partner is squeamish around dead people," Steven said in a soft, reverent voice.

"Not like the two of us."

I grasped the handrail, thinking about taking the steps two at a time, but I didn't want to fall and by some fluke be stuck here. Even though I had a head start, Fab was seconds behind me in slamming the car door. I waved out the window as Fab threw the SUV in reverse.

"What do we tell GC?" I asked.

"Order a copy of that death certificate and slip it under his door, now that we know where he lives—case closed." At the end of the block, Fab eased off the gas and downed the rest of her water, rubbing her eyes. "The bedroom was decorated for a little girl. The mural on the wall was forest-themed, with a woman sitting on a throne, complete with a crown, surrounded by animals. It wasn't creepy until I caught sight of the dead person propped up in the bed. Snapped a couple of pics and got out as fast as I could."

"Except for living with a dead body, he seems to have his life together." Fab did a double take to see if I was serious. "I did wonder what would happen to him if Merry was taken away. Weird, I know."

"You're right—you are weird." Fab humphed. "I couldn't come up with a single law the man broke—handling the body after the fact, but even that's a stretch. There's no indication he harmed her in any way."

"I'm not sure if it's all the sunshine or what, but I know a couple of people in Florida that live with dead bodies. It wouldn't occur to me." I shuddered.

"I can't make fun of you, since I know those same people."

"I need a margarita or six," I said.

"Make that a martini and I'm in."

"The toast: true love."

Chapter Thirty-Two

Creole dropped a kiss on my cheek and left the house for another day of working on the docks. He'd told me that the project was close to completion and they were working on the final punch list.

Hanging over the kitchen sink, staring out the garden window, I watched as Creole made his way down the driveway, coming to a halt in front of a woman in her forties, dressed in a suit, briefcase in hand. I was certain I'd never seen her before.

They stood talking for several minutes, and it appeared amicable. I cranked open the side window, hoping to catch a word or two, but they were too far away. Turning back to the house, Creole ushered the woman to the door, knocked, and opened it.

Fab came downstairs at the same time, pausing in the entry.

"Mrs. Kennedy from Social Services." Creole introduced her to Fab and me, then backed out the door.

"Mr. Baptiste introduced himself." She smiled and crossed the kitchen to the island.

It surprised me that Creole had used his real name, Luc Baptiste... or part of it anyway. Creole had been his street moniker, which he continued to use.

Before I could invite her into the living room, she set her briefcase on a stool and turned to the patio doors.

Fab had doubled back and met Didier as he walked inside, looking every inch a CEO in suit pants and a button-down shirt. Fab introduced Didier to Mrs. Kennedy, and my stomach clenched, wondering what the woman would think.

"Nice to meet you." He deepened his accent and smiled in a way that would melt any woman. "I forgot my briefcase." He pointed to the coffee table. "I'll be emailing you a list of safety changes," he told me. "If you have any further concerns, you have my number." He turned slightly and gave me a wink only I could see.

"How many people live here?" Mrs. Kennedy asked.

"Two," I said. "Fab and myself."

Fab, who'd waved Didier off at the door, opened the fridge and pulled out a pitcher of water stuffed with fruit and a bottled water. She held them out to Mrs. Kennedy with a smile. "We also have soda."

"The fruit one looks good—I've never tried it that way before."

"Fab's fiancé is the healthy one. He's always suggesting ways to put fruit and vegetables in everything." I laughed. "Would you like to sit out on the patio?"

"This works perfectly." Mrs. Kennedy gazed around the kitchen and living room before reaching into her briefcase and pulling out a folder. "I'm happy to hear that you've given consideration to safety precautions. Here's a list of the required ones. Once I'm done checking out the rest of the house, there may be a few more."

"Would you like a guided tour or would you prefer to check it out yourself?" I asked.

Mrs. Kennedy stood. "It won't take me long." She turned towards the stairs and paused to pet the cats.

"Should I sneak out?" Fab whispered.

"We're going to act like we have nothing to hide… because we don't. Do we?" I arched a brow.

Fab pointed at herself. "Why ask me?"

"Stick around and let's get this over with."

"Take a breath." Fab refilled my glass. "You're going to do fine."

Mrs. Kennedy returned. "You have a cozy home." She slid back onto a stool, making a couple of notes. "Once you fulfill all the requirements, it won't take long before Mila will be coming home. There will be an inspector calling to make an appointment to make sure all safety issues have been addressed. And in the future, there will be regular visits by CPS."

"I appreciate everything you've done to make this such a smooth process," I said.

"Although healthy, Mila has emotional issues that you'll need to address, which I know you've been made aware of. Here's a list of health recommendations." She pulled another file from her briefcase, flipped the page over, and circled something. "This is a local child counselor you can work with to make the transition go smoother."

"That would be helpful." Emerson had also given her recommendation—it was Brad's intention to find someone that Mila could relate to.

"I was happy to hear that your visits with Mila have gone smoothly and she's warmed up to you. I've noted in the file that you can arrange unsupervised visits that are convenient with the foster mother." She gathered up her paperwork, putting it back in her briefcase. "It was nice meeting both of you." She stood. "I think Mila is a lucky girl to have found family that's eager to give her a home. Wish it was always this easy."

Fab walked her to the door and, after closing it, leaned against the frame, letting out a long sigh. "That went well."

"We have Emerson Grace, whirlwind attorney, to thank. She said she'd accelerate the case as much as possible, and she's followed through." I pointed to a stool. "Fill your glass and get comfortable. I've got some family updates."

Fab frowned. "Am I the last to know?"

"No," I huffed out a breath. "Brace yourself, though—one of these times, you're going to be. It's happened to most of us, and you're not always going to be an exception."

"Just know that I won't be gracious about it."

"No!" I made a shocked face.

Fab flicked water on me.

"Brad called—he's broken the news to Mother. At first, she was understandably shocked, then angry that he dragged his feet about telling her. He smoothed that over by telling her he didn't want to get her hopes up and then find out Mila wasn't his. Now that she's recovered from finding out that she has a three-year-old granddaughter, she's excited." I sighed. "It's the sweetest thing. Brad brought her a framed photo of Mila—one of your shots."

"Madeline's going to be annoyed with us."

"We'll smooth it over with a girl lunch and take her to the gun range," I said. "Although I'm certain she'd rather we take her to an active crime scene."

"I can't promise that."

"Happy to hear."

"Don't forget I've got the first shopping trip."

"You can duke it out with Mother. My money's on you, girl." I air-boxed. "There's more. Brad told Phil about Mila, and she told him flat out that she was 'not interested in instant motherhood.'"

"Good riddance to that one."

"You do realize that we're going to have to tame down our lifestyles?" I said as we stared at one another for a long moment. "Number one on the list is not getting arrested."

"You need to threaten your employees and tenants that if Mrs. Kennedy shows up, they damn well better be on their best behavior. Mac's the best one to corral the herd at The Cottages."

"That would be a feat. If Mrs. Kennedy decides to check out the property, I'll be adamant in telling her that not only will Mila never live there, but she won't be visiting either."

Fab held up her right hand. "I, for one, vow to be on my best behavior."

"For how long?"

Chapter Thirty-Three

Once Fab had gotten RSVPs from everyone in the family for dinner with her father, she went into whirlwind mode to organize all the details. Don't know why she waited — as if anyone would turn down the opportunity to helicopter out to a private island and meet her elusive father.

Fab — arms crossed, foot tapping — was the only one standing in the driveway next to the limo that her father had sent to take us to the chopper pad. She was waiting on the last arrival, who would be late in another minute.

Liam careened around the corner. Unfortunately for him, he'd get a lecture from everyone present about easing off the gas. He jumped out, looking like an ad for an upscale men's shop. "Sorry," he yelled, running across the street. He kissed Fab's cheek and waited while she climbed in, then followed her, announcing, "The life of the party is here."

Brad shook his finger at Liam as he sat beside him. "You know 'on time' isn't acceptable," he said in mock irritation. "You need to be early."

"Anyone have any personal announcements to make, do it now," Mother ordered. "Any

unpleasant issues whatsoever can wait. Got it?"
She stared at each of us until we agreed.

"Surprised you showed." I stretched my leg
out and nudged Brad's knee. Brad, Liam,
Mother, and Spoon shared one bench seat. Creole
and I sat opposite them, and Fab and Didier on
the end.

"And miss out on a helicopter ride? Then
there's the agony of listening to the retelling from
every single one of you." He rolled his eyes. "No,
thank you."

"Tell us about Caspian," Mother said to Fab.

"He's just an ordinary billionaire who thinks
about little else except making money," Fab said,
a teasing glint in her eye.

"Caspian's not the least bit pompous," Didier
said. "When we first met, I found him easy to
talk to—after he asked a million questions to
determine if I was good enough for his little
princess. He's a regular guy." He laughed at Fab,
who raised her eyebrow.

"One with his own island," Spoon teased.

"Is anyone else surprised that Fab didn't insist
on driving?" I asked.

That brought a round of laughter.

"On the way back, I bet I can get the driver to
relinquish the wheel and challenge someone to
take on this tank in a drag race," Fab said.

Didier's arms tightened around her, and he
whispered in her ear.

"I'll let the driver do his job," she squeaked.

* * *

It was a short drive to the helicopter pad, where we all got buckled in and donned headphones. The lift-off over the water was a bit nerve-wracking, but the ride was a short one. The view from the air was breathtaking, the water clear blue, with visibility to the bottom. The island itself was lush and green. When we landed, a golf cart awaited to take us to the house at the opposite end of the island. When we pulled up in front of the house, sunshine glimmered off the endless row of windows that wrapped around the building. A uniformed man met us at the bottom of the curved stairway—a couple dozen steps that ended at an ornate wood-and-glass front door.

From the open door, Caspian waved, dressed in boat shoes, shorts, and a tropical shirt that reeked "expensive." He looked every inch the affluent gentleman.

"Have you met him?" Brad asked as Fab ran up the stairs and threw her arms around her father, Didier close behind.

"Chasing his limo down the highway was as close as I got," I said.

"You know how to make a good impression," Brad said.

"At least she didn't shoot the tires out," Creole said, and they laughed.

"Shh, you two," I said. "Time to trot out our party manners. I know Fab wants her father to like us all."

"We'll charm him. You didn't bring a gun, did you?" Brad gave me a one-eyed stare.

I smoothed my hands over my black dress with a full skirt and fitted top. "It's just a tad too short; the gun would stick out from under my hem."

"That means you thought about it." Brad shook his head.

We got to the top, where Fab stood next to her father, and she began introducing us.

Caspian ushered us inside. "It's nice to meet all of you — I've heard a lot of stories." He led the way into the cavernous living room. Off to one side, there was a bar the size of the one at Jake's. At the opposite end, double doors that opened into the dining room. The custom table could easily seat a couple dozen people.

"It's such a spectacular day, I thought we'd sit outside." Caspian crossed to a set of open pocket doors, where another man in a uniform stood.

The patio was an open-air space equal to the size of the living room. In addition to the tiki bar, it had its own large kitchen, with every appliance anyone could want, and an island top with barstools. It didn't lack for seating — chairs and couches that wrapped around an enormous fire pit, all arranged to take advantage of the endless view.

Another man appeared and took drink orders.

When the drinks arrived, it was hard to pull myself away from the railing, where I was admiring the view, to take a seat. Another man appeared, this one apparently a guest, as he acknowledged Caspian in a familiar way before turning for more introductions. He and I made eye contact, and I gasped.

"It's you," I shouted and jumped up.

"You crazy bitch."

Creole, Didier, and Spoon were on their feet.

"Apologize now," Creole growled.

The man stepped behind Caspian's chair. "That's the woman I told you about."

"Now," Creole roared and advanced on the man.

"Sorrrry," he stuttered, his hands in the air.

"You can do better than that." Spoon advanced on the man from the other side.

"Sorry. Satisfied?" The man looked scared but wasn't smart enough to appear contrite when facing three angry men, each bigger than his puny self.

Mother was on her feet. Liam wrapped his arm around her middle and pulled her back into her seat.

Fab turned on the man and demanded, "What's going on? Caspian, who is this man?"

"Rodney Naple. He works for me." Caspian waved us back into our seats. "Now, if you'll all calm down and take a seat, this can be explained rationally.

"Works for you?" I asked in confusion and turned to Creole. "I'm sorry. I forgot to tell you at the time, and so much has happened since that it slipped my mind."

"I'm thinking we got gypped out of a good brawl." Brad laughed, which earned him a couple of frowns.

"*Everyone* sit," Caspian said. "I'm partially to blame. I planned this big surprise for Fab, and it's not going off as smoothly as I'd hoped."

Spoon was the last to sit, glaring one last time at Rodney, who—after a whispered word with Caspian—pulled up a chair next to him.

Creole hooked his arm around me.

I whispered to him, "He's a pushy, annoying realtor that said he had a buyer for the beach house. It's all on security tape."

"You are in so much trouble with me." His eyes flashed with amusement before his cool demeanor returned. "Later."

Caspian stood and toasted, "Welcome. This is an unusual way to start a party, but I'd like to avoid any *brawling*." He shot Brad a hard look. "I wanted to do something special for my only daughter, and since she's getting married, getting the perfect gift is important to me."

Mother, who sat next to Fab, smiled at her, patting her hand.

"There's a strip of land that runs parallel to the

Overseas, all waterfront, where only a couple of houses have been built. When Fab shared that she'd looked at one of the houses and was interested in buying it, I got the idea to buy all the homeowners out and give it to her. That's where my realtor comes in." Caspian waved absently to the man by his side. "I got a report back about how the visits to the properties went and was surprised to find out that there had been an altercation of sorts at one of them. I assume that was you." His focus shifted to me, as did as everyone else's.

"He..." I jabbed my finger at Rodney. "...showed up, cruising through the neighborhood—a private area, I might add—and went from house to house, ringing the bells incessantly." That was exaggerated, as I only knew the nuisance he'd made of himself at Creole's, but I didn't feel the least bit bad.

"I certainly did not." He appeared ready to jump up, but changed his mind when Creole moved to the edge of his seat.

Caspian cut him off with a wag of his finger and motioned for me to continue.

"I told him..." I stood, hands on my hips. "I wasn't interested in selling my house—not ever. Did he leave? No. Heck no. Instead, he crept around the property, taking pictures." A tug at the hem of my dress made me sit back down. "He scared me to death." I heard a chuckle in my ear.

"Your house?" Creole said, only loud enough for me to hear.

"You didn't change your will, did you?" I whispered back.

"No, I didn't, you mercenary little thing. But I'd have to die for you to collect."

"That's not happening anytime soon." I winked.

Rodney cleared his throat, dragging our attention back to him. His face was an unpleasant shade of purple. "That's not all she—"

"What's a girl to do?" I cut Rodney off, staring at Caspian and feigning innocence. I noticed that his lips quirked. "I confronted him, ordered him off the street, and told him not to come back."

Caspian broke out in a big smile. "Didn't you wave a gun in Rodney's face?"

"I did not." I glared at Rodney. "Waving is dangerous; I only pointed. My message finally sank in, and he left."

"I'm sure it did, my dear." Caspian continued to smile.

"It's an amazing wedding surprise," I said, ignoring my family's shaking heads. "If you do end up buying all that property, I suggest securing the entire area with security fencing. Fab is the perfect person for all your security needs." I beamed at her.

"You're nervy," Creole whispered.

"It's hardly a surprise," I whispered back, "if Fab's finding out now. I'll have to come up with another great idea."

"Hold on a second." Fab wiggled away from Didier's arm. "It's a great idea. Madison and I can live at opposite ends of the street, hike down the beach for morning coffee."

"Or meet in the middle." Even I had to admit it was a good idea, but I still wasn't fond of the changes that would be happening.

"Since it's your father's surprise, he should be the one to decide," Didier said.

Fab scowled at him, making it clear she didn't like his idea.

"I've not been invited to Creole's house," Mother huffed. "So I have no clue where you're talking about."

"I've got a general idea; I'll drive you by it," Spoon offered. "If a wild redhead comes running out brandishing a Glock, we'll know we're in the right place."

"It appears, Mother, that we're the last two to know," Brad said with a smirk.

"Three." Liam raised his hand. "I want in on the drive-by."

Rodney spoke up, irritated at being labeled the bad guy. "I thought you owned the property."

"Warning still stands." He didn't need to know whose name was on the deed, and I knew he couldn't garner the information from a records check, as it was held in trust.

"Once you get Rod dealt with, it's my house again." Creole nipped my ear.

"Are the other neighbors interested in selling?" Spoon asked Caspian.

He inclined his head toward the realtor.

"The owners of the house Fabiana is interested in are eager to sell, especially when they heard the word 'cash.'" Rodney rubbed his fingers together. "The other two are vacation homes, and I managed to track them down. There's interest."

"Tell Caspian your plan, the one you shared with us," I said to Fab.

She hesitated until Didier nudged her. "I got to thinking that it was the perfect spot for a family compound." She detailed her plan.

Brad's laugh conveyed *not interested* without having to say the words.

Caspian tapped Rodney's shoulder. He leaned over and said something, and Rodney stood. "Good night. Nice meeting all of you." His tone didn't hold an ounce of sincerity. He didn't run, but close, and took the outside stairs down to the bottom.

Another uniformed man appeared and whispered in Caspian's ear. He stood, saying, "Dinner's ready. Shall we go inside?" and led the way back into the house.

* * *

After dinner, we were ushered back to the patio. The fire pit had been lit, lanterns lined the perimeter, and more lights crisscrossed the sky overhead.

Caspian signaled for our drinks to be refilled. "I'd like to learn more about you and get to know all of you better."

Everyone shared an abbreviated bio. Caspian's interest perked up when he found out Spoon owned JS Auto Body, and he spent the majority of the time engaged in conversation with Spoon, peppering him with questions about cars, mostly vintage, moving on to boats and aircraft, and inquiring about his experience.

The only person to not share a bio was the man himself.

I was certain everyone noticed, but no one spoke up and said, *Hey dude, what about you?*

Eventually, Creole held out his hand, I stood, and he found us a spot overlooking the water that wasn't bathed in light. He brushed his lips over my cheek.

"We can't smooch like teenagers." I laughed at his frown.

"I wanna go home," Creole whined. "The problem with being helicoptered out here is we can't just get up and leave."

"Another reason we're perfect for one another—I'm ready to go home too."

"Good news: Just got the thumbs up from Didier, and Fab's talking to Caspian, so I'm thinking we're close to being out of here." He clasped my hand, and we joined the others.

Caspian took out his phone, ordered the helicopter to be made ready, then turned back to Fab. "What kind of morning appointment?" His voice was laced with suspicion.

It was fun watching the two of them together. Heaven help both of them if they decided to get into a stare-down.

"Three drug dealers rented sports cars and failed to return them." She held up her hand. "No, I'm not going to chase them down. I've got a guy who enjoys that kind of work. He only complains when he gets shot at." She smiled, not quite "crazy girl" but a definite taste, and Caspian wasn't amused.

His head snapped around to Didier. "I hope you're keeping a close eye on my daughter."

Didier half-laughed, his irritation on the rise. "That's a job for three men. If you think it's easy, I dare you to try."

Creole and Brad had their heads down, shoulders shaking. Everyone within hearing distance knew what a sneaky handful the woman could be.

"Oh, calm down." Fab stamped her foot. "I'm doing much better."

Liam rolled his eyes. Mother chuckled.

"Our helicopter awaits us." Taking charge, Fab waved her arm and led the way.

The ride back seemed shorter.

Once back in the limo, Fab said to Mother, "Girl lunch. You decide the day."

"Wait until my police scanner arrives," I said. "Then, after lunch, we'll see if we can locate a crime going down and speed over. Won't that be fun?"

"Like hell," Spoon growled.

"Pranked you." I laughed at him.

"That's not funny."

Mother whispered something that tinged the man's cheeks pink.

Brad crossed his fingers in front of his face.

Chapter Thirty-Four

The security gates opened, and after a car count, I determined that Fab and Toady were the only two there.

Early on, GC had sent over another report detailing Patty's history, including details about her family, which I'd failed to follow up on. Instead, I'd shoved the file to the bottom of the growing stack. Once we learned about Mila, I knew I had to do something about it immediately. If there were more family members like Patty, I didn't want them showing up on my doorstep to make a claim on Mila.

Feeling guilty for dragging my feet, I'd caught Toady with a few days' downtime and asked him to make the trip to Charleston to check them out. He'd just gotten back and summoned me to Fab's office.

I parked and hiked up the stairs. Annoyed when I turned the knob and found it locked, I kicked the bottom of the door with my heel. "Open up," I yelled.

Toady threw the door open, grinning. "Come in, sweet Madison." He flourished his arm in a wide sweep.

"You're obviously not going to break the door, so I can't get a new one out of you," Fab said. "You get dirt on it, you pay to have it repainted."

"I'll ask Didier nicely, and maybe he'll take one of his guys off the job site to come over and take care of it for you." I bet I'd never hear another word on the subject.

I grabbed a chair and started to drag it across the concrete floor, pausing to make sure I hadn't left skid marks. Toady ran over, picking it up and setting it down next to Fab's desk.

"In the future, it would be nice if my chair didn't get moved all around," I told Fab in a lecturing tone.

Fab shook her head. "You're annoying today."

"Can't get out of practice."

Toady cleared his throat. "Just finished emailing you a copy of my report. Would've done it sooner, but I just got the address from Frenchie. These reports aren't my strong suit, so don't expect no thesis. Anyway… good enough excuse to come over and be close to my one true love." He flashed Fab a one-toothed grin. "You got any questions?"

Fab's face was a mask, not showing what she thought of being the object of Toady's affection.

"You're in one piece, so that's a good sign," I said.

"The Thorsons are nice people," Toady said. "Patty, the youngest of their brood, was a normal, healthy, happy child growing up. In her first year of college, she had a break with reality, the doctors called it—went crazy, I say—and never really recovered. The family did everything they could to help her, but she resisted at every turn. They were relieved when she packed up and left one day."

"I imagine they felt guilty," I said. "Not knowing how to help her and running out of patience."

"Since Patty didn't stay in touch, they knew nothing about what she'd been doing. Then they got the notification of her death and hired someone to investigate." Toady sneezed into the crook of his arm, taking a deep breath. "When they learned everything that Patty had put Brad through, they figured he couldn't take it anymore, snapped, and killed her. They felt sorry for him, understanding how he could be pushed to the brink."

"I don't suppose you've got a smoking gun in your pocket?" I asked. "Anyone mentioned other than Brad?"

Toady shook his head. "I was upfront and told them I was there to investigate any other potential suspects. They had nothing but did wish me luck on my way out the door. They don't want the wrong person behind bars."

"Think they were truthful?" Fab asked.

"They weren't hiding anything; I'd have ferreted it out. They were a nice middle-class couple, good neighborhood. They had pictures all around—saw a few of Patty, cute kid, and even more of their grandchildren. It was clear they doted on them kids. I left, happy for Patty's parents that she wasn't an only child."

"It's sad that Patty didn't want help," I said. "Her life might've taken a different turn."

"Frenchie told me about your visit to Cardio. I'll go interview him—I've got a way of getting info out of people." Toady cracked his knuckles. "And that woman friend of Patty's you located. Women are attracted to the Toads; they're putty in my hands."

I did my best not to squirm at the sight of his fur-splotched hands, sizing him up in his usual beater shirt and, for a change, shorts and hiking boots. "There's one more guy that befriended Patty that we've yet to locate. Folsom Diggs. They lived together before she met Brad."

"I say unleash Toady on all of them." Fab's lips tilted up at the corners in a hint of a smirk.

"You need to be careful," I told Toady. "Cardio is odd, to say the least. As for the waitress, she wanted money, and I'm not adverse to another pay-off for good information. You'll be reimbursed." I liked the idea and hoped that it might yield something we hadn't been able to get.

"Okay, ladies." Toady stood and bowed.

"You're forgetting your other update." Fab motioned for him to sit again.

"Oh yeah, the dead guy." Toady threw

himself back down, almost toppling the chair over. "The good news is that he's still dead."

"Dow Gibbons?" I shook my head at Fab. "I thought we were investigating that case."

"We were... until the only address GC could come up with was some backwoods weed patch north of here. Tell her the rest."

"Dow's got a brother, Dex — not identical, but you can tell they share DNA. He was in prison when his brother died and shortly after got released and assumed his identity, living off the largess his bro left behind."

"Now what?" I asked.

"Leave him alone," Toady said in exasperation. "He's not hurting nothing, fishing every day. You tattle to the gravediggers, the cops will get involved, and Dex'll go back to prison, when he shouldn't have been there in the first place."

"Do I dare ask why he was incarcerated?"

"Double murder," Fab said, a note of glee in her voice at being the one to share.

"He was exonerated," Toady hissed. "DNA got him off."

"As far as I'm concerned..." I brushed my hands together. "I didn't hear any of this and however you close out *your* case is up to you." I proceeded to glare at Fab, whose smirk vanished.

"You upset Frenchie," Toady growled.

I growled back.

Toady jerked upright. A smile curving his lips,

he gave me the once-over, as though we hadn't met before.

Eww.

"Don't you worry none; I'll take care of this." He attempted to pat Fab's hand and instead made contact with the desk. "I'll head over to the hot dog stand and tell the diggers that Dow is dead, which is the truth, and that he did have a nearly identical bro who disappeared after he got sprung. I'll leave my card in case of another sighting. How's that?"

Fab clapped. "Call me if things don't go as planned."

"Don't you worry your pretty head." Toady motioned to Fab as though asking if he was good to go. She nodded. "I'm getting right on this, and don't think I've forgotten about those other two. You think about my offer." He gave Fab a lecherous wink.

I squirmed. To her credit, Fab remained emotionless. Another trick I needed to hone.

Once the door had closed and his boots clunked down the stairs, Fab lowered her head to her desk, covering it with her arms. After a minute, she turned her head to the side. "I think Toady knows this Dex character. It wouldn't surprise me if he's already relocated to a new patch of weeds."

I stuck my fingers in my ears. "I'm more interested in the offer he's talking about. Don't tell me nothing."

Fab sat back up. "Toady wants to work for me exclusively."

"Do you have enough work?" It wasn't a bad idea—the man had proven to be an asset and never balked at danger.

"I would if I took Brick's lowlife cases. Apparently, he can't keep a reliable team. Imagine that."

I groaned at the mention of Brick's name.

Fab ignored me. "The recent case, the cars—three in total weren't returned on their due date and the client's phones were disconnected. I suspect burners." She leaned back in her chair. "Toady rounded the cars up in a day and a half. Brick was so impressed that, for once, he stopped hounding me to come back to work."

"That was fast. No problems?"

"Well..."

Oh, I don't want to hear this.

"There was an exchange of bullets, nicked Toady in the thigh. Shooter wasn't a very good shot."

"Since Toady was just here, and I didn't see bandages, I'm assuming no long-term recovery was prescribed."

"Just a flesh wound. He carries a first aid kit and 'don't need no trip to any hospital.'" She used air quotes.

"The others... I'm assuming they're the drug dealers you mentioned to Caspian?"

"They're not the smartest criminals. Cops got

called and found drugs in the trunk of one of the cars. Hauled them all off to jail with added charges for guns and such. One actually resisted arrest, which won't go well for him in court."

"And the Toads?"

"He had legit paperwork, and once again, cop friends of his showed up—he must know the whole force. Anyway, it made the process go smoother. Here's an interesting tidbit—when Brick's name got mentioned, the cop acquaintance told Toady to watch his back. His parting shot was, 'Screw Brick at your own peril.'" Fab knew that firsthand, which was one of the reasons she'd finally distanced herself from the man.

"That's a heartwarming story, but what does it have to do with you having enough work for a full-time employee?" I asked.

"Toady would still be independent, but I'd be his only client. He's got other income that pays his bills."

I tapped my finger on her desk. No way was I asking what. I didn't have to know everything.

"Brick wants to snag him from me, which is not happening. But in order to keep that from happening, I'd have to take over all the problems with bail jumpers, rental cars and, I suppose, anything that goes wrong at one of his pawn shops."

Brick loved businesses that screamed cash.

"Don't forget the occasional stripper

hightailing it out of that club of his."

"You know there's almost always a wretched boyfriend in the mix. So far, Brick hasn't been directly involved except to ride to their rescue. Modern day Galahad." Fab rolled her eyes.

"He gets credit for paying whoever he hires to do the 'saving,' since he never gets his hands dirty." We'd tracked down a couple of his girls, who were neck-deep in trouble that included illegal activities. Brick had them relocated. "Your plan is turn Brick jobs over to Toady. Keeps you in good with Brick and, at the same time, out of trouble with Didier. Do I have that right?"

"I'm thinking about making my company a boutique agency."

"That means… what exactly? Catering to rich clients who don't have the… nerve to go commit their own felonies? You know how that goes — you get caught and they've never heard of you."

"Putting it like that makes it sound so common."

I leaned back in my chair and laughed. The annoyance on her face made me laugh again.

Chapter Thirty-Five

A grey sedan pulled into the driveway and parked. Mrs. Kennedy opened the back door and reached inside, lifting Mila out and setting her on the ground. She grasped one of Mila's hands and, with the other, grabbed a small suitcase.

I'd visited Mila as often as her foster mom, Holly, would let me. It wasn't long before I resorted to bribery, offering to include all the children in story time. As it turned out, they chose to run around in circles, yelling—no quiet voices outside.

During all the time I'd spent with Mila, she still hadn't spoken. She eagerly sat on my lap and let me hug her, and the last visit, I got to kiss her cheek. I always left with promises to be back. Holly confided that I'd made more headway with Mila than she had in the six months the little girl lived in her house. She'd mentioned the two other homes that Mila'd been placed in before hers but hadn't offered any information as to why they didn't work out, and I'd been hesitant to ask.

Mila clearly enjoyed our one-on-one time, and I planned to make sure she had more of that.

Every member of the family was eager to meet her, and she'd soon find herself showered in attention.

It took business acquaintances and favors to expedite the paperwork, all of it accomplished by Brad's attorney. Creole, Didier, and Brad had installed all the required safety features, plus a few that Fab suggested, and the house passed inspection on the first visit.

Mother had bought child safety seats for everyone's cars. "We couldn't all share one?" I asked, and she scoffed at me. Mother and Fab had already had a spirited discussion about who got to take Mila shopping first. They both lost. Brad, who'd overheard, put his foot down and told them not to spoil his little girl outrageously—*he* would do that, and he'd be taking his daughter shopping first.

I raced to the front door, slowed, then walked out calmly. I waved and motioned for the two to come inside. Mrs. Kennedy let go of Mila's hand, and she ran to me, grasping mine. The three of us walked back inside.

"Would you like something to drink?" I asked.

"That won't be necessary. I'll do a walkthrough before leaving, and you can expect a visit in a couple of days."

"Any questions, we'll be right here." I picked Mila up, hugging her, and sat down on the daybed, setting her on my lap. "I'm not sure if you knew, but you're going to be staying here with me." I kissed the top of her head, wanting to smother her in hugs and at the same not overwhelm her even more, though she seemed calm.

Snow jumped up and pawed her way across the pillows, slid down to nestle against Mila's side, and went to sleep.

Mila reached out tentatively, patted the cat's head, and jerked back. A huge smile lit up her face, and she did it again. Her smile got even bigger, and she petted Snow again, looking up at me, as though for approval.

"That's Snow, and she loves being petted." I pointed across the room. "That's Jazz. They're friends." I'd have to keep an eye out to see how the cats adjusted to having a child around. Probably the same way they reacted to everything else—a sniff and a nap.

I wished Fab hadn't snuck out, so she could capture these sweet moments in pictures. If Mila was camera-shy, Fab would have her over that in no time.

Mrs. Kennedy came back downstairs, went out to the patio, and wasn't out there longer than a minute before coming back inside. "You have my card if there are any problems, but I don't anticipate any."

"Thank you. I appreciate everything you did to make this happen. I promise Mila will have a good life."

"If I didn't think that, I would have never

signed off on the file." She waved and left.

Mila didn't seem to notice, as her attention was focused on Snow.

I took out my phone, snapped a couple of pics, and texted Fab. "Coast clear." It wouldn't take long for her to get back from the beach.

She slipped through the side fence a few minutes later—unknown to most, there was a path running from the front of the house to a set of steps that wound down to the beach.

"Mila needs to learn to swim," Fab announced, walking through the patio doors with a big smile on her face and waving to the little girl. "I'm your Auntie Fab." She curtsied, which brought a smile to Mila's face. Fab approached her, hand out. "Do you want to see your new home?"

Mila stared intently, and after a good minute, she clasped Fab's hand. "We're going upstairs." Fab pointed.

Mila slid off my lap onto the floor.

"For now, we're going to walk up one step at a time. Later, I'll show you all the cool ways to get up and down." Fab smiled conspiratorially.

I cleared my throat.

"I said later."

They went up the stairs. I heard doors opening above me, Fab giving short explanations as they moved down the hall. Mila came back downstairs with Fab, wide-eyed, paused on the last step, and jumped.

I stood and watched as Fab took Mila out to the patio, pointing out where the pool toys were kept.

"We need to get you a bathing suit, so you can play in the water," Fab said, coming back through the French doors.

I sat on the floor, reached under the coffee table, and pulled out a basket of newly acquired toys that Brad had raided the toy store for, taking suggestions and adding a few choices of his own. Next came a pile of picture books that I'd had fun choosing from the Cove's bookstore.

Letting go of Fab's hand, Mila came over and sat down, staring at the toys. I shifted the basket in front of her. "These are your toys, and they'll always be under here for you to play with."

Fab crouched down and sat on the other side of her.

Mila reached for a doll, hugging it and petting her hair, much the same way she did Snow.

"Now what?" I asked Fab and snapped a pretend camera. "We can't just sit here and stare at her." I kept an eye on Mila to make sure she wasn't paying attention to my attack of nerves. I got a tear in my eye at the clucking sounds she made in the doll's face. "Do we unleash the family on her? That could be overwhelming."

"We're both getting a crash course in parenting." Fab pulled her phone out of her pocket. "We're going to ace it." She walked around the room, snapping pictures from every angle.

A few minutes later, several issues were settled — what to do next and when to call the family. The front door opened, and Mother and Spoon came in. They had shopping bags with a familiar name on the front looped over their arms and a stuffed bear every bit as large as the man carrying him.

"Hiii." Mother waved.

Mila looked up, then went back to staring into her doll's face.

Mother took the bags from her husband's hand and headed to the kitchen. I stood and knocked Fab's foot as I passed to help Mother. "More pictures."

Spoon set the bear on the daybed and lay on his side on the floor across from Mila. "Is this Mila?" he asked the doll. "Tell her I'm happy to finally meet her after hearing so much about her from her Auntie Madison."

Mila stared into Spoon's face.

"I'm Spoon, well, Jimmy Spoon. I'm married to your grandmother over there." He waved in the direction of the kitchen. "You can call me Grandpa, Grandfather, whatever you like," he rambled. "I'm your go-to person if you need a good listener. Better than a talker."

I smiled and left the man to talk Mila's ear off. I'd tell her later that she was to be congratulated, as I'd never heard Spoon so chatty. I hoped that

Fab, who'd stepped off to one side, was now capturing every minute on video.

"You didn't forget dessert, did you?" I hugged Mother.

Mother snorted. "Would you stop squeezing the life out of me?"

"You're an amazing mother, and the only one in the family with parenting experience." I kissed her cheek. "You're going to be the go-to chick for endless questions."

"I'm fairly certain I haven't been referred to as a chick before." Her eyes filled with amusement.

"And a hot one too." I admired her spaghetti-strap sundress. "I need to call Brad."

"He's on his way. I called him when Fab texted that the social worker had left. He was worried about overwhelming Mila, and I told him nonsense, he's just scared."

The front door opened, and Brad poked his head into the kitchen.

I pointed to the living room, and Mother and I craned our heads to see father and daughter's first meeting.

"Hey Mila, nice to meet you." Brad waved and bent down, setting a Hurricanes baseball cap on her head and a football in her lap. He nodded to Spoon and sat cross-legged next to her.

"Have you given your doll a name?" Brad asked, fluffing the doll's hair.

"It's Mila's new friend. They met on the beach, and she brought her home," Spoon improvised.

Mila giggled.

My eyes filled with tears. Until that moment, I hadn't heard anything out of Mila except gurgles, huffs of air, and a sigh or two.

Chapter Thirty-Six

Mother, Brad, and I worked out Mila's schedule. She spent mornings with Mother while Fab and I took care of business, and Brad arranged his schedule so that he ate breakfast and dinner with his daughter and stayed to tuck her into bed.

Mila learned quickly how fun the guys could be when they went all out to impress a three-year-old. Creole introduced her to coloring — the first night, he came to the house with coloring books, a gigantic box of crayons, and a blank pad for her own inspirations. She learned to dance from Didier, who waltzed her around the kitchen and living room while she stood on his toes. Spoon had been instrumental in overcoming her shyness around the men. The first morning at his house, he coaxed her onto his back for the ride of a lifetime around the house. Brad couldn't sing, but apparently no one had pointed that out to him. Armed with plastic microphones and a video of children's songs, Mila perfected some wild moves that Brad encouraged as he sang along.

Afternoons were Fab's and my time to entertain Mila. Today, Fab had met Didier at the office and they made plans for a late lunch, so I hurried home to change before Mother brought Mila home. As I turned the corner, a silver BMW cruising slowly up the street caught my attention. Instead of turning into my driveway, I passed it and pulled over in front of a house three down from mine. What had made me so suspicious? Possibly overreacting, thanks to the kinds of cases Fab took, which kept us constantly on alert. I expected to be laughing at myself at any moment if the car parked in a driveway and turned out to be a neighbor. The driver made a u-turn and passed me again, the tinted glass making it impossible to make out anything more than that there was a man behind the wheel. Ready to snap a photo of the tag number, I realized the car didn't have a license plate.

A few minutes later, it had turned the corner and vanished. I turned around and went back home, parking in the driveway. I poked my head out of the car, looking one way and the other. All was peaceful. *Just overreacting.*

The house was quiet. Even though Mila was a toddler and still unnaturally silent, her presence filled the house. Not to mention the adults who stopped by to entertain her. I never minded having a house full of guests. Creole and I enjoyed finding ways to sneak off and enjoy alone time. I loved him more, if that was possible, for never complaining. "It's good practice," he said the other night when we slipped down to the beach.

Pouring myself a glass of flavored water, I took every report GC'd sent me concerning Brad's case and set them on the island, then hopped up on a stool, planning to go over them one more time. If I'd missed anything before, I was determined to find it now. The trial was several months off, and we needed to come up with either the real murderer, a viable suspect, or exculpatory evidence. The body in the car was not an insurmountable hurdle but close. Ruthie had told Brad that there were no fingerprints found on the body bag.

Hearing a rustle behind me, I asked, "Hungry?" not expecting more than a meow or howl.

"Maybe next time," a male voice laughed. "But there won't be a next time."

I spun on my seat, staring at the man who'd entered through the patio doors. Setting down two gas cans on the living room floor, he reached behind him with one hand, closing the doors. The other pointed a gun at me.

"Cardio. I didn't think our meeting went so poorly that you'd want to shoot me." I maintained eye contact, trying not to show fear. How had I missed the vacant dullness in his crazy eyes? He hadn't left me feeling that I needed to keep one eye peeled, gun ready, after the meeting in his dingy apartment. "I'm sure we can work something out."

"If it's any consolation, you were not my first choice. I'd rather it was your brother."

"I don't understand what you're talking about. Maybe you could fill in the details."

He only took his eyes off me for seconds to scope out the rest of the room. Not enough time for me to reach the gun in the junk drawer, and even if I could, it was now kept locked. My fingers itched to drag my phone closer, but that wouldn't go unnoticed.

"You're a smart girl, or so you think; you'll figure it out. Maybe." He laughed, sending a chill up my spine. "Thought about having you call Brad over on some pretext or other, but figured you'd tip him off, so I decided to settle for second best for now. I'm thinking I might get a kick out of attending your funeral to watch Brad suffer. Then set a trap for him."

Cardio's eyes locked on a framed photo of Brad and Mila. He grabbed it off the shelf, his face filled with rage. "What's *he* doing with Patty's daughter?" He covered the glass in spit. "She had a good home. Patty had plans to get her back."

I shuddered at the thought of Patty ever getting her hands on Mila. "Name your price. In exchange, you go far away and neither of us mentions this meeting to anyone." I didn't have anything else to bargain with, and even if the option were available, I sure as hell wasn't going to set Brad up to be killed when he walked in the door. That would end in two dead people, as Cardio couldn't afford to let me live. My guess was that he knew that already, but I'd try anything. There was running... but then he'd probably shoot me in the back.

"Money, money, money. Some people think it's the answer to everything, and you're one of them." He sneered. "My mission is to avenge Patty."

"But I never had anything to do with Patty." Now wasn't the time to mention that I was instrumental in her last arrest, and I hoped he didn't know. "Brad didn't kill her, I promise you."

"I know. I did," he said, matter-of-fact. "You're thinking 'then why does Brad have to die?' Because..." Fury filled his face. "He lured Patty in with pretty words and empty promises, and gutted her when he walked out." He calmed himself somewhat. "Patty and I loved each other. We had plans to move up to the panhandle, settle down, and have a few kids of our own."

"You murdered Patty, and it's my brother's fault?" My eyes fluttered, a wave of dizziness hitting me. I forced myself to bury the fear.

"Your worthless brother swept Patty off her feet, and she never gave another thought to her true love, Cardio." He thumped his chest. "Brad this, Brad that, was all she yammered on about. You'd think that brother of yours walked on water."

Mentally, I ran through anything useful in my kitchen. The knife holder sat on the stove on another wall. And bringing a knife to a gunfight equaled loser. "How can you blame Brad? The relationship didn't work out; it happens." I had to keep the man talking, but Mother would be there anytime with Mila. I shuddered at the thought of the two of them getting caught in the middle. Cardio would kill Mother. Mila? Coming face to face with Patty's child, would he kidnap her?

"You know Patty had finally been cured?" he spat out.

I flinched at the word "cured." The chances of that in her case were nil.

"When she got out, I asked Patty to marry me, and she proudly wore my ring." Cardio stared down at the ring he was wearing. "We were happy. But she had to see Brad one last time, and there was no talking her out of it. The bastard fixed her good, had her arrested, and we knew if she was deemed mentally fit, she'd get transferred to the county jail to await trial. So she went back to the hospital. I still kick myself for not dragging her out of town when I had the chance. Away from his influence, she'd have come to realize that my love was enough for her."

"The reason Patty got arrested was because she drugged and kidnapped Brad and held him against his will."

"Your brother lied," Cardio spat. "Patty told me the truth. He proposed, bought her a house, then when she told him about Mila and that she wanted them to be a family, he turned on her. Said that no way was she going to ruin his future, then cooked up that stupid story and had her arrested."

The sheer inconsistency of his fiction about how Brad had treated her made my head spin. I shook off questions about how Brad could simultaneously want to marry her and not want to have a child with her and instead said, "I promise you, had Brad known about Mila, he'd have never turned his back on either one of them."

Cardio scoffed at that. "Your promises aren't worth spit."

"Your problem is with Brad, why come at me?" I eyed the gas cans again and could only guess at his plans. In that moment, I decided that if he took a step towards me, I'd make a run for it. I'd rather take a bullet than go up in smoke. "Would you mind shoving my cats out the door?" I pointed to where they both lay on the floor close by.

"Filthy things. If they're that important to you, your family can bury you together." He laughed at the idea, sounding even more unstable.

I squeezed my eyes shut, and pain shot through my chest as I sent a mental *I love you* to my family and friends.

"You're never going to get away with this." I didn't have to look around to know my options were few. I'd have to make a run for the front door and take my chances on him being a poor shot. "If my family gets their hands on you before the cops, your death will be slow and gruesome. If the state gets you first, they'll set your hair on fire." The electric chair had malfunctioned a couple of times in the past.

"I'd like to do slow and gruesome with you—more guilt for Brad to deal with—but I can't hang out here all day." He tapped his watch as though he had someone else to go kill. "You won't suffer long once I blow this place sky high. Maybe not at all. You'd be surprised what a bullet can do to a gas can. Fireworks." He threw one arm in the air. "You'll either burst into flames along with the house, or possibly die of smoke inhalation—not sure there'll be time for that before you catch fire." His eyes glittered. "Saves your family some dough—I'm thinking there won't be much to bury."

"How did you get in anyway?" I didn't care—anything to slow him down.

"Excellent security system." He saluted. "Had to be careful. Got me a ladder and waited for the neighbor to leave, threw a rope over one of their tree branches, swung over like Tarzan, and managed not to touch the fence. Landed hard, got a sharp pain in my ankle, but that wasn't going to stop me. Pays to have a high pain tolerance."

"How did you find me?"

"Unfortunately, it was a lot easier than finding your brother, which is why I changed my plan to zero in on you. Patty saved an old article where they profiled you and that dump bar of yours. You're not much for regular hours, and it got tedious waiting for you to show. But finally, got you! Followed you home. You're not much for picking up a tail."

I must have been driving that day. "That was you in the BMW, wasn't it?"

"Rich people." He shrugged. "Not even an alarm on that baby. Got a buyer for the parts who's meeting me later with cash. Now there's a lucrative business. The perk of my job is that I get to drive one swanky ride after another."

"Surprised you didn't get pulled over with no tags."

"Not as unobservant as I thought. But where did it get you? Here. With me." He laughed again, pure evil emanating from him.

"There's no reason to kill the cats. It's not like they can finger you." I glanced down, blinking back tears—I wasn't crying in front of this cretin.

"That it bothers you is reason enough for me. Another perk of the job. Let's get this show started. When I get my face-off with Brad, I'll tell him that he can be proud you didn't grovel or beg for your life. Or better yet, tell him you did both of those things on your hands and knees."

I hoped Spoon was the one to track Cardio down, and when he got his hands on him, that he'd cut him up one small piece at a time and flicked them to a nearby alligator.

"Thank me," Cardio demanded.

"For what?"

"Killing you before setting the place on fire. Thought about it—can't run the risk of you escaping somehow."

Here's your thank you. I gave him the finger.

"Bye-bye." He grinned and pulled the trigger.

Pain blossomed first near my left shoulder, then seared through my chest and the rest of my body as I hit the floor. *Terrible shot.* I kept my eyes shut, not daring to move an inch, no matter how much it burned, wondering how long I'd be able to fake death. At the sound of liquid being splashed around, I risked a peek under my eyelashes and tried to calm the panic as I watched him carry out his threat to turn my house into an inferno.

I'd been shot before, and it hurt like the devil. I lost the fight to stay still and began twitching— so much for not attracting attention and another bullet that would finish me off.

Cardio finished slinging the gasoline around the lower level and threw what was left of the one can on the stairs. The other, he picked up and placed in the middle of the living room. He kicked open the French doors and backed out.

"This has been sheer pleasure." He laughed manically and put a bullet in the remaining can.

The can exploded, flames of gasoline shooting out, igniting the carpet and licking across the room.

I struggled to my feet, grabbing the countertop, and scanned the corners of the room for the cats. If they hadn't taken off at Cardio's first shot, they were gone now—upstairs would be their only option, and my heart sank as the fire swept up the stairs. The flames flicked around towards the front door, blocking the exit. Grabbing a broom, I leaned over the kitchen sink, ripping out the garden window shelf and sending it flying to the floor. I jammed the handle into the double-paned glass. The inner pane shattered, but the outer remained intact.

I wrapped myself in the kitchen rug and eyed the flames that engulfed the French doors. I didn't like my idea at all, but I had no choice. It would take a miracle to survive.

As I struggled to breathe, the last thing I remembered was falling.

Chapter Thirty-Seven

My stomach hurt. It felt weighted down. Cracking my eyes open, I wanted to laugh at the familiar head of black hair, forehead resting on my navel, just below where my chest and left arm were bandaged. What came out was a crackling noise. The panel on the machine that was hooked to my other arm remained lit up and silent, which I took as a good sign and the reason for my pain-free state. So I'd made it to the hospital. I wiggled my fingers and examined all the parts of my arm that I could see—no burn marks or scorched skin.

Happy that no one had closed the blinds, I gazed out the window. I surmised that it was early morning, as the sun was just making its appearance.

Vague recollections swirled about. Being lifted into the arms of a fireman—or so I assumed, as he was dressed in yellow from head to toe, a gigantic mask over his face. Laid on a stretcher, loaded in an ambulance. An air mask covering my face, and then nothing.

Jazz. Snow. I whimpered, tears rolled down

my face. My cats had died in the fire. Everything in me hoped that they were overcome by smoke and died that way. I couldn't bear the other. I moved my hand across the sheet, twining my fingers in Creole's hair.

He jerked up. "You're awake." He kissed me lightly, his fingers wiping away my tears. "No crying. You're alive, and that's all that matters. I love you."

"Wuv…" I tried to tell him and got cut off by a coughing fit.

"Ssh…" He brushed my hair back. "Rest and I'll do all the talking." He reached for the water cup sitting on the bedside stand, sticking the straw in my mouth. "Drink," he ordered. "You're going to need your strength when your family comes flocking through the door to see for themselves that you're okay. I kept them at bay, except for your mother."

"How long—"

"Overnight. Even that was too long," he said gruffly.

The door opened, and Dr. A sauntered in. He flashed his most wolfish smile, picking up the clipboard at the end of the bed. "I was here earlier. Did you wake up for me? No. I tried my best. Very happy to see those beautiful brown eyes of yours."

If looks could kill, the charming doctor would be laid flat out on the linoleum and Creole wouldn't feel the least bit of remorse.

I coughed out a half-laugh and opted for a wave.

"My favorite patient is doing well." Dr. A winked. "I'm personally going to see that you're on your feet and out of here before you get bored and get into trouble." He turned to Creole. "You want to get out of the way?"

Creole growled at him and reluctantly moved to the other side of the bed, grabbing a chair and bringing it closer.

"I'm Madison's *doctor*." Dr. A laughed. "Besides, I tried long ago to steal her away, and she turned me down." He perused the chart, digging his stethoscope out of his pocket. "You're lucky, my dear. Lean forward. You know what to do—we've done this before." He pressed the stethoscope to my back, and then front, and listened to my breathing amidst the coughing. "Much better." He picked up the water cup and handed it to me, waiting patiently while I drank. "More?" When I shook my head, he took it back and set it on the table. "The more you can drink, the better. Along with plenty of rest, and no jumping out of windows… for now." He teased. "The firemen rescued you just in time, saving you from more serious injuries. You're suffering from smoke inhalation, which we're treating, but thankfully no burns."

"You're the best," I coughed out.

"You know I make house calls." He laughed as though we shared an inside joke, which we did. He had treated more than one person at my house who'd refused to go the hospital, mostly because they didn't want to end up explaining to law enforcement how they got hurt. "Once you're released, I'll stop by the house and check on you."

"How many patients do you do that for?" Creole asked sarcastically.

Dr. A thought for a moment. "Two, maybe three," he said with a smile before becoming serious again. "Are you up to talking to the police? I can hold them off for a bit, but they want a statement about what happened."

"Did they take Cardio into custody?" I asked.

"Who, babe?" Creole patted my hand.

Cardio got away. That wasn't possible… or maybe it was. Panic set in. "K-killed P-patty." I struggled to breathe. "Brad. Protect Brad."

Dr. A pulled me into a sitting position. "Easy. Breathe. Watch me." He demonstrated slow breaths, which I copied.

Dr. A and Creole stared at each other, and I had no clue what message they sent between them.

"I hate to be the pushy one," Creole said with a look of remorse, "but… Did this Cardio fellow start the fire?" I nodded. "You're going to need to answer questions so we can get this creep behind bars." He took out his phone. "I bet Fab knows this weasel."

"Bastard!" Dr. A growled.

"Madison's awake," Creole snapped when she answered. "Brad's in some kind of trouble. Find him and don't let him out of your sight. Then get over here—we need your help." A few seconds later, he disconnected. "You're not to worry. With Fab and I working together, Cardio will be begging to go to jail."

I reached for the water cup and came up short. Creole pushed my hand away, picked it up, and held the straw to my mouth.

"I'm off on rounds," Dr. A said. "Take it easy. You feel a panic attack coming on, breathe through it. Doctor's orders. I'll be back to kick you out when you're well enough. If you need *anything,* here's the magic button." He held up the cord tied to the side of the bed, then left with a wave.

I teared up again.

Creole thumbed them away. "What are you thinking about?"

"Jazz, Snow," I whispered.

"Rescued by a fireman." He grinned. "They weren't very happy with his methods, but they're safe at my house. He found them in your bathroom, grabbed pillowcases off the bed, stuffed them inside, and handed them out the window. Fab went to the pet store and got everything they needed."

"My house?" Looking into his eyes, I could see the terror and anger he'd felt.

"When I thought I'd lost you..." He closed his eyes.

I traced my finger over his lips.

"Took out the first floor, the staircase."

I could see him picturing what he'd seen as he described what was left.

"There might be something salvageable from the second floor... maybe. Not sure how it'll smell." He sniffed. "Didier and I are going to oversee cleanup. Once your insurance gives the okay, it can be rebuilt when you're ready. Emergency fencing is currently being installed to keep out lookie-loos."

"So happy Mila was with Mother."

"Me too. Something like that would have traumatized her — wiped out all the progress she's made. Mila laughs a lot now that she's coming out of her shell, and it's fun to see. I think it has to do with the attention she's getting, all of us trying to outdo each other. Hands down, I think the top vote goes to Spoon — he's become her very own chauffeur and she loves to ride on his back. Her next favorite thing is rolling around on the floor."

"It's fun to watch the two of them together. Actually, all of you."

Kevin stuck his head in the door, saw I was awake, and walked in. "Woke up this morning thinking 'what would heal Madison faster,' and it came to me — a visit from my smiling face."

I coughed.

Creole and Kevin engaged in a stare-down, followed by a nod.

"Hear the food sucks," Kevin said, pulling up a chair. "I volunteered to come ask questions, seeing as how close we are—you know, friends."

"Your sarcasm appeals to me," I said. "How did they find me in time?"

"You've got your neighbor to thank for that. He wasn't happy when he came home and found a ladder leaning against his fence and a rope dangling from the tree. Called the cops. Did you know that's what most people do when they have a problem?"

"Save your lectures for never," Creole gritted out.

"Anyway... The cop that came to investigate saw the smoke and called it in. Fire department made it in record time. What I want to know is, what the heck happened? Fire, I got that. Pretty sure you didn't put a bullet in the gas can yourself. Fire Marshall reports that as the cause of the fire."

"You've got to find Cardio Gates," I rasped. "He killed Patty and tried to kill me. He's not going to be happy when he finds out I'm not dead—he'll be setting a trap to kill my brother." I detailed what happened.

"That chick just doesn't go away, not even in death." Kevin grimaced. "Has me rethinking the women in my life."

"Now's not the time to be telling us about

351

your love life," Creole said evenly. "I'm certain there will never be a good time."

"No?" Kevin faux-pouted. "Good thing, it's not exciting right now. I don't want to put a crimp in this bonding moment, but to get Brad off the hook, we need this Cardio Gates alive. Corral your posse. Let the state set fire to his ass."

"If you wait a few, Fab will be here, and she'll have a picture of him," Creole said.

Speaking of... the door burst open, and Fab flew in, tugging on Didier's hand. She rushed to my side, bending and enveloping me in a hug. "Who did this?" she growl-whispered in my ear.

I grasped her top and whispered back, "Cardio Gates. He murdered Patty and he's after Brad. We need him alive."

"I'm going to sic Toady on him." Fab's eyes darkened with sadness and anger. "He's a motivated man, since Cardio clubbed him over the head, leaving a bump the size of an egg." She took her phone out of her pocket and headed back out the door, Kevin on her heels.

Didier took her place, leaning over, kissing my cheek, and whispering in my ear.

"That Frenchy talk is better than medicine," I said. "If that was something about me looking beautiful, you're fibbing."

"Your being naughty means you're getting better."

Chapter Thirty-Eight

Release day at last!

Dr. A had kept me an extra day.

I got discharged with admonitions to rest, which I needed after the endless round of visitors, most peering down at me mournfully and not listening when I told them I was almost recovered. That morning, Crum, Joseph, and Svet had dropped by and settled in for a long visit, jabbering between themselves until I closed my eyes and feigned sleep, and no, they didn't get the hint.

Finally, the door opened, and I peeked under my lashes as Creole came to an abrupt halt. "What the devil?" he said, startling the two men who were camped on the settee with the blowup doll. "Get out." He pointed to the door.

At least it wasn't the window, as the room was on the ninth floor.

Crum and Joseph left, taking Svet with them and grumbling all the way. As soon as the door closed behind them, I opened my eyes. "I owe you."

Creole leaned down and gave me a noisy kiss.

Behind him, Liam cleared his throat. "Stop. I

have a young, impressionable mind."

"I didn't see you standing there." I threw out my arms. "Just happened to be in the area?"

"I offered my brawn." He flexed his muscles, then leaned down and hugged me. "I'm here to help spring you from this joint, and I'm driving, so get ready to hang on." He made a revving sound, which earned him a glare from Creole.

I'd planned to recuperate at Creole's, but Mother wasn't having any of that. She'd invited Fab and Didier to stay at her condo, which they accepted after telling her that it would only be for a couple of days. Mother also ordered Creole to relocate the cats to her place. I wanted to go to Creole's, but I also wanted to see Mila and that won out.

"Your mother's a smart one," Creole told me when he learned of her plans. "She made it impossible for anyone to say no—first the doe eyes, then the subtle guilt. She didn't overdo it, but she got her message across. We all caved."

"On my way out, I heard Grandmother on the phone, ordering all your favorites, so be prepared for food overload."

"Did she call the liquor store and order tequila?"

Liam laughed. "You might want to stay sober. You never know what she has up her sleeve."

The nurse came in and delivered me to the curb in a wheelchair limo. Creole opened the back door and lifted me into the back of an SUV I hadn't seen before, a loaner from Spoon probably. That didn't bode well for the Hummer. Creole climbed in after me, hooking his arm around my shoulders. I nestled my head against his chest.

"Where's Brad?" I asked.

"Just got a text." Creole read: "'Holed up on Spoon's boat.'" He shoved his phone in his pocket. "Didier is purchasing new disguises as we speak. Spoon swapped out your ride and Brad's—he got a beater truck with tinted windows and bars across the front, and this is yours until Cardio is picked up. The Hummer escaped damage, but I decided to leave it parked in the driveway."

"I want to see Brad."

"Figured you would." He brushed a lock of hair behind my ear. "He'll be around later, once he's certain he's not being followed."

"Spoon's got a couple of his guys on round-the-clock parking lot duty at the condos," Liam said over his shoulder.

"Watch what you're doing," Creole barked. "Stick to the speed limit."

"Yeah, yeah." Liam stopped at the security gate, then followed the car in front of him inside. "Don't overthink the living situation." He turned to me after we parked and got out. "Treat it like a vacation rental with way too many people. You're not staying forever, just until you decide what's next."

"Good advice." I nodded. "I was feeling overwhelmed."

Creole hit the buzzer on the security panel in the front of the building. "Open up."

When the elevator doors opened, Spoon stood in the doorway. "Welcome home." He kissed my cheek as we entered.

Mila stared, wide-eyed, from the opposite end of the hallway, next to the kitchen, as we crowded into the condo. I'd worried that my being away for a few days would leave her thinking I deserted her, but Mother had assured me that wasn't the case and brought me one of her drawings in the hospital. Mila jumped up and ran to meet us, hugging my legs.

Spoon scooped her up and leaned her toward me. I kissed her cheek and gave both of them a one-armed hug. He put her down immediately. "Mila enjoys a hug as long as it's short. At first squirm, she wants down."

Mila whirled around and ran back, plopping down in the midst of toys and books.

Mother held out her arms, and I walked into them. We held onto one another for the longest time. "So happy you're here." Her eyes filled with tears. "I should apologize for being so sneaky. Should."

"Don't cry." I sniffed. "Because I'll cry, and how will we explain happy tears to Mila?"

"Take each day as it comes." She shook her finger at me, tapping the tip of my nose. "Rest.

Relax. Overeat. Don't be bashful about asking for whatever you want."

I looked down as fur wound its way through my legs. "Oh…" I reached down and petted Jazz, kissing the top of his head. He meowed his annoyance and walked over to Snow, curling up next to her. "I know you, Mother—when is everyone getting here?" I looked around. "No Fab? Didier?"

"Everyone will be here for dinner, and no one better be late." Mother sighed in exasperation. "Fab's hunting down Cardio. I admonished her to be careful, for all the good that did. Was she listening? Half-heartedly." Mother shook her head. "I reminded her twice that we need Cardio alive."

Chapter Thirty-Nine

Two days later, there hadn't been a single sighting of Cardio Gates. I was on edge, jumping at any little sound, and called Brad fifty times before he finally asked Creole to take my phone away.

Creole and I set up a temporary office on Mother's patio. We commandeered her table and worked every connection we had, sending photos. Thank goodness for Fab's penchant for photographing everything, no matter how trivial. It surprised me that she'd been able to get a couple of shots of the man in that dreary apartment of his — I hadn't been aware she did it and, judging by the pictures, neither had Cardio.

Fab had left early for the office, promising to call in every favor owed her. "That bastard will not get away with this."

The only new information GC had uncovered was that Cardio used an alias he'd managed to keep separate from his true identity. Folsom Diggs. That meant there was never a second man in Patty's life — there was only Cardio.

Creole appeared in the doorway, pocketing his phone, a grim look on his face. "Cardio is dead.

There was a shootout in central Miami. Thankfully, he didn't take any officers or innocent bystanders with him." He ran his hand through his hair in frustration.

"Who tipped off the cops?" I asked.

Mother and Spoon came out, and Creole pulled out a chair for her. Spoon distributed drinks, knowing our preferences without having to ask, and sat next to his wife. I only got water until I was off pain meds, my arm out of the sling.

"Toady." Creole took in a deep breath and let it out slowly. "He caught sight of Cardio on a motor scooter, of all things, and followed the man, who ditched his ride behind a dumpster and hotwired a car in a grocery parking lot. Tracked him to an abandoned house that he holed up in. Patrol cars rolled up to the house, but before they attempted to make contact, Cardio started shooting."

"Damn." I threw my head back against the chair cushion. "That screws Brad. It's now just my word, and I'm the accused's sister."

"Screw me again, did you?" Brad came through the doors, his lips quirked in amusement.

"You need to eavesdrop better," I said. "Fab could give you some pointers." I was surprised the neighbors hadn't called the cops—they must not have seen Brad in his grungy beach attire, cap pulled down over half his face, aviators covering the rest.

"Fab and Didier are on their way," Brad said. "She called with the news that Cardio's dead, and I relayed it to my lawyer. Waiting to hear back from Ms. Grace." He ruffled my hair and sat down next to me. "How's your arm? You're not coughing as much." He stared, giving me the once-over.

I slugged him in the arm—not very hard, since he half-laughed. "Stop blaming yourself for me getting shot. He was as psycho as Patty—now there was a match." I sighed. "You know what's scary? He was trying to track you down to kill you, and we had no clue. How do you protect yourself from that, from someone you didn't even know?" The first night at Mother's, I'd gotten a few minutes to have a private conversation with Brad. He'd never heard of Cardio Gates.

"That's why you've always got to be aware of your surroundings. All of us do," Creole said. "Truth is, it's darn near impossible."

"I'm just thankful Mila was with Mother and Cardio didn't get his hands on her." I shuddered.

"Thank you. For everything you've done through all this." Brad gave me a lopsided hug. "Can't say that enough. You were there and listened, and that helped immensely."

Spoon refilled our glasses.

The front door slammed.

"If Fab wakes up Mila, she's going to hear

about it from me," Mother grumbled. Her eyes reflecting her irritation, she kicked back her chair to go check on her granddaughter. "Not one word until I get back," she said over her shoulder.

Fab made her entrance, Didier at her side. "I've got news." She dropped her tote on the concrete. "But I've been ordered to wait."

Didier held up a bag from Jake's. "Cook wouldn't let me order. He sent over one of everything on the menu." He pulled containers out of the bag and lined them up down the middle of the table.

Spoon left and came back with dishes and silverware and tossed a roll of paper towels at Creole's head.

I leaned toward him. "I'll kiss it and make it better."

Creole winked.

Mother came back, Mila's hand in hers. "She was playing with her doll, so she'd been awake for a while." She eyed the table. "I'm not sure there's anything here that Mila will enjoy."

"That's why I got a grilled cheese." Didier held out the container.

Brad reached out to Mila, who went straight to him; he lifted her and put her in his lap, then ripped off a long string of paper towels and wrapped it around her shirt. "She can sample whatever she wants — if she spits it out, we know she doesn't like it."

I smiled, wondering how big a mess the two of them would make. Fab had her phone out, snapping pics. I'd tell her to forward them to me later.

"Now that we're all here," I said to Fab. "What's your news?"

Fab cast a glance at Mila, who had snubbed the sandwich in favor of a taco and was wholly focused on her meal. "Tossed Cardio's hellhole and found a detailed, handwritten journal, laying out his relationship with Patty from day one, right up until the day he killed her. Love at first sight." She wrinkled her nose. "The final straw came when Patty went off on a rant about her love for Brad, and Cardio couldn't take it anymore. Realizing she'd never be his, he choked the life out of her. Did his ramblings stop? Oh no. He left an exhaustive list of all the things he did to find Brad and his plans for his demise." She grinned at her find. "I'm no lawyer or judge, but I think it's enough to clear Brad."

"Please tell me you left it where you found it?" Creole groaned.

"Who do you think you're talking to?" Fab asked in her snooty tone.

I nudged Creole's leg to remind him she was family. "Sneaking around behind Didier's back again? I can't imagine him sanctioning that visit. You weren't crazy enough to go by yourself, were you?"

Didier tipped back in his chair, a big grin on

his face. "You tell her," he said to Fab.

"He was my lookout." Fab flashed him her sexy smile. "After I persuaded him that the best place to do that was from the parking lot and not Cardio's doorway."

Spoon clapped him on the back.

Creole shook his head.

"Fab's dragged you over to the dark side," Brad said, enjoying the dirty look he got.

"There's more. I made a copy of his computer files and have them on a drive in my bag."

"Nice job." I held out my knuckles, which she ignored.

"How is it that you beat the cops out to his place?" Creole asked.

"He rented it under an assumed name, and since he hadn't been arrested of late, it wasn't listed in any records we could find," Fab said. "When Toady called and asked if I wanted him to search the place, I told him I'd do it and call him when I was done, and that he was to be ready to pass the information along to one of his friends on the force."

"That's why we're late," Didier said. "We parked down the street and waited until the cops showed. It didn't take long, and then we were out of there."

"Can't wait for this case to just go away," Brad said. "I'd like to stop looking over my shoulder, waiting for the cops to beat on my door." He brushed Mila's hair with his fingers.

She smiled up at him, her face covered in sauce and bits of food. A true Westin—she enjoyed her tacos and rice.

"I have an announcement of my own," Brad said. "After everything that's gone down, I grew a pair and politely ended my relationship with Phil. It was exhausting, pretending an intimacy we didn't share." He shook his head and continued, "Had a sit-down with Bordello, and we're terminating the partnership once the project is finished, which should be within the next month. His informing me he was moving to Chicago made the decision easier."

"So everything is amicable between the two of you?" I asked.

"The man's a hard read. He might've had a different reaction if he didn't have one foot out of town. But he needs me… or the ability to split himself in two. He needs someone he can trust to see the project to completion and not screw him. My opinion is: he was as relieved as I that the breakup was drama-free."

"Now that I'm feeling better, I can get back to meddling in your life." I smirked at him. "Bring your talents back to the Cove and find a partner here. You could end up owning the top of the Keys. Besides, you've got a daughter to raise and family trumps strangers helping you."

Mila held her arms out to Spoon. He scooped her up and carried her into the house, saying, "Someone needs her face washed."

"Pretty certain Mila would agree—she has her favorites." Brad laughed.

"It's the sweetest thing." Mother stared after them.

Chapter Forty

Wedding week had arrived. Leave it to Fab to need a whole week. To be fair, the extra time was necessary to include all of Papa Caspian's plans. He invited the family out to the island for final preparations, which included a night out for the guys and a dinner the night before the nuptials for family only. In a few hours, we'd be arriving to start the festivities.

I felt bad that I'd been barely any help, nursing my arm and not able to shake off the nightmares of Cardio. My arm was now out of the sling, Creole helping with the exercises the physical therapist had given me.

Conjuring up images of the condition of my house wasn't adding to my mental health. I needed to mourn the loss and move on. A few pictures had been salvaged, which I treasured. But I'd been told there wasn't much else left. I had a plan. Today was my day to escape everyone's watchful eye and sneak out of Mother's to do a drive-by and check out what remained.

I backed into the hallway with one last glance. Mother's voice talking to Mila could be heard in the kitchen. I turned and yelped. Creole was leaning against the front door, arms across his chest, tapping his foot. He held out his hand. "Ready?"

Chagrinned, I closed the space between us, putting my hand in his. He jerked me hard against his chest, leaning down and searing me with a kiss. I'd lost my touch, but I should've known I would never succeed. I hadn't been able to get by the watchful eyes of my guards even once, not even to go down to the strip of sand this place called a beach by myself.

"Don't think I wouldn't have tracked you down. And then." He sliced a finger across his throat.

A giggle escaped me. "Sorry." I stuck out my lower lip in a faux pout. "I just wanted... I don't know... to be the old, take-charge Madison for a few."

He opened the door and crossed to the elevator. "When you go through a traumatic situation, you have doubts about getting back into fighting shape, but you will. Look at me." He flexed his muscles.

We stepped into the elevator, and instead of pushing the button, Creole swooped me into his arms, bending me back for a kiss.

"Think of me as your personal driver. I'll take you wherever you want to go." He kissed me again.

The man knew how to kiss.

The door opened. "Ick," a kid yelled. "They kissing." He smacked his lips.

"Behave, David," said an older woman who'd come around the corner, a young girl by her side.

Creole swept me off my feet and into his arms. Winking at David, who made a face, he carried me to his truck. "Where to?" he asked, sliding me onto the seat.

* * *

As we drove up to my house, the sight of it sucked the air from my lungs. The exterior was a blackened shell. The bottom floor gutted, the second only partially but deemed unstable, the property had been red-tagged. Tears ran down my face, and Creole wrapped his arms around me. More than a few thoughts ran through my head. It could've been worse. The cats and I had survived. Possessions could be replaced. I peeked around Creole's shoulder, thinking about my aunt—she'd want me to rebuild, and I would, but the thought of living here again didn't appeal at the moment. It wasn't the first time I'd had my house invaded by intruders, and I wanted to make certain I was never caught off guard again.

The question of where to live loomed. Thus far, I'd split my time between Mother's and Creole's. We'd steal away and spend the night at his house, returning before Mila woke up. I wanted to take her with us, but there wasn't enough room and she'd settled in at Mother's.

As my tears dwindled, Creole wiped the rest away. "I know what you're thinking. I've worked up a plan."

I groaned, and he laughed.

"We're eloping and finding a bigger house — I'm thinking one that's more secure, short of living out in the middle of the water."

"If you're waiting for me to disagree, I'm not." I leaned my head against the seat and looked up at him. "I'm exhausted just being a part of the wedding plans, and I don't want to turn around and do it again. Besides, we'd need seat fillers. Do you suppose Dickie and Raul could get us wedding guests from the same retirement homes they get the mourners?"

"No freakin' way," he growled and tickled me.

"No, nooo," I squealed. "Mean," I squeaked out.

"Love your laugh." He pulled me into his arms. "Do you want to get out and have a look around?"

"How's the pool area?"

"It's another gut job."

I nestled my head against his shoulder. "I've seen enough. When does cleanup start?"

"Next week. Didier and I will be overseeing it and will run every decision by you first. Then we can talk about what you want done after that."

"Such a mess. The neighbors will be happy when they don't have to look at the eyesore." I shook my head. "Hamburgers? My treat."

"Drive-thru or are we going inside?"

"I'm thinking staying in the truck—that way, I can put my feet on the dash."

Creole burst out laughing. "You're lucky you're with me, young lady," he said sternly. "Your bestie would never allow such behavior."

"I'm very lucky."

Chapter Forty-One

It had been arranged for the family to be taken out to the island by boat. Fab and Didier had made the trip two days previous. Everyone— except for Liam, who'd arrive the night before the wedding—was packed up and standing on the dock, awaiting the arrival of "*Caspian*," the new yacht purchase, to make the short trip across the water. I'd heard from Fab that, in addition, a pontoon boat had been rented for the big day to shuttle guests back and forth.

Brad normally made himself scarce for these types of events unless nagged at and jerked by the ear by Mother. His incentive this time was Mila—she was the flower girl, and wherever Brad's daughter was, he wasn't far away. He'd taken to fatherhood as though they'd never spent a day apart. Mila's eyes lit up and she ran into his arms every time he came through the door.

I'd found parenting books on his desk and teased him, covering the fact that the sight of them had me choked up with happy tears.

"After reading a dozen or so, I'm done. I figure if I can't get it figured out, I'll call Mother. She raised us after Dad died, and we didn't turn out half-bad," he mused. "I never miss a chance to tell Mila I love her."

I left Mother and Creole at the bar with Spoon serving drinks, and found Brad in the bow of the boat, Mila on his lap. She was dressed in the pink tutu and leotard I bought. Mother and Fab were a bit annoyed that I managed to sneak something so cute by them, and even more so by the pair of flip-flops that came out of the bag too. I'd called the store where I'd seen the outfit in the window and had everything delivered. The ever-vigilant father had purchased a life vest, sunscreen, and also picked out a pair of mermaid sunglasses to match the tote bag she loved.

"How's your custody case going?" I asked, sitting down next to him.

"Sweet Emerson. When Ruthie got the charges dropped, she didn't waste a second filing the paperwork. Both of them are excellent lawyers — thank you." He turned his head and whispered, "I hope Cardio's churning in h-e-l-l, knowing that in the end, he helped get the charges dropped."

"Is it going to take long?" I sighed.

"It's a waiting game. I'm trying to be patient. But looking forward to being a full-time dad." He kissed my cheek. "Found a therapist. We've been to two appointments so far. 'Baby steps,' she keeps reminding me. I took Mila to the condo and gave her a tour. Showed her her new bedroom, all in pink. Thank you for that tip."

"How did that go?"

"She took it all in without much of a reaction. I figured I'd overdone it and told her we just stopped to get ice cream and would be going back to Gammi's house. Mother's new title, by the way."

"Liam told me." I laughed. "He wanted to make a bet about how long it would be before she changed her mind, and I passed."

"I sat Mila on the island and got out the ice cream. I fed her, she fed me, and we got it all over our clothes. Reminded me that she needs a change of clothing at my house. When we got back to Mother's, she gave us the once-over, both of us sticky messes, but didn't say anything."

"Afterward, she was probably sorry she didn't get a picture."

"I'm going to pay someone to organize all the pictures that we've accumulated and make sure everyone gets a copy." The motor started, and Brad stood Mila on the bench between his legs for a better view. "We're going that way." He pointed. Mila clapped. Without taking his eyes or hands off her, Brad said to me, "When the docs are signed and sealed, I'm going to have her spend the night, like a sleepover, until she's comfortable with me and her new digs."

"She's already comfortable with you. I love that she's responsive, making noises and attempting to talk."

Brad laughed, looking embarrassed. "I repeat

'Dad' over and over and point to myself."

"I'm going to miss little Miss Sweetness here." I brushed Mila's hair with my fingers. She rewarded me with a smile.

"We'll be seeing each other every day when we all move into Fab's hotel."

"Hotel?"

"First she suggested being neighbors, and I thought that idea sucked." He mouthed the last word. "Now she's talking about all of us under the same roof." He rolled his eyes. "I know I'm going to be ganged up on, and I'm telling you now — not giving up my condo."

I banged my head on his shoulder. "Haven't heard a word about these new ideas. You already know this, but if Mother and Fab unite on an idea, heaven help us both."

Chapter Forty-Two

Fab had insisted we have lunch out on the patio as she went over the checklists one more time and didn't get an argument from me or Mother. Creole and Didier were engaged in a fierce game of basketball in the pool, water flying everywhere.

Brad had inquired if Caspian had a harness so he could take Mila on a bike ride. He clearly didn't know what Brad was talking about, but one showed up the next morning. With Mila strapped to his chest, dad and daughter had gone for a ride around the island. Brad had gotten a packed lunch from the kitchen and planned to stop and eat on one of the grassy areas.

The family dinner had originally been set for Friday, and it was at my suggestion that it was moved to Thursday so we could get our drunk on and not show up hung over for the wedding. The men had set the bachelor party for Wednesday. Invitations to a private club had been secured, and there would be top-shelf liquor, an array of the finest cigars, poker, and scandalous entertainment to enjoy.

"That's a terrible idea. The guys should have

their party here," Mother said when I told her of the new schedule. Spoon, who'd been standing behind her, smirked, but it vanished fast when Mother looked up. "You should've told me."

He held out his hands. "I could hardly say no. It's all for a good time, and won't get out of control." He winked.

"We could take a vote," I challenged. "Let's take a vote. Spoon's vote counts five, as he'll be voting for the guys. Caspian can cast his own vote."

"I'm abstaining." Caspian laughed.

"That won't be necessary," Mother said. "I'm stressed over nothing."

Fab hugged her. "Anyone would be stressed with a million things to think about. We both deserve a drink."

"We do, don't we?" Mother smiled.

They'd bonded more than ever over the wedding details, and I felt less guilty when I thought of running away. I needed to follow the advice I gave Creole and tell Mother how I was feeling. If anyone could come up with a plan to please everyone, it would be her.

A tray of flavored water and glasses showed up. I suspected it was Caspian's way of saying he didn't want us getting our drunk on. So much for the pitchers of margaritas I'd envisioned. I looked up at him, wanting to glare, but managed to behave. He grinned, sensing my frustration.

"I've been thinking about entertainment for

the family dinner. I'm thinking a fight." I air-boxed.

"You got a good reason to start one?" Spoon asked.

I shook my head. "I'll ask around and see if anyone's got any grievances to air."

"If not, I'll come up with something." Fab laughed. "You've *so* corrupted me."

"Pot!"

"I'm Kettle," Fab said, slapping her hand down on the table.

"No. You are not."

"Children, please." Mother patted the space between our hands.

Fab smirked.

It felt good to sit here in the sunshine without a care. "At least Brad's not bringing Phil." I did a double take at Mother's expression. "What's that look on your face?"

"Me?" she said with so much sweetness, it made my teeth ache.

I looked around the room. "Who else? You want me to yell, 'All mothers raise their hands'?"

"Madeline fixed him up, but he doesn't know it yet," Fab answered with a shrug, letting Mother know it was going to come out sooner or later.

"No. No. I'm putting my foot down." I lifted my leg. "This one right here."

Caspian cleared his throat.

"I know that look," I said to him. "If we were

children, you wouldn't let me play with your precious princess."

"I didn't get where I am by being dumb. I'm staying out of this conversation. But I'm warning all of you that if a brawl breaks out at my dinner table, you won't like my reaction." Caspian wagged his finger at us.

"Who's the woman?" I demanded.

"It's not a date. It's so we have the right number of people. Even Liam is bringing someone," Mother weaseled.

I pushed my phone across the table. "Cancel now. Stranger hookups at weddings are weird."

"Do you want me to tell her?" Fab blew out an exaggerated sigh. "If my opinion counts, and it does, your mother chose well."

"Oh, all right." Mother paused, waiting for our glasses to be refilled. "It's Emerson. And... I was honest with her, even told her I wasn't sure whether I'd warn Brad in advance."

"Which means you won't," I said, picturing the twosome and liking it.

"The best part is Emerson laughed at my nerve. Told me it would be way more fun than being Ruthie's date. Then suggested that I sandbag her mother — her word, not mine — with a surprise date." Mother fairly gloated.

"Hmm... a date for the lawyer extraordinaire," I said. "I have no clue."

Spoon had left to snag a beer, no water for him, and showed up in time to hear the last part of the conversation. He settled in a chair next to Mother. "I can get her a date."

Fab laughed at him, letting him know she highly doubted that he could.

"Youuu…?" I said.

"I know respectable people," Spoon growled, not amused that we were grinning at him.

Caspian flipped down his sunglasses. Did he think no one would notice him still sitting there?

"You know, Mother, Mr. Dumont here is single." I looked over, and his body stiffened. "Just a thought. Keep your eyes open for some nice little lady that might catch his eye."

Caspian made some indecipherable noise, clearly not happy at the turn of the conversation. "Nice little ladies aren't my type."

"No kidding," Fab said.

Okay. "Where's the food?" I said, loud enough to cut the uncomfortable silence that had descended.

Chapter Forty-Three

Another perfect day dawned on Caspian Island—in fact, throughout the Florida Keys. The soft scent of the salty gulf wafted through the air, a slight breeze providing relief from the warm, rising sun.

The water crashed against the rocks and cascaded over the white sand in the distance as seagulls squawked overhead, forming the perfect backdrop for the wedding.

The curve of the island, an area still within walking distance of the house, had been chosen as the venue and staged for the ceremony. It was decorated precisely to the bride's requirements, and it was apparent no expense had been spared. Trenches were dug on either side of the main aisle and lined with hot-pink rose petals. Seashells and large starfish hung by ribbons from the sides of the white chairs set up for the guests.

At the end of the aisle, there was a small pedestal that formed the altar. The altar's arch was built of bamboo, and a sheer fabric draped over it for a canopy, decorated with colorful tropical flowers—the peonies, roses, and orchids giving off an intimate feel.

Didier stood to the right of the altar, talking with the minister as he awaited his bride. Behind him stood Creole and Brad, his groomsmen, both dressed in white tuxedos. Theirs were the best seats in the house. With the exception of Caspian, the parents of the bride and groom hadn't flown over. Instead, plans had been made for the couple to honeymoon in Bordeaux and renew their vows. Mother and Spoon were as excited about Fab and Didier getting married as if they'd been their own children.

Strains of soft music drifted through the crowd as guests arrived to take their seats on either side of the aisle. It was easy to see their net worth displayed in the designer clothes and accessories they wore, dressed in the highest fashion but comfortable enough for the beach. Remarks—about the decorations, how romantic the scenery was, and how they were eagerly looking forward to the main attraction: witnessing the stunning bride—floated upward.

"Did you rent all these people?" I asked, staring down at the beach from the window. "Don't tell me that..." I made a quick calculation. "...hundreds of people are your best friends. After me, of course."

"Didier put his foot down at a hundred." Fab sighed. "They're business friends of Didier's from the old days and, of course, Caspian's friends."

"And how many of these people do you actually know?" I asked with a hint of a smirk as she glared at me. "Knowing how you are with names, I can't wait to hear how you address all these… strangers."

Fab covered her face with her hands. "I know," she squeaked and then laughed.

"My advice? Forget names — it would be the talk of your tight-knit group if you called someone by the wrong one."

Fab threw her arms around me. "No getting a new bestie while I'm on my honeymoon."

"Zero chance of that. Besides, Creole promised me a few days away, down in Key West."

Fab moved to stand in front of the floor-length mirror, turning from side to side and staring intently, as though there might be a flaw. "Do you think Didier's going to like this dress?"

"You look absolutely beautiful," I said.

Her white gown floated around her. "I almost don't recognize myself. I feel like a glamorous actress."

I'd listened to hours of endless planning by Fab and Mother, and even Caspian had had his say. Everything had gone according to plan. Everything was *perfect*.

Fab rubbed her stomach. "I've got the worst case of butterflies."

"It's nerves and excitement," I reassured her.

"I can't believe this day is finally here. For months, I've been afraid to look forward to it, afraid I'd do something to jinx it and Didier would tire of my antics and walk away. Now that it's finally arrived, it's moving too fast and I'd like to slow it down." Fab put her arm around my shoulders, pulling me close and turning me towards the mirror. "You look amazing." She hugged me hard.

We stood side by side, looking in the mirror. "I'm so happy for you both." I smoothed the front of my emerald-green sheath dress. I didn't argue when Fab insisted she'd be choosing my dress, and as it turned out, I didn't have a thing to worry about. She'd also insisted that I pile my hair loosely on the top of my head. "Ready to get this show started?"

Fab nodded with a smile and turned to check herself in the mirror one last time. I interrupted her to hand her a carefully crafted bouquet of peonies and orchids.

"Have you got the ring?" Fab asked, raising an eyebrow.

Fab kept worrying that I'd lose it, misplace it somehow, even though I'd assured her that wouldn't happen. She'd gone so far as to attach the ring to my bouquet with a ribbon, assuming it would be hard for me to lose something the size of a bouquet.

"Oh no... I can't find it," I said, picking through the flowers.

"You what?" Fab asked in shock.

"I'm kidding." I laughed. "Time to breathe. I'll

show you how." I demonstrated. To calm her fears and wipe the frown off her face, I held my flowers out so she could see the wedding band secured tightly to the bouquet. "Your ring is safe... I've got this." I gave her a quick hug before taking her arm and leading her outside.

Fab tried to relax as she said, "That wasn't even a little bit funny."

I chuckled. "On the contrary, I thought it was quite funny."

She smoothed her dress in a nervous gesture. "I wasn't this anxious on Didier's and my first date."

Mother waited at the bottom of the stairs, Mila by her side, looking like a princess in her white tulle flower girl dress, a basket over her arm. Mother was in an A-line princess V-neck tea-length chiffon dress in a shade similar to my own. I took my place behind her. Mother kissed us both, whispering, "You both look so beautiful." She gave Mila last-minute encouragement, then was ushered to her seat by Liam, who sat next to her in the front row.

Creole and Brad kissed Fab's cheek, told her how beautiful she looked, and wished her and Didier every happiness before joining me, one on each side.

The minister stepped forward and asked everyone to stand, and Fab knew it was time. Soon, all eyes would be on her. The music changed, and Brad bent down, whispering to

Mila. Creole and Brad hooked their arms through mine and walked me down the aisle.

When I finished my walk, Fab whispered to Mila. The music began again, and Mila ran, then slowed and stumbled down the aisle, lining the path with white rose petals as she saw fit. She ran out of petals halfway down the aisle and decided to hurry and skip the rest of way, making her trip end faster. When she made it to the end of the aisle, the music stopped. Mother motioned for her to come sit by her side. Mila got halfway, then turned—her eyes zeroed in on Brad, and she ran to stand beside him. He scooped her up, holding her. A few chuckles could be heard amongst the guests.

All eyes turned to the dazzling bride.

The intro to the traditional bridal march started to play, and down the aisle came Fab. Her strapless wedding gown was embroidered on the bodice, with rhinestones and pearl beads sewn into the skirt.

Didier smiled at the sight of his bride, who'd stepped into view and had taken a couple of steps before she was met by her father. They exchanged whispers and kisses before he tucked her hand into the crook of his elbow and walked her down the aisle, leading her to her groom. The walk seemed longer than it was in the rehearsal. The guests stared at her in awe, taking pictures, waving, and smiling.

Didier stood with his shoulders squared, his

eyes on the love of his life as she walked towards him.

Fab was all smiles as she and Didier made eye contact.

"He will always be the love of my life," Fab had whispered to me the night before. She faltered a step. I was sure her nervousness had kicked in again. Her father must have thought so too, because he squeezed her arm gently.

I wanted to tell her, "Only ten more steps to go — you've got this, Fab."

After what seemed like years, Didier walked out to greet his new father-in-law and wife-to-be. When he met them, her father stopped and pulled her to him, hugging her. "I'm proud of you," he said with a smile before presenting her to her future husband, placing her hand on Didier's. As a way of welcoming Didier to the family, Caspian patted Didier on the shoulder before stepping back. Didier and Fab exchanged smiles.

"You're gorgeous," Didier mouthed, holding her gaze, and Fab blushed. They held each other's hands and walked the rest of the way down the aisle, until they stood in front of the altar.

"You may now be seated," the minister said to the guests, and everyone followed his direction. "Dearly beloved," he began.

Didier held Fab's hands, gazing into her eyes. They exchanged vows, promising to take each other as spouse, constant friend, faithful partner, and lover from that day forward.

Fab's voice shook with emotion as she told Didier how much he meant to her.

Didier smiled, watching her with all love and adoration.

It wasn't difficult to see the love that Fab and Didier shared—it brought tears to my eyes. I'd been there since day one and had shared their journey.

After they took their vows, Creole and I presented the rings. Fab placed Didier's ring on first, and then he put on hers.

The minister nodded in approval before saying, "If there's anyone who objects to the marriage, they should speak now or forever hold their peace."

I held my breath, but no one said a word, as expected. You never knew, though. Creole winked at me, and I knew he'd read my thoughts.

The minister continued, "With the power vested in me, I now pronounce you man and wife. You may kiss the bride."

The guests roared in approval as Didier swept Fab into his arms. His fingertips skimmed her cheek, guiding her face to his. His lips met hers full on, and he bestowed upon her a possessive stamp of ownership. Fab clutched at him, pressed herself against him, and centered herself in his embrace. The kiss was rough and passionate, and yet shockingly sweet, all at the same time.

The guests clapped as Fab and Didier walked together up the aisle, holding hands.

PARADISE SERIES NOVELS

Crazy in Paradise
Deception in Paradise
Trouble in Paradise
Murder in Paradise
Greed in Paradise
Revenge in Paradise
Kidnapped in Paradise
Swindled in Paradise
Executed in Paradise
Hurricane in Paradise
Lottery in Paradise
Ambushed in Paradise
Christmas in Paradise
Blownup in Paradise
Psycho in Paradise
Overdose in Paradise
Initiation in Paradise
Jealous in Paradise
Wronged in Paradise
Vanished in Paradise
Fraud in Paradise
Naive in Paradise

Deborah's books are available on Amazon
amazon.com/Deborah-Brown/e/B0059MAIKQ

About the Author

Deborah Brown is an Amazon bestselling author of the Paradise series. She lives on the Gulf of Mexico, with her ungrateful animals, where Mother Nature takes out her bad attitude in the form of hurricanes.

Sign up for her newsletter and get the latest on new book releases. Contests and special promotion information. And special offers that are only available to subscribers.
www.deborahbrownbooks.com

Follow on FaceBook:
facebook.com/DeborahBrownAuthor

You can contact her at Wildcurls@hotmail.com

Deborah's books are available on Amazon
amazon.com/Deborah-Brown/e/B0059MAIKQ

Made in the USA
Coppell, TX
01 August 2024

35476190R00223